D0008369

LIGHT YEARS

LIGHT YEARS

Emily Ziff Griffin

SIMON PULSE
New York London Toronto Sydney New Delhi

SIMON PULSE

An imprint of Simon & Schuster Children's Publishing Division
1230 Avenue of the Americas, New York, New York 10020
First Simon Pulse hardcover edition September 2017
Text copyright © 2017 by Emily Ziff Griffin
Jacket photograph copyright © 2017 by 123RF/photo5963, Thiti Adeong
All rights reserved, including the right of reproduction in whole or in part in any form.
SIMON PULSE and colophon are registered trademarks of Simon & Schuster, Inc.
For information about special discounts for bulk purchases, please contact Simon & Schuster
Special Sales at 1-866-506-1949 or business@simonandschuster.com.
The Simon & Schuster Speakers Bureau can bring authors to your live event.
For more information or to book an event contact the Simon & Schuster Speakers Bureau
at 1-866-248-3049 or visit our website at www.simonspeakers.com.
Jacket designed by Erin Alexander
Interior designed by Mike Rosamillia
The text of this book was set in Adobe Garamond.
Manufactured in the United States of America
2 4 6 8 10 9 7 5 3 1
CIP data for this title is available from the Library of Congress.
ISBN 978-1-5072-0005-6 (hc)
ISBN 978-1-5072-0006-3 (eBook)

For Charlie Ziff, my father
For Phil Hoffman, my mentor
For Nick Griffin, my husband
For Wren and Zephyr, my life

"The most beautiful thing we can experience is the mysterious.
It is the source of all true art and all science. He to whom this
emotion is a stranger, who can no longer pause to wonder and
stand rapt in awe, is as good as dead: his eyes are closed."
—Albert Einstein

"The Self is everywhere. Bright is the Self,
Indivisible, untouched by sin, wise,
Immanent and transcendent. He it is
Who holds the cosmos together."
—Isha Upanishad [8]

CHAPTER 1

It was that time of day, when the light hits everything sideways. The sun was casting its final gleam of golden warmth and the sky was going from blue to purple. We went down to the beach, my young mother smiling and laughing, her dark chestnut hair falling down her back in wavy curls, and my father carrying me in his arms. We braced against a sheet of wind that hit with the force of a clanging church bell when we cleared the top of the boardwalk and saw the ocean spill out before us.

My mother ran ahead, flinging her sandals onto the sand and stripping off her emerald green dress. My father set me down, grabbed my hand, and we ran after her. I was all of two or three years old, but I remember. The waves seemed like mountains, but as my mother charged into them, they shrank. My first lesson in scale and perspective. My father pulled his T-shirt off over his head and stooped down to my level: "Stay here, lamb. Okay?" I nodded and watched him go.

The two of them sank under the warm summer sea, then reappeared, kissing, as I stood on the wet beach, the frothy water rushing up and over my feet. I smiled and took a step toward them. And another. They looked back at me and began to swim to shore. I took another step. Suddenly a wave rushed in and knocked me down. I felt the water all around me, filling my ears and pulling me as the wave ebbed. And then, my father's hands, lifting me to him and my mother swooping in. She grabbed me and held me as I cried. I don't know if I cried from upset or relief. But I cried and my mother kissed my face, wrapped me in her green dress, and carried me all the way home. That is my first memory.

The sound of the city dissolves into a hum. I stare up at the gleaming glass tower and a torrent of blue pours down. The building's edges blur against the cloudless sky—nature and the man-made becoming one. Blue always tastes like chocolate when I'm nervous, and I'm nervous. I swallow, then will the sensation away with the sound of my own voice.

"This is it," I say to my father as the white-gloved doorman beckons us inside. We enter the marble lobby and the temperature drops about twenty-five degrees. A rush of magenta sweeps across my eyes. My skin erupts in goose bumps and the trickle of sweat that has been nagging its way down my spine dries up in the cold air.

I step toward a bright-eyed man behind a reception desk. "How can I help?" he asks.

"I'm Luisa Ochoa-Jones," I reply quietly. My father mops his sweaty brow with a handkerchief.

"Yes, of course," the man says, nodding. "Seventy-fifth floor."

"Thank you." I turn toward the long, mirrored corridor that

leads to the elevator bank. I've been blonde for exactly nine hours and even though I'd never felt more like myself as when I stepped out of the shower with my new hair, my reflection is kind of a shock. I guess I'm still getting used to it.

My father and I arrive at the elevator. I glance down at my black lace dress and chunky, high-heeled ankle boots. I press Up and focus on the shape of the arrow on the button. It's short and squat. A fat little arrow.

"Before a concert," my dad says as we wait, "I like to think about how the music isn't for me; it's for someone out there listening, someone who needs it. That always makes me less nervous."

Okay, that's nice and all, but Thomas Bell doesn't need anything from me. It's the other way around.

The elevator car shakes gently against its surrounding walls as we rocket up the seventy-five stories to the penthouse. My ears pop and my stomach rolls over on itself. I clutch the handrail, wanting both to get there and never arrive. A *ding* as we level off. I shift my posture, tilt my chin slightly upward, roll my shoulders back. *Breathe*, I tell myself. The doors open with a wave of cold air. Another flash of pink reminds me that I am not at ease.

These sensory misfires have been with me all my life. When my emotions run high, my senses get muddled. It's like the wires get crossed and my brain sends the wrong messages to my body, or vice versa. Smells come with flashes of color, sounds have tastes, sights bring the sensation of temperature or touch. Certain people and places can spark complex reactions. My grandmother is the same way and all her life everyone has treated her like she's crazy. She doesn't seem to mind the condition, but I do. I keep it hidden. Most of the time, I can think my way back to normal. Most of the time, I can keep my feelings in check.

We come out into the hall. The walls are papered in ecru velvet and lit by small chandeliers that look like they were salvaged from the Titanic. A light-haired, boyish-looking man stands waiting in crisp khakis and a white dress shirt. "Hello, Luisa," he says. "And good afternoon, Mr. Jones. I'm Joe Anderson, Special Assistant to Mr. Bell." He shakes our hands and leads us to a door at the end of the luxe hallway.

We step through. Below us, Central Park's lush meadows and plump trees spill out, surrounded on three sides by the gray and beige concrete of an older New York, the one that existed before the skyline was swallowed by glass and steel. I stand and look down from this 200-million-dollar apartment nearly 1,000 feet in the sky. I feel like I can hold the entire world in my palm.

My father takes in the space. "Jesus," he mutters. It's easily twenty times the size of the biggest room in our house. Leather sofas. Thick, plush rugs. Two walls of floor-to-ceiling windows, a third with a series of closed doors, and a fourth covered by a massive painting of a shirtless figure superimposed over a satellite image of a city.

"Is he falling or flying?" I wonder aloud.

"What do you think?" replies Joe. His expression is unnervingly flat. "Please sit," he offers after a moment. "Something to drink?"

My father clears his throat. "I'd like some water, please." Now he's nervous. Which somehow makes me calmer. I watch Joe move briskly to one of the doors, then vanish behind it with barely a sound.

My watch buzzes with an incoming text. My mother: **In a cab. Be there ASAP**. She's late, like always. I sit down and look over at the wall of closed doors. How many rooms are back there? Who's in them? What does Bell keep in his fridge?

I cross my legs and direct my anxious mind to the scar on my knee from when I fell horseback riding in Mexico. My grandmother says it looks like Our Lady of Guadalupe, the Mexican Virgin Mary. She says it signifies my closeness to God. Like I said, people think she's nuts. Maybe she is.

I rub the scar with my thumb. My shrink, Dr. Steph, says that the more I can engage my senses deliberately, the less they will take on a life of their own.

"She's late," I report.

My dad shakes his head. "I told her, not today. Not to this."

"I don't care," I respond quickly. "It's better she's not here. She'd only make me more stressed."

He sits down and hooks his steady green eyes to mine. "You have nothing to lose here, whatever happens. You just be yourself and let go of the results."

But I have everything to lose.

Thomas Bell is the most brilliant and successful tech entrepreneur in the world and the Avarshina Fellowship means funding, mentorship, and most important, freedom. Yes, the fact that I've made it to the final round will most definitely help get me into college, if I wanted to go to college. But I don't. College is just a bubble, a delay.

I want my life to start now. Five minutes ago. I want to know what it's like to turn the lock on my own apartment door, to work all night and sleep all day if I feel like it, to not have to explain myself to anyone. Plus, my mom would be paying for college and I don't want to owe her anything.

"Mr. Bell is ready to see you." I look up. Joe is back. He sets a crystal-clear glass of water on a heavy coaster. I watch the liquid settle in the glass. I look down again at my scar. All the days between splitting my knee and dyeing my hair are imbedded in my cells like bits of rock in a mountainside: my body as time capsule.

My father and I stand.

"Sorry, the meeting is between Luisa and Mr. Bell," Joe says.

I hesitate. My father looks at me. His eyes are searching, uncertain, then they shift.

"You're very tall in those shoes," he says after a moment. I soften into a smile. I grab my bag and follow Joe to the wall of closed doors.

My watch buzzes again. My mother: **In the lobby**.

I quicken my pace. My pulse quickens with it and my mouth becomes so dry I imagine any words I form will come out as imperceptible gasps. I take one look back at my dad and cross into the next room.

The door clicks behind me and a wave of bright yellow gives way to pitch-black. As my eyes adjust to the darkness, I see a large desk at the center of the room. Two slick black chairs stand next to it facing a monitor that seems to float on the surface. Joe leads me to sit and a moment later I am alone.

My chest constricts. A hissing sound envelops me, like I'm surrounded by snakes. *This isn't real*, I tell myself. But my body doesn't believe me.

EMILY ZIFF GRIFFIN

I leap to my feet. My eyes search for the door. I have to go. I have to get out. I take two clumsy steps and the screen lights up behind me. I turn back. The Avarshina Industries logo fills the void: an abstracted image of a flaming match.

I struggle to draw breath. I zero in on the match's orange tip. Orange: bright, harmless. I track the edges of the match from one end to the other and back again. I start to relax. I remind myself that 2,300 people applied and only five of us made it this far.

I picture the apartment I will have. It's one big room. Bright light and a couch for reading. A place to work, a bed. All grays and white. I'm making coffee in the morning quiet. Maybe there's a bird on the window ledge. Maybe it chirps like it understands the value of solitude.

I go back to my seat. I wrap my hands around the armrests and wait, steeping in the amber glow of the monitor. Moments later, I am overwhelmed by the smell of roses. I sense a figure standing in the corner. The room brightens. The figure is Bell.

He's tall and wiry in a navy suit and pale-blue tie that mirrors the electric color of his eyes. All the blue pools in my mouth like one big chocolaty lump.

He smoothes his jet-black hair across his forehead with a gentle sweep of his hand and takes the chair next to mine.

"Hi," I murmur like I'm at the doctor's office, naked under a paper gown.

"Hello, Luisa." I have to lean forward to hear him. "You look different from your picture."

"I changed my hair," I say.

He nods. "I'm a problem solver," he says after a moment. "That's my—quote—thing. Could the same be said of you?"

I press my hands into the smooth sides of the chair's armrests. "I think so," I reply.

"Oof. Ambivalence," he scoffs. "I'm not a fan."

I rush to clarify. "Yes. I am a problem solver."

He crosses his long legs and clasps his hands over one knee. "I knew I was a problem solver at eight years old. My mother was cooking breakfast. I remember bacon. My father was in the next room reading the paper, as he did every morning." He half smiles at the memory, but his voice is distant, like he's telling someone else's story.

"Suddenly, we heard a noise. It was like a thud and a gasp and the clatter of broken pottery all at once. I looked at my mother, who called out my father's name. 'Jim?' No response. I followed her into the dining room. His enormous body lay in a twist, and his hands were at his chest. He was gasping for air."

I bring my own hand up to my throat, dizzy with Bell's scent. I tap my heel on the floor three times. Another of Dr. Steph's tricks.

"My mother ran to the phone. I looked down and saw a broken vase. Purple flowers scattered around. A trail of water running toward the door. I locked eyes with my father. And then, his focus went soft. His face seemed to melt. He was gone. The moment was—" He stops, smoothing back his hair. "Intolerable."

We sit in silence.

"I decided that was the last unsolvable problem I would ever face."

I nod. "It's a powerful story," I finally blurt out.

"Yes," he says.

The armrests again, cool under my sweating palms. "I'm sorry about your father."

"My mother was so upset by his death that she left me on the doorstep of an orphanage with a note and a paper bag full of my things." He looks down at the carpet. "She was not a problem solver."

"She couldn't handle her feelings," I offer.

He stares right through me. "No. She couldn't."

Does he know about my condition? I bring my hand to rest under my chin. The familiar scent of my lotion masks the flowery stink coming off him.

"Did you tell this story to the other finalists?" I regret the question the second it flies out of my mouth.

"Would you feel special if I said no?"

He's mocking me. I don't respond. Instead, I use every cell in my body to keep from flinching.

"What were you doing at eight years old?" he asks. "Was it all princess dresses and magic wands?"

"There might have been a wand," I reply. "But mostly I was swimming laps in the pool and wondering why my dad was such a jerk." I pause. "He's an alcoholic," I add. "In recovery now." If I can't win his respect, maybe pity will do.

His eyes seem to point at me like lasers. "He's alive," he replies.

"Yes," I acknowledge. Three more taps on the floor.

He glances at his watch. "We have a few minutes left. Show me LightYears."

Finally. I push Bell's keyboard aside with my shaking hand and pull my laptop out of my bag. I bring up the home page of Front Line News.

"Okay so," I begin. "This image." I click on a photo of the president wearing a hijab on a trip to Indonesia. Then I open my LightYears demo site and paste the URL for the photo into the search bar.

"LightYears takes any piece of online content and tells you in real time how we feel about it, collectively." I click *Mine*. "As the algorithm scans the Internet for responses to this particular image, different descriptors will occupy the field of 'pervasive sentiment.'"

We watch as a text cloud emerges. Words like *Admiration* and *Love* appear, along with *Outrage* and *Disgust*.

"The size of the word in the cloud indicates the pervasiveness of that particular reaction. See, as the data is being mined, right now *Anger* is dominating at twenty-two percent, but it looks like *Respect* is also vying."

I watch the analysis build and I get lost in the cloud—a tangible expression of other people's emotions. Word after word: concrete, quantified. In those moments, I forget to feel nervous. I forget to feel anything at all.

Bell stares at the screen. "And the data can be sorted according to location?" he asks.

"Exactly." I click on *Geo* and a drop-down appears. "You can search by continent, country, state, province, city, all they way down to postal code."

He turns to me. "And what problem does it solve, amassing this data of our feelings?"

"Well, I'm not sure I think about it in terms of solving a problem necessarily," I reply.

"You said you were a problem solver."

"I know how to solve problems, yes, but—"

"Ambivalence again." He chuckles like I'm an idiot. "It's a waste of energy, Luisa."

"What is?" I snap. "My ambivalence or my work?"

His eyes are like daggers. "Both."

I can't help it this time. I flinch.

"The world has more data than it can ever possibly know what to do with," he challenges.

"I don't disagree that data has no inherent value. I guess the question is what can it be translated into? What kind of tool can it be?"

The lights in the room suddenly grow brighter, like the show's over.

"And? What's the answer to that question?" His gaze falls to the scar on my knee.

"That's what I want to find out," I reply.

He doesn't seem to hear me. He's just staring at my scar. I reach down to cover my leg. He looks up at me like he's seen a ghost. "What?" he mumbles.

"That's what I want to find out. That's why I want the Fellowship."

A clicking sound. The door. Joe's back. "We done here?" he asks.

Bell nods and stands up. Then, without another word, gesture, or even a glance, he slips out.

"Shit," I murmur. I pull out my phone. Dr. Steph suggests I keep a log of my significant sensory reactions. She says it helps diminish their power. I enter *Thomas Bell. Smell. Roses.*

"This way," Joe says. He's holding open the door that leads back to the living room.

The hiss of failure falls over me like a veil. "That's it?"

He avoids my gaze. I walk slowly, willing time to elongate.

My mother is waiting by the window. Her black stiletto–clad toes graze the glass as she peers straight down. Her bright white scent hovers in the air. I swallow the lump of defeat in my throat, and with it, the urge to cry.

"Hey," I say as coolly as I can manage. My mom looks up and we lock eyes.

"*Ay Dios, qué hiciste?*" she barks. She looks horrified.

"Is that a rhetorical question or do you actually need an answer?" My insides sink down even further.

"It's blonde," she says.

"Yes, I'm aware."

"I think it looks great," my dad says.

My mom turns to him. "Did you give her permission to do this?"

"It's just hair," he replies. "When I was sixteen I was riding a motorcycle across Italy with an ounce of weed in my pocket and a guitar strapped to my back."

"Yes, which worked out so well for you," she snaps. My dad may be a recovering addict with five years of sobriety under his belt, but my mother is a recovering martyr with two decades of resentment under hers.

"It's just hair," my dad says again.

"Thank you for coming," interrupts Joe, who's been waiting for us to finish bickering.

"No, thank you," gushes my mother. She reaches out to shake Joe's hand as he leads us to the door. "Please tell Mr. Bell I hope to have another opportunity to meet him myself. My lab is doing some amazing things in neurochem right now."

"I'll let him know that, ma'am," Joe says. He smiles like a golden retriever. I am mortified on multiple levels.

"Thank you," I offer quietly.

"A pleasure, Luisa." Joe takes my hand and looks me straight in the eye. For a moment, I think I can smell roses in his smile, but it passes. I follow my mother down the hall. Her manicured finger rings for the elevator.

"We'll deal with the hair later," she says.

"Or not," I mumble as the doors open. I step in and leave Bell's otherworldly world behind, along with my dreams of escape.

CHAPTER 2

"So?" my mom inquires.

The elevator shoots down. I grip the handrail. "So it was fine."

"If it didn't go well, you can tell me."

"Why would you assume it didn't go well?"

"I know how you get when you're nervous." She turns to my father. "You shouldn't have let her go in alone." They've been separated since he got sober, but she still loves to throw a little blame his way.

"That was the only option," I insist.

"If I had been there on time—which I was going to be, but the idiot cab driver took Broadway even though I told him that was going to be slower—I wouldn't have let you go in alone."

"I don't think that would have mattered," I say.

"So it didn't go well!" she exclaims like some kind of lawyer catching me in a lie.

"I didn't say that. It was just a normal conversation."

"Look, it's fine, sweetheart." I perk up at this unusual display of compassion. "It's better that you don't get picked." Right, that's more like her. "Getting to the finals is all you need for colleges to pay attention. You don't need to make an enemy of Thomas Bell."

"What do you mean, make an enemy?"

She smirks. Her smell, a bright white haze that makes me squint. "If you were to turn him down. You're too young. And you need to go to college."

Are you fucking kidding me?

"Wait, I'm sorry. So all that work and you were planning to try and stop me from going?"

The elevator *ding*s. The doors open. A flash of purple: anger. I almost forget to get off.

"You're too young to be on your own," she says, walking away. This from the woman who moved out and calls me maybe once a month.

I step into the magenta chill of the lobby in a daze. The sun blasts through the window, casting a blinding rectangle of light onto the marble floor.

"Dad?" I murmur.

He looks at me with a helpless expression. "Lena, let's maybe see if she even gets it before we make any decisions."

My mother says nothing as she disappears onto the street.

We walk to the train in silence. I try to focus on the warm summer air against my skin, the clacking of my footsteps on the pavement. My entire body aches from trying to keep my shit together, and I'm so tired I want to crawl into bed for the next, maybe, week.

But then as soon as we reach the subway stairs, I'm back on alert. Even though it's been five years since the Blackout Bombing, I can't go down these stairs without feeling just a little bit afraid.

My mother hands me her MetroCard. "I only have enough for one fare," she says as I pass through the turnstile.

"No problem," my dad says. He swipes his own card and glances down at the digital display. "Shit." He turns and hustles to the refill machine as our train thunders into the station.

"Hurry up!" my mother calls. "The train is here."

"I do have two working eyes, and ears. But thanks!" he calls back.

New York, Chicago, and Boston. Someone hacked the electric grids, cut the power, and set off bombs on twenty rush-hour trains. They never figured out who did it and 6,000 people died.

We hurry down to the platform. I stare hard at the other people shoving to board the car. I imagine against all logic that if one of them is a terrorist, I will sense it and intervene.

A mother pushes through with a stroller. A gauzy sheen of sweat covers her skin. Her infant is asleep with a pacifier in his mouth. Does her diaper bag contain explosives?

A Front Line Peacekeeper steps up. "Let's back it up, now," he says, making space for people to exit. I smile at him without meaning to. After Blackout, when everything was chaos, a bunch of college kids in Boston started a group to do all the stuff the FEMA people couldn't seem to manage—food distribution, transportation, supplies, even funeral arrangements.

By the end of the year, Front Line was in a dozen cities and now, they are everywhere. There are more Peacekeepers on the street than actual cops. They are one good thing that came out of something horrific. My dad getting clean was another. It was like realizing we all could have been killed shocked him into getting sober.

The woman struggles to get her stroller over the lip of the doorway. My dad rushes up and he and the Peacekeeper both lunge forward to help. She nods her appreciation but declines the open seat in front of me. I let my mom have it and squeeze into an empty pocket by the door.

The train lurches forward. I put my headphones in. I close my eyes and disappear into a recording of an Italian physicist. He's talking about Einstein's vision of the universe, how Einstein understood before anyone that interstellar space swells and falls in waves, like the ocean. He describes a wave as a "disturbance."

My body rocks with the motion of the train. I steal a look at the stroller. A flash of yellow. How quickly would the blast move from there to the surface of my skin? Would there be a nanosecond of recognition first or just oblivion? These questions encircle me like wreaths of smoke.

I return to the physicist's rolling Rs and pinched-nose vowels. I ignore the meaning of his words and just listen to the sounds. My fear fizzles.

Suddenly the train whips around a curve. I lose my balance and look up. The train slows. We are at Canal Street. People's attention turns to the platform. Conversations quiet.

It's mostly been cleaned up. It's just the missing tiles where the station's name used to be written in mosaic. But we can't help straining to see what can never be seen: some evidence of what it was like for the people who were right where we are when the bombs blew. We are looking for ghosts.

My dad glances up from his phone. On the day of the bombing, I might've wished he'd been on one of the trains. Not really, but kind of. In the abstract. I used to think about things like that. Like maybe he'd drink too much and die. It seemed like it would be a relief. But it turns out I didn't want him to die; I just wanted him to stop being that version of himself.

Four more stops and we're in Brooklyn. We resurface into the quaint charm of the Heights, with its large-leafed trees and immaculate brownstones. It's my brother Ben's high school graduation tonight. I'm psyched for him. He actually gives a shit about going to college.

My dad stops on the way into the church. Some of the other music teachers want to chat. I turn back and watch him. He looks out of place. He's older. His face is etched with all the years of not taking care of himself. His tawny hair has thinned and his sloping shoulders make him look like he's sinking.

But then he smiles at someone's joke and a silver swell of love washes over me. I feel his smile like the sound of wind blowing through the trees. It's familiar. It's like my scar—memory embedded.

My mom and I find seats along the aisle about halfway back. I try to adopt a casual pose, but my eyes are darting everywhere. The small orchestra tuning its instruments. The school chorus dressed in black at the back of the stage. Someone's ancient grandma inching forward with her walker.

And then I spot him. Kamal. Up in the balcony with Des Frank and George Keenan from swim team.

His broad shoulders and smooth, dark skin are like a magnet only I can feel. I steal a long look at his almond-shaped eyes glittering in the chandeliers' light. I hear his voice in my head. His English accent melts like honey in hot tea. My legs tingle and a swirl of fresh pine sweeps around me.

Kamal has been my brother's best friend since he moved from London in eighth grade. The night before he left for Harvard last summer, he and I stayed up all night watching movies after Ben went to bed.

We went out into the backyard at dawn. I could hear the inky morning light—a heavy drone like the earth churning through the cosmos. We walked past the massive maple that fills the view from my bedroom on the second floor and settled at the table at the end of the garden.

"It's almost too late to sleep," he said. He pulled a silver flask from his pocket and took a sip. "I might have to just stay up."

"Forever," I added.

"Never sleep again," he said, handing me the flask.

The scorch of bourbon hit my throat with a hum like an old basement's fluorescents. I squeezed the edge of the table to keep myself steady.

"I'd like to be one of those people," I said. "The ones who need, like, three hours of sleep a night. They always become president or something."

"Yeah. My dad is one of those." He looked down at his watch. "He's probably getting to the office right now."

I eyed the raspberry bush along the fence. My parents bought our house in Bed-Stuy when they got married. It was a shitty house in a shitty neighborhood back then, but it was what they could afford and my mother fell in love with it because of that bush. She once cared about things like that.

"He's not taking you up to Boston?" I asked, getting up to pick berries.

"Nope."

"Your mom?"

"She's in London. Some courier service is taking my stuff and my dad's plane is taking me."

Silence between us. The sky continued to brighten.

I put a handful of berries on the table and sat back down. "God, you're just so . . ."

"What?" he asked.

"Rich."

He laughed. "I'm not rich. My parents are rich."

"Well, I'm not rich either," I said, smiling.

"So we're both not rich. Probably a good thing. I see what my father has to do to keep up with his cash and it's a type of happiness, but it's not the one I want."

"What's the one you want?"

"The kind that has to do with people. When you have serious money, you see everything in terms of money. People stop mattering and you can't be free because you become a slave to your own wealth." I followed his gaze to the surrounding brownstone rooftops. They seemed to be getting darker as the sky grew light.

"Most people would say the opposite," I countered. "That money assures freedom." I took another sip from the flask and passed it back.

"I'm not most people." He exhaled a big breath. "My last few hours in Brooklyn."

I grabbed some berries and leaned toward him, just an inch. The smell of pine needles and that prickly sensation only I could feel. It made me wish he could exist in my strange universe, just for a minute.

"Yeah, it must be weird." Three taps on the grass beneath my feet. "What will you miss?"

"A lot of things," he said. His hand was suddenly resting on my knee. He was looking straight at my face and my legs were growing numb. I wondered if they were disconnecting from my body and then I felt his fingers press against my bare skin. "I'm gonna miss a lot of things."

I grabbed the edge of the table again and forced myself to hold his gaze even as the garden seemed to revolve. For the first time maybe ever, the feeling of too much was also the feeling of not enough.

"Yo," my brother's gravelly voice cut through the air like sharp peppermint. Kamal quickly pulled his hand away. Three more taps on the grass as my heart threatened to burst. Holy shit.

"What's up," Kamal called out. His voice was calm and even. I looked at Ben. He's tall and lanky like our father, but his nose is flat and wide and his brows are dark and thick, like our mother's. He was coming toward us, his mountain of wavy brown hair piled in a mess on top of his head—peppermint dulling the pine.

"I couldn't sleep," he said, taking a seat. Kamal offered him the bourbon and I retreated into the thought of Kamal's hand on my leg.

I placed my own hand where his had been, like I could trick myself into believing it was still there.

I don't know who said what or what time it was when we finally said good-bye. I was just trying to act cool as Kamal walked out our front door like nothing had happened. A few hours later, he left for school.

Now he's sitting up in that balcony.

I distract myself with the program and find my brother's name. Benjamin Ochoa-Jones. Such a strong name. I breathe in pride, anticipation.

"Next year, it will be you," my mother whispers as the lights dim. Is she trying to piss me off or does she genuinely not get it? My father slips in next to us and gives my arm a squeeze.

I sneak a look at Kamal. Our eyes meet for a fraction of a second. He looks away, but he saw me. Definitely. A rush like little pinpricks as the room goes silent.

The familiar notes of "Pomp and Circumstance" reverberate across the church. We rise and turn to greet the first pair of graduates. They appear like bride and groom at the back of the chapel and two-by-two the whole class walks. Beaming. Finished and about to start over.

I replay the moment Bell stood up and walked out. "A waste of energy." His words echo in my head. My heart sinks. I know my life could be way worse. I shouldn't complain. But it gets old being smarter than everyone and hanging out with rich kids when you aren't one. It gets old trying to hide the thing that makes you different. Also, if I'm honest, I don't like to lose.

Here comes Ben in his black suit, checked shirt, bow tie, and fedora. He chose to walk with his ex, Annalise Hastings. She's the kind of girl that comes to school in a chauffeured car and carries a Chanel bag. Like, instead of a backpack. But she's a serious actress, the star of every school play and on her way to Yale.

In March, she told Ben they should break up since they were heading to different colleges. I've never seen Ben so drunk as he was that night. He woke us up banging on the door because he couldn't hold the key steady enough to fit it into the lock.

The next morning he ditched school, dug an old wetsuit out of the basement, and took the train to Far Rockaway. It was like twenty-eight degrees out. He swam two miles in the ocean and never said another word about it. By the end of the year they decided they were friends. But I know he still loves her because when he says her name, his voice catches in his throat.

He winks at me as he walks past. He looks happier than I've ever seen him. Silver tears fill my eyes, peppermint swirls around my head. I roll the program into a tube and wrap my hands around it. I think about how smooth the paper is instead of how much I love my brother.

When the ceremony ends, everyone files out into the street. I stand on tippy toes and crane my neck.

"Do you see him?" my mother asks.

"No," I reply, secretly searching the crush of faces for Kamal, not Ben. "Oh wait." I spot Ben and wave him over. "He's coming."

"Congratulations, *cariño*," my mother says. She pulls him into her arms like she may never let go. When she finally does, she's looking at him like she used to look at us when we were kids—no judgment, no harshness.

My dad steps forward for his own awkward hug. "B." His voice cracks. "God. That was so exciting. To see you up there. I'm so totally proud of you."

My mother wipes tears from her eyes and whatever softness I glimpsed vanishes. "Yes we are. Very proud," she echoes. Ben glows.

My dad pulls out his phone. "Let's get some pictures." He snaps a few of me and Ben, then makes us all get together for a group selfie.

"How about dinner?" offers my mom. "Chinese?" My father looks at the photos.

"Love to, Mom, but grad party," replies Ben. He's already texting his friends.

"Well, soon," she says. "I'll call you both tomorrow and we can make some plans." I don't expect her to call. And I don't particularly want her to either.

"Is Kamal here?" I ask, avoiding my brother's eyes.

"He already left." Fuck. "We should go too," he adds.

"Hey, hey." My dad puts his hand on Ben's shoulder. "This is a big deal, what you've accomplished. I know I've created a lot of struggle for you. Both of you," he looks at me. "I'm going to be making up for that for a long time. And I don't deserve much credit for this moment, but I'm beyond happy to be here to see it, to see you." Tears well up in his eyes, Ben's too. I look down at the cracks in the pavement.

"Thank you, Dad," Ben says.

"Love you both." My dad smiles at us. Wind rushing through trees. A deep breath.

We say our good-byes and Ben and I get in a cab. We're going to an old warehouse in Queens. The one the seniors rent every year for graduation night. The television in the backseat is blaring news about forty-one people dying of some kind of mystery flu.

I mute the volume as a text comes through: my dad. It's the photo of the four of us. We look happy. I wish I could climb inside the picture and stay there forever. I glance back through the rear window, catching one last glimpse of my parents together on the street before they disappear.

"Dad's such a softy," Ben says, looking at the photo on his phone.

"Yeah." I flash to the time I found him passed out on the kitchen floor at six in the morning. I knelt down and put my hands on his chest. I wanted to check that he was breathing. He snapped awake and yelled, "Get the fuck away from me." So, there's also that.

"And Mom," he continues. "I literally haven't heard from her in like three weeks and she shows up and is all crying and 'Let's go out to dinner'?"

"Yeah," I mumble, but I'm focused on the TV. Camera flashes fire in the background as a basketball player's massive body glides through the air in slow motion like gravity doesn't exist. My heart flies into my throat as I watch the ball leave his hands, then slip gently through the hoop. Two points. Deep satisfaction in that moment, even though I couldn't care less about the sport itself.

This is what my mother studies. How the chemistry of our brains makes watching other people do something as exciting as if we were doing it ourselves. It's why we like sports and movies and social media. It's why we are interested in other people at all. It baffles me that she studies the part of us that cares about others when she barely seems to care about anyone besides herself, but hey.

"Hello?" Ben snaps. I look at him. "Have you talked to her lately?"

"I got a text from her three days ago asking for Bell's address. Otherwise, no. And she was twenty minutes late, by the way."

"Of course she was. She's worse than Dad ever was and at least he had an excuse."

"She also told me if I get the Fellowship, she won't let me accept it."

"Um, sorry. What?"

"Yeah." I press my hand against the window. The cool glass, an antidote to the anger bubbling purple in my field of view. "It doesn't matter anyway. I'm not going to get it. Bell told me my work was a waste of energy."

"Is that a quote or are you doing that thing where you act like someone hates you but actually they think you're amazing?"

"Direct quote." I press the glass harder. "And I don't do that."

Ben looks at me in a way only my older brother can. "Yes you do. But anyway, listen. Fuck that guy. Fuck him. You don't need that guy." The question of Bell's value is now settled in Ben's mind. He goes back to his phone.

Yeah. Fuck Bell, I think to myself. But I don't mean it.

We pull up to the party and get out of the cab. Missy Allegheny is puking behind a Dumpster. She is one of the most popular girls in my class, but this is not the first time I've seen her slumped over in some corner trying not to get vomit in her hair.

"Are you okay?" I offer. She nods and then doubles over. She gives me a thumbs-up as she wretches onto the concrete.

Inside, it's dark and loud. Music, warm bodies, the smell of liquor, weed, and beer. If it weren't for the chance to see Kamal, I would never have come.

"I'm gonna go find Des and George. You cool?" Ben asks. I nod and he disappears toward the bar. I weave through the dimly lit crowds. I pass Clara Adams and Cicely Dormer, wasted and dancing their faces off. I pass Matt Kenner and Dan Fryman ripping bong hits. Nathalie Spencer, Dave Rothman, and Zoe Kalember are in a corner decked out in VR goggles and gloves.

These people are not my friends. Ben likes their world even though he isn't from it. He's popular because he doesn't care what they think. But I do. Dr. Steph says I should try getting to know them, and let them get to know me. She doesn't see that they only like people like them. Rich, normal. They do not like weird. And a girl on a scholarship who can taste colors and hear smells would definitely be considered weird. Mostly, I just keep to myself.

I turn back the way I came and stop at the dance floor. I scan the crowd of bodies frozen midmotion in the pulsing light. I'm looking for the particular shape of Kamal's shoulders that is permanently lodged in my brain. And then, like an anchor to the ocean floor, my focus falls on her—straight red hair, a poppy-colored pout, and smoky eyes. She's walking right toward me like she owns everything on earth.

Who is she? Why can't I stop looking at her?

Then, as her path veers, I see him. Kamal. Right behind her, his hand on her back. He guides her forward and they melt into slow motion. My mouth is suddenly dry with the taste of salt as a hot flash of realization travels up from my stomach and out the sides of my face. They are together. This stunning girl is Kamal's girlfriend and I want to die.

I turn away before he can see me. I practically run to the bar, where I find Ben. Breath is barely escaping my lungs. Waves of purple light mix with brown. I get the attention of the freshman behind the bar and order a vodka and orange juice. I drink it down in about seven seconds. I feel better. I order a second.

"What's wrong?" Ben asks. I just shake my head as the drink arrives. I lean against the bar and wrap my hands around the icy cup. The cold helps a little. Then I feel that tingle run up my legs. I practically gag on a torrent of pine. I don't have to move to know he's standing right behind me.

"Hey stranger." His voice and all its proper Englishness. I clutch the cup tighter. I take a sip and turn around. "Lu," he says. I stare at him, wordless. Thoughtless. Blank.

The girl extends her hand.

"Hey, I'm Phoebe," she says. She is like the teacake that makes Alice shrink to the floor. I let go of my drink just long enough to shake.

"Phoebe just graduated," Kamal says.

"High school?" I blurt out.

"Harvard." Her white teeth twinkle like Christmas tinsel. I shrink another two inches at least.

"So the world is pretty much your oyster," remarks Ben. He's

EMILY ZIFF GRIFFIN

using the deep voice he reserves for beautiful girls and their parents.

"The world is everyone's oyster, if they step up to crack it open," she replies, hopping to the bar. The taste of salt again, so strong my mouth feels like it's withering into dust.

"Phoebe's working for Front Line," Kamal adds.

"Oh. So you're a hippie, or a communist? Excellent," Ben says playfully.

Phoebe laughs. "I guess we are like hippies. If hippies were, like, the most tech-savvy, organized, and democratic power structure in the world, doing shit that the so-called government never could with all its bullshit bureaucracy and antiquated aversion to anything grass-roots and actually effective."

Ben smiles. She's right. Five years after Blackout, Front Line is practically like a second government. Plus they have their own news network and all those Peacekeepers.

She orders a vodka soda with a lime and her arm grazes mine. I grab a piece of ice from my cup and squeeze it. Cold water drips down my hand as her lips surround her straw with a heart-shaped pucker.

I want to kill her and be her all at once.

She turns to Kamal and puts her hands on his chest. "Let's dance!" she exclaims and sails off. I shake the water from my hand and attempt to slink away unnoticed.

"Hey," Kamal calls. I stop and turn back. I feel so invisible I wonder if he can actually see through me. He walks up and pulls me toward him. His leather jacket dulls it, but his scent wraps itself around me like a cloak. My legs buzz.

"Hey," he whispers. He tucks my hair behind my ear and lets his face linger close, the theory of relativity proving itself true in this moment that seems to last a thousand years.

"Welcome home," I manage to say.

"Thanks." He steps back. "I'll see you around." He turns and walks off toward Phoebe. A second later, he turns back: "I like the hair!"

I gulp the rest of my drink and text Janine: **U here? Need u**. She writes back instantly: **Upstairs, couches**.

Janine is basically my only real friend and the only one at school besides Ben who knows about my condition. She comes from money, but you'd never know it. She makes beautiful photographs of what's left on the table after people eat. She says they are portraits of time—its passage, but also how it creates memories that become part of us, like how our food becomes part of our bodies. She reads books. She sees movies in movie theaters. She talks about philosophy and religion. And sex. And she makes me feel like it's normal to be not normal.

I count my steps as I stumble to the stairs in a haze of internal sensory chaos. I find Janine sipping tequila and telling one of her epic stories to a freshman named Francis.

"And then I took the knife and slit its throat from one end to the other." Francis watches her mouth form each word. "The blood drained into the earth and I realized: I've never seen an animal die. I could actually feel the energy shift, like when a cloud covers up the sun and everything feels totally different for a second? And then, it was all normal again. Just like that."

"Whoa," Francis murmurs, mesmerized. And stoned.

"We ate the pig that night."

He gasps.

"I need to talk to you," I say. I pull Janine toward me, signaling that Francis's time with this beguiling older woman is up.

Janine hands Francis her cup. "Would you?" she says. He trips over the couch and leaves. Janine turns back to me. "Okay, what's up?"

"Kamal is here."

"And?"

"And he's with some girl. Like a superhot, smart Harvard girl who just graduated and is practically model-pretty only real-looking and she also seems really nice and it's making me—" I don't need to explain.

"Ugh," she replies. "Let's go." She grabs my hand and I follow her. My woozy mind struggles to touch down amid a kaleidoscope of thumping music and flashing lights. Her long black hair becomes my runway.

We make it outside and walk to the nearest intersection. The streetlights buzz above us as Janine lights up a half-smoked joint and takes a hit. Smoke swirls around her like dancing phantom serpents. We are comfortable in silence.

"Henry and Bay," she tells the driver as we get into a cab.

"Dude," I say. "We can't."

"Oh c'mon. We've done it like a hundred times."

"Yeah and last time we almost got busted."

"But we didn't. Look, you want to feel better. This will make you feel better."

I roll my eyes. But she's right. She lowers the window and spits onto the street. I gaze through soft focus at the passing lights, the storefronts, the people busy in their lives. This silent movie lulls me as the vodka and adrenaline wear off and sleepiness sets in.

"Hey," she says after a while. "You didn't even tell me. How'd it go today?"

I don't say anything.

"Hello?"

"Sorry." I sit up straighter. "It didn't go well." She doesn't press me, thank God. "My mom loved my hair, though." She shoots me a look. "Kidding."

"Your hair is amazing," she says.

"I know. And thank you."

We arrive at the Red Hook Pool. In summers during middle school, my dad would take me and Ben here every Sunday morning and drill us on our strokes. Half the time he was still drunk from the night before, but I loved it. I loved his voice booming from the side of the pool, and his attention, which was rare then.

I quit the swim team after freshman year when I started building LightYears, but Janine and I still sneak in on warm nights to swim laps back and forth across the dark, cool lanes.

There's a break in one side of the fence and there's never anyone around, except for the one time when a cop saw us coming out. He decided not to chase us when we ran.

We climb through the fence and come out onto the concrete deck. With no lights on, the pool looks black and bottomless. We strip down to our bras and underwear.

"You have the best boobs," Janine says, staring at my chest.

"Your skin is like white lilies in the summer sun," I tell her, stifling laughter as I dive in.

The moment my skin breaks the surface, I am home. The weightlessness, the quiet, the smooth pull of the water along my body. This is where challenges, disappointments, and uncertainties slip away. All I have to do is exhale and move forward. If I were to have a church, this would be it.

I take the whole length underwater, my eyes open, and come back up as the murky wall of the far end comes into view. Janine arrives next to me a moment later.

"I'm so bummed about this girl," I say, catching my breath. "I mean, it's obviously not like we were together at all; we never actually even kissed. And of course I couldn't expect him to go to college and not meet someone amazing. But I somehow still thought there was something there and that he'd come back and—I don't know."

"Who is she?" Janine asks.

"Her name is Phoebe. She has, like, insane red hair. And she has bangs, really good bangs."

"No!"

"Yes. Perfect bangs. And she's smart."

"But not as smart as you," Janine says. I smile. This is most probably true. "Why do you like him so much anyway?" She floats on her back. I consider the question.

"He has every reason to be just like all the others, to just be rich and into himself and boring. But he knows that, and he doesn't want to be that. That night in the garden, my senses were all over the place,

but it wasn't entirely terrible. It was kind of the opposite of terrible."
I push off the wall and float next to her.

"I've never been in love," she says.

I am quick to clarify. "I am definitely not in love with Kamal."

"Why not?"

"I think of love as something mutual," I say.

"Mutual? Um? Unrequited love? That's, like, a thing. That millions of songs and poems and books and movies have been written about. Most love is the opposite of mutual."

"Well, I still wouldn't say I love him. I don't even know what love is."

"We are born of love, love is our mother. I read that on a teabag," she says.

"Not my mother," I reply, laughing as Janine disappears underwater. I look up at the muddy gray-black sky. All the ambient city light makes the stars invisible. They are there though. Blocked by the light, but they are there. And I can feel them.

EMILY ZIFF GRIFFIN

CHAPTER 3

Bell is the first thing on my mind when I wake up the next morning. I check my e-mail hoping for a message from him or Joe or anyone involved. Nothing.

I go downstairs. My dad's making banana bread and watching CNN. I can't speak or even think until I have coffee. I pour myself a giant mug. The words BREAKING NEWS scream across the screen like they always do. It's the mystery flu. The same one from that headline in the cab.

"The Centers for Disease Control and Prevention have issued a statement confirming that the number of fatalities attributed to this emergent illness is escalating rapidly and they have yet to determine the cause." The reporter sounds overcaffeinated.

My dad stops mixing the batter and turns to watch.

"Also unknown to them, according to the statement, is how this flu is being transmitted, as there is no apparent connection between the victims."

I wrap my hands tightly around my warm mug. "That's creepy," I mumble.

The newscaster is replaced on-screen by a press conference setup and a polished-looking older woman at a podium. A CDC placard and an American flag stand behind her. Her name, Dr. Rosemarie Timmons, comes up at the bottom of the picture.

"We are calling it ARNS, or Accelerated Respiratory and Neuro-degenerative Syndrome," she says. "The first cases emerged across the U.S. approximately three weeks ago, and the CDC has been monitoring the trajectory of the infections thus far. We have seen forty-one fatalities and the pattern is consistent."

"Let me stir," I offer. I grab the spoon—the nearest distraction.

"Patients complain of flu-like symptoms, which worsen over a period of hours or days. The nervous system ultimately fails, leading to paralysis and death."

Her voice softens as she says "death," like she's run out of air, like she's hoping that one word will be too faint to reach us. I see a burst of yellow. I continue to mix.

"We've seen complete deterioration occur in as little as one to two days, but it can take a week or even longer. We have not yet seen evidence of the symptoms reversing." I am stirring vigorously. "Our current theory is that ARNS is transferred by a new type of flu-like virus, by the exchange of bodily fluids, but we cannot confirm that at this time."

My father starts chopping onions for a frittata. The smell bombards me like a beating drum.

"Can we turn this off?" I ask, motioning to the television.

"Oh, I'm sorry," my dad replies. "Of course. I should've realized." He fumbles for the remote as the doctor from the CDC tells us not to panic. She tells us that the ordinary flu kills over twenty thousand people a year, so this is not that big a deal. Yet.

We turn it off. Relief. My dad stares at me with a concerned look.

"I'm fine," I say. "The onions were a little . . . loud. But it's really fine."

"Sit down over there, lamb. Take your coffee. I'll put on some music. Yes?"

I nod and go over to the chaise by the garden door.

"Jazz?" he asks.

"That's fine." I curl up on the chair. The bright, relaxed notes of a Bill Evans track fill the room. I close my eyes and listen. I wish I were musical like Bill Evans, like my dad. I'm sure I could master the playing part if I worked hard enough. But the expression, the feeling behind the music, that requires a language I don't speak.

"You know the news likes to make everything so much more dramatic than it is," my dad says after a bit.

"I know. Are you worried?"

"Not worried, no." He clears his throat. "I think it's just the normal media hype thing." The piano trills. The un-oiled hinge on the oven door whines as he puts the banana bread in. He throws the onions into a hot pan. They smell like onions, nothing more. I exhale a deep breath. "I think the real concern is how late Ben is going to sleep and whether we should save him any breakfast."

"I vote no," I reply.

"I heard that." Ben is lumbering down the stairs.

"You do realize it's still morning?" I tease.

"I'm a high school graduate now. It's time to start living responsibly." He flashes his crooked smile and grabs three plates from the cupboard.

We all sit and dig into a steaming plate of eggs and chopped veggies.

"How was the party?" my dad asks.

"Fine," Ben answers.

"Yup," I echo.

"You know that answers like that are described in the parenting handbook under the heading 'Be Concerned When.'"

Ben rolls his eyes. "Good one, Dad."

My dad turns and whispers to me: "Did you think that was funny?"

I whisper back: "No."

"Huh," he mutters to himself. "But I know. Why should you tell your lame dad anything? Your childhood wasn't exactly filled with reasons to trust me."

"It's not about our childhood," Ben snaps. My father swallows his food, stung.

"What's your problem?" I demand.

"Nothing. Sorry." He softens. "It was just a party. It was fairly lame. There's nothing to tell."

"We met Kamal's girlfriend," I blurt out.

"Who, Phoebe?" Ben asks.

"Is that her name?" As if I could possibly forget even the tiniest of tiny details about her, let alone her name.

"She's not his girlfriend. I mean, he probably wishes she were, but they're just friends or whatever." I stuff my mouth with food to keep the smile from exploding across my face. They are not together.

"I always liked Kamal," my dad says. "Your mom thinks he's a spoiled—"

"*Un mequetrefe, bueno para nada,*" I interrupt.

"That's right." He laughs. "But I always liked him." A flash of silver like metal glinting in the sun. He's looking at me as if he knows the whole story, even the part that hasn't happened yet. No, he wasn't always around, he wasn't always nice, but when he looks at me like that, he sees a part of me that no one else can. And I love him for it.

"Dad, you're sweating," I say, noticing beads of moisture along his hairline.

"Hot stove." He wipes his face with his napkin as Ben's watch buzzes.

"It's Mom. She's asking if we saw the news?"

"There's a flu going around," I say. "They're warning everyone to be careful."

"And they're making it seem like the world is coming to an end, right?"

"Pretty much," I reply. Ben believes the media has only one goal: terrorize as many people as possible to drive up ratings and make money.

He pulls his phone out of his pocket. "LA, Seattle, Austin, Detroit, San Francisco, and New York." He looks up from his screen. "Seems like a lot of places."

"Fifty people have died." My father begins clearing the dishes.

"Forty-one," I correct him.

"I'm with you, Ben. I think it's mostly hype," my dad says.

Ben gets up and heads toward the stairs. "I'm telling Mom we're ordering HAZMAT suits on Amazon."

"She'll love that!" my dad calls back. I start loading the dishwasher, then catch him staring at Ben's empty seat.

"What?" I ask.

"Hard to believe how fast it goes. I can see him five years old sitting in that chair. I close my eyes for a second and he's going to college? Not possible."

I smile. "Now you're stuck with me."

"That's the good news," he says.

I go upstairs to my dad's bathroom looking for a thermometer. I take my temperature. Normal. I stare at my father's toothbrush by the sink. I picture the millions of microscopic germs swarming all over it. Gross. I look at my throat with a flashlight in the mirror. It seems fine. I don't look sick. I don't feel sick. I go to my room and lie down on my bed. My eyes drift shut.

They started to arrive, one by one, with their parents carrying gifts. Sarah, Morgan, Bridget, Lizzie, Missy, Molly, and Janine. It was August and we were out in the yard. There was lemonade on the table and little sandwiches. The raspberry bush was bursting with fruit. We made a game of shaking the pear tree's branches, unleashing a shower of small white petals. We spun around underneath, becoming covered in a kind of summer snow.

My mother had gone to the bakery. Even at eight years old I knew she had been gone too long. She came back looking flushed and flustered.

EMILY ZIFF GRIFFIN

My father couldn't seem to look her in the eye. Something had come up with work, she said. She'd had to take a call, she said. She was lying and I knew it. I sat with Janine at the table. I watched through a haze of brown as the other girls picked berries and my dad drank whiskey over ice. I wished they'd just go home. Janine put her hand on mine and gave it one short squeeze as the sky began to darken.

It was time for the cake. My mother brought it out proudly, lit with candles. Everyone sang. Then, the first few drops on my cheek and ear. They were heavy and wide—big splats of water. And then the lightning, followed by the unnerving boom of thunder that made us all jump. The rain came swiftly and we ran inside, the adults grabbing what they could and the girls shrieking gleefully with each explosion in the sky.

I watched the pear tree through the window, the branches and leaves shaking violently, its trunk still deeply rooted. My mother came over and stood next to me. She smoothed my hair. The soft, white wave of her scent swirled around me. I took it in, her smell and her touch. Then I turned and walked away.

Missy lives in a typical Brooklyn Heights brownstone with the kind of living room no one ever actually sits in. Except when there's a raging high school party happening, in which case every surface is covered in plastic cups and beer cans. I head immediately to the backyard to find the keg. My brother's friends Des and George are next in line.

"What's up, Luisa?" George asks, handing me a cup.

"Not much. What's up with you?"

"Chilling. Ben here?"

"I think he's coming later."

"Cool."

"Is Kamal here?" I ask. "Ben wanted me to let him know."

"Nah, he's not around tonight." My chest deflates. Des steps up to the keg and offers to fill my cup. The whoosh whoosh of the pump. We all watch the beer flow from the spigot. We have absolutely nothing else to say to each other.

I lift my foamy beer to meet their empty cups. "Cheers," I say like an idiot. I turn and head off into the garden. My brother's ex, Annalise, is holding court at the picnic table.

"Hey Lu." Her friends all turn and look at me. They have the guts to wear things like bright scarlet blazers and green floral dresses. Their skin drips with gold jewelry and their lips glisten with gloss. I feel flattened by their glow in my denim cut-offs and "Models Suck" T-shirt, which seemed cool when I left the house.

Annalise beams at me. "Is Ben coming out tonight?"

"Later, I think." I tap my foot. I wish they'd stop looking at me.

"Thanks, honey." She turns back to the table, taking the spotlight with her.

I find Janine sitting on a wooden tree swing. She's head-down with her phone and she looks pissed.

"What's wrong?" I ask. I sit and pick up an empty cup. "This yours?" She nods and I pour in half my beer.

"I didn't get it," she says. She swallows the whole cup in one gulp. "He said it was down to me and one other photographer, a guy of course. And they chose him."

"That blows."

She brightens slightly. "Whatever. Their loss, right?"

"One hundred percent," I tell her.

"I'm gonna have to go to Europe with my parents now."

"Oh, poor baby."

"I know. I know! I'm an asshole. But I was so psyched to be here this summer, alone, doing my thing. Working. And I know most people would kill to kick it in a Tuscan villa for two months, but like, how many pictures of laundry hanging from a rustic clothesline does the world need?"

I laugh. We swing back and forth. I sip my beer. "Thomas Bell told me my work was a waste of energy."

"Whoa," Janine mutters. "Did he really say that?"

"Yeah." I stare off into space. "So I guess I know how you feel."

"We are, like, total failures," Janine announces.

"Yup." I knock back the rest of my cup. "Washed up at sixteen."

"Washed up and out of beer," she adds. We can't help smiling.

We make our way back to the keg. We fill our cups and suddenly there's a horrible sound. Even though I feel pretty even, I see it for a split second before I hear it: red. I whip around. Clara Adams is kneeling on the deck. She's coughing her brains out and she sounds like she is dying.

Some other girls stand around her. No one moves or says a word. It's too intense. Then, my stomach rolls over on itself. Another flash of red light. I tap my foot to get a grip.

Janine drops to the floor next to Clara, brushing her hair off her face and patting her gently on the back.

"Hey," snaps Kelly Printz. "We're her friends. We'll help her."

"Seriously," adds Rose Gerson. She pushes Janine out of the way.

"Careful, Rose," whispers Madison Dewy as Janine stands up. "Didn't you see the news? That flu thing."

"Whatever," Rose replies. She rubs Clara's back. The coughing dies down. "Clara's not *sick*."

"Let's go," I say. I grab Janine and pull her into the house. I look back at the girls. A woozy Clara is trying to stand. Her friends offer her another drink.

Janine and I find a bathroom. We lock ourselves inside and she sits down to pee.

"I'm, like, not good enough to help them? What the fuck is that? None of them moved a muscle until I did."

"They suck," I say.

"And what flu? What are they talking about?" Janine looks at me in the mirror.

"There was some stuff on the news about a new flu. Like forty people died." A burst of red. "Clara was probably choking on her drink though. Just wash your hands, you'll be fine." Janine stands up, flushes, and gives her hands a rinse.

"Let's get out of here," she says, heading for the front door.

I stop in the den, looking for a pint of something we can take. I grab a bottle of whiskey, then stop. A familiar voice: "Hey you."

I freeze.

Alex Murphy is sitting against the open window swirling a rocks glass in one hand. A chill runs up my back.

We kissed last New Year's. We were at Shane Franklin's party, upstairs in his little sister's bedroom. Alex had never said two words to me and suddenly we're lying on a little girl's pink carpet making out. I kept one hand on the floor, my fingers moving slowly over every single loop of that rug's yarn. That was the only way I could handle how good his body felt on top of mine.

"What's up?" I say, not moving.

"Come here." He winks at me.

"Don't do that." I try not to smile, and fail.

He winks again. "Just come over here. Just for a minute." I look across Missy's den at him. His legs are spread wide. One arm is resting on a bent knee. He's as confident as anyone has ever been. "Just for a minute," he says again. Another shiver.

I put down the bottle. The sound of it hitting the bar, a tether to the ground as I start to float away.

I walk over to him. His breath is heavy. His stare doesn't break.

"Blonde, huh?" he whispers.

"Yup."

"It's hot." He reaches up and traces the neckline of my T-shirt with his fingers. My chest rises against his hand as I inhale. He presses his palm against me. My head whirls with golden light and we start kissing. Slow and sticky. The warm air bleeds through the open window with a low, heavy tone. I feel for something to grab besides him. Something steady, heavy.

He shifts onto his feet, lifting me up and swinging me to the arm of a couch. His full weight moves against me, the piece of furniture a counterforce. My hands feel for the fabric. Velvet, soft. I keep my mind there as best I can, but it starts to be too much. Plus, Janine is waiting.

"I can't," I say, pulling back.

"You said that last time," he whispers.

I smile. "Well. It's still true. I have to go."

"Tragic." The warmth of his voice burrows deep in my ear.

"Yes," I agree. He steps back and lets me pass. I pick up the bottle and walk out, counting my steps until I feel normal.

Janine is waiting on the stoop. She looks at my face. "Uh, what the fuck is up with you?"

"Sorry, I got held up for a minute."

"You look like you just swallowed a pocketful of M." We head down the steps and out into the quiet, cloudless night. "Did you? Swallow a pocketful of M?"

"I ran into Alex," I confess.

"Ah. So pretty much the same thing. And? How is he?"

"Hot," I tell her.

"He's so damn hot."

"So hot. So weird and so hot."

"So what, you, like, just boned him in the bathroom?"

"God. No. We just kissed a little. And then I left. Because my best friend was waiting for me."

"Mistake!" she yells, laughing. "Big mistake. Shoulda boned him in the bathroom!"

"Damn it, you are so right." I fake a smile as I worry that I'll never be able to handle anything more than thirty seconds of making out.

We head to the long promenade that faces New York Harbor. We find a bench hidden from the streetlights under the shadow of a tree. We open the whiskey. We sip. She takes out her tiny point-and-shoot camera.

"Oh Jesus, no," I say. I put my hands in front of my face.

"C'mon!" She starts snapping pics. "Drop your hands."

I look up at her. "You know a single image being a true record of anything is an impossible idea, right?"

Janine looks stricken. "Shit. Really? We better tell people. Maybe they can start, like, a camera buy-back program so everyone can get rid of these useless pieces of junk." She struggles to keep a straight face.

"You are the worst."

"If by the worst you mean the best." She fiddles with the settings on the camera.

"Don't you feel like sometimes we forget to have actual memories and just have photos instead?"

"Give me a sex face," she says.

"Oh. You're not interested in my brilliant insights. That's cool, whatever."

She looks up from the camera. "Art is not optional," she says. Her authority is like a face full of cold water. This is why I love her. "Sex face, please."

I give her the finger and sip from the bottle.

"Let's see what you looked like tonight with Alex."

"Shut up!"

"Or think about Kamal," she yells. Kamal. I had almost forgotten about him. But I'm fully drunk now, so I don't care. I don't feel.

"You are truly insane," I protest.

"Do it!" she cries, bringing her camera to eye level.

"Okay, okay," I say. I close my eyes and I think about Alex's hands on me. I think about Kamal's voice in my ear. I open my eyes with a start.

"Hot!" she squeals.

"I love you!" I yell.

"I love you too!" We collapse in a torrent of drunken giggles.

If I were going to look back and point to the last hours of my old life, when I was still my old self, it would be that night, laughing and posing for stupid pictures with Janine. Because by the next morning, nothing would ever be the same again.

CHAPTER 4

I lie in bed for a long time thinking about last night, about Alex sitting in that window, his hands on me. I think about Bell and where our meeting went wrong. How I can only go so far with people that matter before my senses make it impossible for me to focus or connect.

I think about what Dr. Steph will say when she gets back from vacation. How she'll tell me to be patient with myself. Patient and kind. "Would you judge a friend so harshly?" she'll say.

I look out at the big maple swaying in the sunlight. It's already afternoon. Eventually I get dressed. I follow the sound of the television blaring downstairs. Before I even hear what they're saying, I feel it. There's an energy in the air, a charge. It was like this on the morning of the Blackout Bombing.

I stop at the doorway of the living room. The reporter says they were off base about the number of flu victims. It's more like three thousand people dead, not forty-one. They say officials are scrambling to make sense of it.

My father notices me standing there.

"You should go back upstairs," he says. But the room is already starting to take on a dandelion hue. Before I can decide what to do, the news cuts to a clip of Bell speaking from his company's headquarters. His blue eyes coat my tongue with the taste of chocolate.

"The fact that the outbreak has gotten to this point without the public being informed, without any sort of protocol being put into place, just shows what so many of us have known since day one of her administration: Joan Cartwright lacks the leadership skills necessary to protect our national security." Even though he's talking about the president, I feel his attack like it's directed at me.

I look away as the newscaster returns. "That was tech tycoon Thomas Bell speaking from his California campus, where he says the world's top scientists and engineers are working around the clock to determine the cause and eventually develop a cure for ARNS."

"I hate to say it," my dad says. "But he's right. This is a big fuckup."

"Yeah," I mutter. I try to focus on the idea of the government making mistakes instead of three thousand people being dead.

"Which is not to say I want Thomas Bell to be our next president," he adds. Everyone expects Bell to run next year. And a lot of people think he can win.

My dad switches the TV to Front Line News. I take a seat next to him. He gives me a look.

"It's okay," I say. "I'm okay." Right now my imagination would be worse than whatever is actually going on.

On the screen, a cool-nerd interviewer is introducing a pudgy man known as Merz. Just Merz. Like Beyoncé. His face is flecked with acne scars. His voice is confident and clear and it makes my mouth pucker with the taste of sour apple.

"The government's response on this is like an elephant trying to dance *Swan Lake*. It's not pretty," Merz says. "Front Line has already activated its massive network all across the country to respond to ARNS."

A banner appears at the bottom of the screen: WWW.FRONTLINEARNS.COM.

"We are on the ground, we are on the streets, assessing what is needed and delivering it. Food, care, information, preventative supplies, we're doing it. The government is not. This is the Blackout Bombing all over again, and we will be the ones who make the difference in terms of saving lives and getting the country back on its feet when this is over."

The interviewer pauses for effect. "Will it be over? Seems unlike anything we've seen."

"Everything ends eventually," Merz replies.

The camera cuts back to a newsroom set. A young anchor stands in the center.

"That was Front Line representative Merz speaking from our headquarters in Brooklyn. We're going now to the streets of San Francisco, an area that has seen numerous cases of ARNS over the past twenty-four hours. Volunteer correspondent Trisha Huff is on the ground. Trisha?"

The screen cuts to a young black woman standing outside a grocery store describing, in her words, chaos. The camera shows empty shelves and long lines for food and water.

I stand up. "What do we do?" Flashes of yellow are coming one on top of another. I begin to pace.

"We wait and see," my dad says. I count my steps. "The most important thing is that we stay calm. We don't need to panic about food, so that's good." My mother put a serious stockpile of canned supplies in the basement after Blackout in case something like that ever happened again. "And really, this is what the news does. They scare everyone so we keep watching. I don't think it's as dire as they are making it seem."

"Okay," I say. I want to believe him.

"I left a message for your mother," he adds.

"Cool."

"You okay?" he asks.

I nod and go into the kitchen for coffee, then head back upstairs.

I get back into bed and Janine texts me: **U seeing this?** I write back yes. She writes: **Freaked.**

I press my hands against my hot mug and I hear Bell's voice: "Are you a problem solver?"

I go over to my desk and pull up the Front Line ARNS site. They've listed the places where people can go for supplies. They've listed the medical facilities that are receiving victims. And they've posted hundreds of video clips with real-time reports from all over the country.

I click on one from Elizabeth C. in Chicago. It opens with a girl sitting on the shore of Lake Michigan. The wind whips her long brown hair and empty sand stretches out behind her.

"I'm Elizabeth. I'm sixteen and my sister died today," she begins quietly. Tears fill her eyes. "She got sick three days ago. We took her to the hospital today, but it was too late. She was only nine. She liked tap dancing and soccer."

She looks out across the water and then back into the lens. "Her name was Catherine." She begins to sob. I look out the window and count the leaves on the maple. "I haven't cried until now," she continues. "I think my mom may have it too. Help us, please. Somebody please help us."

She clicks off. The video refreshes and begins to play again, as though Elizabeth C. is now trapped in this pleading loop.

I pause it. I put the link into LightYears and click *Mine*. The text cloud starts to build. Words bloom in front of me. *Horror. Pity. Compassion.* Thirty-four percent *Sad.* The abstract idea of what the words mean, and the numbers—they're like a shade blocking out the glare of the feelings themselves.

Wanna chat? The cloud is suddenly obscured by an x.chat window. The sender's handle, Theodore_Nam, glows on the screen in black boldface. It's a name I don't recognize.

Wrong number? I write.

Lu, you're no fun. A jolt of adrenaline. He knows my name.

Who are you?

A friend, he writes and then disappears, dissolving the chat.

I text Janine: *Was that u?*

She replies with a question mark. I look back at my computer.

I pull up Alex Murphy's profile page. There's a photo of him at the Egyptian temple Abu Simbel. He looks miniscule next to the soaring pharaoh statues that guard the entrance to the tomb. His face is inscrutable.

I open a message to him. My fingers hover over the keys. **I'm tons of fun**, I write. A second later, I erase it. I close his page. Elizabeth C.'s frozen face stares back at me, next to the completed LightYears analysis. Pervasive sentiment: Sixty-eight percent *Afraid*.

My grandfather is the only dead person I've ever seen up close. He was eighty-two and I was seven when he died of lung cancer. I remember his hands placed across his belly in the coffin, his thin gold wedding band glinting in the brown haze of my vision and how my mother cried in my father's arms. She kept saying it didn't look like him.

I look back at the tree. I stopped counting the leaves at forty-four. When they all fall off and die in winter, does the tree know they'll grow back in spring?

I go up to my father's bathroom and take my temperature again. Still normal.

"Hey," Ben says, ducking through the doorway.

I jump. "Jesus!"

He zeroes in on the thermometer. "You all right?"

"Yeah. Normal," I say. "Just checking, like as a precaution." I rinse it and put it back in the cabinet.

"Dad's down there, glued to the TV. I'm thinking of heading over to Front Line. Kamal says they need sleeping bags and tents and we have all that crap in the basement."

My legs tingle at Kamal's name. "They're saying three thousand people are dead."

"Yesterday it was forty-one; today it's three thousand. Tomorrow it will be back to ten."

"Yeah. Ten thousand," I say.

"They have to make it sound like the end of the world or else no one will watch."

"True. But what if it is the end of the world? And since when are you so eager to help the hippie communists?"

"Phoebe said they need stuff," he answers plainly, brushing back his eyebrows in the mirror.

"Oh, Phoebe said?" Now I get it.

His face flushes. "Phoebe, Kamal. Whatever. We have like twelve sleeping bags in the basement."

"Uh-huh." I walk out of the bathroom.

"What?" he snaps.

"Nothing. I'm just not sure it's safe to go out."

"Look, you're the math genius. There are nine million people in this city. Even if all three thousand people had been in New York, which they weren't, that's like what, .003 percent? It's more likely that we'd be killed in a car accident on the way over there or gunned down by a leprechaun riding a goat."

"A leprechaun riding a goat. Excellent."

"Don't you want to see what it's like out there, with everyone freaking?" he asks.

Not really. But I do want to see Kamal. "All right, fine. I'll go."

I follow Ben down the stairs.

"Have you ever heard the name Theodore Nam?" I ask.

"Don't think so. Why?"

"Doesn't matter."

The television is off. The door to my dad's music room is closed.

I hesitate. Toward the end, when his using was getting really bad, I would stand in the hall and listen to a strange snorting sound coming from the other side of that door. I realized a few years later it was my dad getting high. But even then, I knew it was something bad because I would hear it like the smell of vinegar. It would sting my whole face to stand there and listen to that sound.

To this day, I hate the smell of vinegar. And I hate that door.

Ben knocks gently.

"Come in," my dad calls. He's sitting at his piano with a sheet of music paper and a pencil.

"Front Line needs some extra camping supplies," Ben says. "So we're gonna drive over and give them some of our old gear. Cool?"

My dad looks up. "Mmm, I don't know. It's getting pretty weird out there."

"It's like a ten-minute drive," Ben argues. "Kamal's over there. Lots of people are there helping out. And we have all that stuff downstairs that could help people. We don't need it all."

"Did I really raise two do-gooders? Imagine that." He glances at me. "You okay to go out?" I nod. "Just straight there and back, yes? Nowhere else."

"For sure," Ben says.

"And don't take anything we might need."

Ben and I go down into the basement. The wall of shelves packed tight with gear oozes with the actual smell of bug spray and wood-fire ash. It rockets me back to our summer trips to Maine, to the top of Mount Katahdin at the head of the Appalachian Trail. We'd roast hot dogs and marshmallows in the fire, tell stories, wish on stars. In the morning, Mom would wake us before dawn so we could be the first people in North America to see the sun rise.

"We have seven sleeping bags and nine tents," Ben says. "Plus all this stuff." He starts digging through a shelf piled with camping stoves, dishes, headlamps, and climbing rope. "But they just said tents and bags. So we keep four of each?"

"Seems right. Why do they need this stuff anyway?" I ask.

"They're expecting a ton of new volunteers to show up at their tent cities, apparently."

We stuff everything into two big garbage bags, then load into the ten-year-old gas-guzzling station wagon that has seen us through so many trips home, so many arguments, so many good times and bad.

"This reminds me of Blackout," I say as we pull out onto the empty street. "When we drove around with Dad."

"Sort of. But that was fucking bizarre. New York with no lights is like another planet."

A wave of white from my mother's smell left behind on the seatbelt. "This is pretty bizarre. It's summer and there's no one on the street."

"Not no one. There's a guy walking his dog."

"Yeah. He's wearing a gas mask."

Ben shrugs. "I was hoping for more of a chaotic feeling. This is just, like, a Sunday morning vibe."

We arrive at the gates of the Brooklyn Navy Yard. A masked Front Line Peacekeeper steps forward holding a tablet. His hands are sheathed in black gloves and my eyes go straight to the gun on his hip.

Ben puts the window down.

"Good evening, sir. How can we help you?" The man's voice is firm.

"We're here to drop off a donation. To Phoebe Lowe."

The Peacekeeper taps his tablet. "Identification, please."

"So official," I whisper to Ben as I hand him my learner's permit.

"Hippies don't trust anyone," Ben jokes. The guard hands us face masks and gloves.

"Make a left at the stop sign and park in spot number twelve. You're going to building D-6, second floor. Put those on before entering the building."

The wrought-iron gates slowly hinge open. We drive through, park, and get out. I put on my mask and gloves. I feel ridiculous.

We unload the bags. I notice Kamal's black Tesla Model X parked two spots over. I glance at my reflection in the window. I sweep my hair off my forehead.

A large three-story building marked D-6 stands in front of us. Just behind it, Manhattan looms across the river. Sharp angles of steel and glass define the skyline—One World Trade Center at the center and a large waxing moon shining down. It bathes everything in silver light.

The buildings. The bridges. From dirt and grass, humans built this city, this civilization, this world full of people making decisions and asking questions, hurting each other, loving each other, laughing, sleeping, living and dying. But the moon, the sun, the earth itself—they don't depend on our existence. They are indifferent to our experience. I close my eyes.

What if when I open them, everything is gone?

We arrive at the door of D-6 as my watch trills with a call: my mother. I tap Decline and we go in.

People are everywhere, rushing, loading up supplies, carting pallets of water and boxes of food. They're talking on phones, typing on tablets. They are electrified by their urgent tasks. And they're all wearing the same black gloves and masks.

"Stairs?" Ben calls out to a guy in a Detroit Lions T-shirt. He barely stops to point us to the right. We make our way up to the second floor. Central air pumps in an arctic chill with a hum. There's a large room with about a hundred chairs arranged in a series of concentric circles. A small army of volunteers watches an orientation video on a multidirectional projection screen. Faceless in their masks, I wonder if some of them will be dead by next week.

Kamal appears with a rush of pine from behind a closed door. His thin gray T-shirt falls perfectly over those broad shoulders, its hem just grazing the top of his low-hanging black jeans. He even manages to make the face mask look good.

We follow him back into a hallway that runs along a glass-walled conference room. Phoebe and three men are inside talking. One of the men is Merz, the Front Line rep from TV. He's not particularly handsome, but he looks like the kind of guy who could talk you into anything. My gaze darts compulsively between him and Phoebe.

"It's the end of days," Kamal says.

"A bit much, don't you think?" Ben replies. "All this fuss?"

"They're pretty freaked. Sounds like it could take down several million people, and quite quickly." Three taps.

"Are you joining the cause?" Ben asks.

Kamal laughs. "Not officially. But I don't really have anywhere else to be. " His eye twitches. "And Phoebe is very persuasive."

"I bet," Ben says. Ugh. We all turn and look at her through the glass. She speaks with her salty eyes, with her body. I can't hear a word, but I feel myself agreeing with whatever she is saying.

"I have to admit though," Kamal says, "I'm scared."

A flash of yellow. "Me too," I say. Our eyes meet. His smell shoots through me quicker than my own pulse.

He grabs the bags from us. "Thanks for these."

I notice a screen inside the conference room. On it is the image of a young boy lying on the ground in the middle of a road. His wild eyes stare straight at the camera. My heart plummets into my stomach with more yellow, then red.

"What is that?" I murmur as Phoebe opens the door.

"Guys, hey. Could you help us with something?" she asks. "We'd like you to watch something and give us your opinion." We file in behind her and she taps her watch.

I eye the door, already wishing I could bolt. Instead, I steady myself against the large table in the center of the room.

The video of the boy starts to play from the beginning. He's walking down a suburban street. A Spider-Man backpack tugs on his shoulders. He's maybe seven or eight. There are birds chirping in the background.

He starts to cough. It's the same cough Clara Adams had at Missy's party. My stomach twists and my vision blurs red. Within seconds, he falls to the pavement. He wheezes. His tiny arms claw the air.

"He can't breathe," I blurt out. I dig my nails into the table and look away. Ben puts his hand on top of mine.

The gasping sound stops. I glance back at the screen. The boy isn't moving. His eyes are fixed open, his mouth agape. None of us says a word. Phoebe taps her watch again and the screen goes dark.

"So," Phoebe begins gently, "the question we're dealing with is whether we release this."

"Are you joking?" Ben charges. "Absolutely not. How is that even a question?"

"People need to see what's happening. This is awful, true, but if this is what we're dealing with, the world needs to know," Phoebe counters.

"It will create hysteria. And who's the asshole who filmed it and didn't help him, by the way?" Ben argues.

"ARNS is creating the hysteria," she says evenly. "The video will save lives by forcing people to take it seriously. And we don't know who shot it; it was sent to me by some untraceable deep web handle. But there was nothing he or she could've done to save this boy and they had to make the tough call to capture something that can help others. If we put it on the air."

"What about his parents?" Kamal asks with a shaky voice.

Merz stands up. "Exactly. We don't know where this came from, if it's real, who this boy is. It's not good journalism in the traditional sense and there could be a backlash." He pauses and turns to me.

"What do you think?" I inhale, looking at the black screen, certain I can make out the ghosted image of the dead boy. I hold the table.

"I think it's horrible. But it's not the first time the world has seen someone die on camera."

"This is a child," Ben mutters.

"But if it can save a life now," I continue, "then maybe he didn't die for nothing."

Phoebe nods. "Smart girl. Look, Merz, these are extraordinary circumstances. I don't think the usual rules of ethical journalism apply."

He narrows his eyes. "Okay," he says. "Push it out for a vote and have it prepped for the ten thirty broadcast in case it passes." The other two guys nod and rush out. "I hope this doesn't bite us in the ass," Merz adds, following them.

Ben shakes his head. "This is not right."

"It's up to the Front Line stakeholders to vote now," Phoebe replies. "It's not just my decision. But I do appreciate your conviction."

"And I appreciate yours, even if you're wrong," Ben says. A flicker of something passes between them. It's like the force of their opposing views combusts into a single charge moving from one to the other and back again before burning out like a dead shooting star.

"I have to get back to work," she says. "Good luck, and thank you for your input. Seriously. It means a lot." She opens the door and struts away like a plane taking off. I want to hate her for being all the things I worry I'm not, but I can't. She's too nice and too smart.

In the hall, a curvy woman with two long braids comes by with a tray of granola bars. Kamal grabs one. "I always imagined my last meal would be a cheeseburger. But I guess this'll do."

"Uh, pretty grim to be imagining your last meal," I tease.

"Also, don't bury me," he says.

"I know, 'cause what if you're actually still alive?"

"Exactly."

"Totally." We stand there like idiots.

"Can we go now?" interrupts Ben.

"We're gonna see each other again, right?" Kamal asks.

"No doubt," Ben replies. "This whole thing will blow over. Trust me." Kamal's eyes settle on me like the double barrel of a shotgun. I freeze.

"Be safe," he says.

"I will."

"I'm serious."

"I know," I say, still immobilized.

"Let's go." Ben heads for the stairs and I force my legs to follow him. We get back in the car and I enter ARNS into my database of sensations. *Touch: rolling stomach. Sight: red light.* Ben pulls off his mask and gloves. I don't.

I watch the old industrial buildings along Flushing Avenue flicker by as we drive. The darkness makes them look like melting candles dripping into the street.

"That Phoebe is . . . I don't even know what to call it," my brother says as we shoot up Washington. "Maddening," he adds.

"I like her," I say. We drive in silence, block after deserted block. "I can't get that boy's face out of my head," I mutter after a while.

"You shouldn't have encouraged them to use it. It's irresponsible and it's going to needlessly torment his family and everyone who sees it. People don't need help panicking; the news is already doing a great job of making sure they do." He's probably right.

I pull up the Front Line ARNS site on my phone. They haven't put it up yet. Maybe it won't pass the vote. I scroll through the thousands of videos, all the faces and titles, then re-sort the pages by number of views.

The most popular by a lot is called "Thorny Rose" by someone named Evans B. in Redlands, California. I click on it and an older woman springs into frame. Her eyes are haunting and translucent like a wolf's. Her skin is paper-white. She's so close, I can see the fine hairs inside her nose. I could swear I've seen her somewhere before.

"This is the information *they* don't want you to have," she says, conspiring with the camera. Her eyes are manic, but her voice has the steady authority of a teacher and it smells faintly like wood-fire. "The more people die, the better. That's what they think. They act confounded, but it's basic. It's simple science. And they don't want you to find that out." She holds up a hospital ID bracelet. "Two days ago, I was locked up like a monkey. They left me for dead. Then I got free and I cured myself. You won't see me on the news, but this is the truth. I can help you."

"What the fuck is that?" Ben barks. "Some crackpot?"

"Yeah, I guess." I shuttle back and freeze on the bracelet. It's got her name underneath the Redlands Community Hospital insignia, the date—day before yesterday. And four letters printed on the corner: A.R.N.S.

We stop at a red light and I look up. The electric orb glows intensely overhead, as though it is calling, stop: danger, do not pass.

It unsettles me, that red. Crimson is now a synonym for ARNS. The light turns green and Ben hesitates.

"Go," I snap.

"Dude. Chill," he replies.

"Sorry."

We pull up to our house. The parking spot we left earlier is still empty. I turn so I can see Ben's eyes. "Do you think we're all going to die?" I ask. He backs the car into place.

"I fucking hope not," he snorts. We go inside. My dad is asleep on the couch with the television on. I watch him. One arm is slung up over his head like a shield. He reminds me of the images from history class of the ancient Romans fossilized by lava from Mount Vesuvius—anguish frozen on their faces for eternity.

I listen to his shallow breath. How did he get here, to this moment, asleep on a couch in an old house in Brooklyn with his daughter staring down at him? My parents' lives are like a mystery novel that's missing half the pages.

I go into the kitchen and pull the tinfoil off the banana bread. I cut a hunk and grab a small bowl of pasta from the fridge.

I pass by my dad's music room. I turn back and linger in the doorway. He left the light on over the piano. I go in. I look at the sheet of music paper he was holding earlier. It was nearly blank then. Now it's filled with notes—his feelings translated into sounds by a language I can't read.

I go up to my room. I pull up FLN on my computer. The anchor is just introducing the video of the boy. The vote was a yes.

I turn off the sound and look away while I wait for the comments to appear. The screen lights up within seconds. Already thousands of people are weighing in.

I open LightYears and put the link to the video into the search bar. I watch. The response morphs along an undulating wave of popular opinion. There's a crest as people question its origins. Who is this boy? Where did this come from? Then the collective view shifts: the hashtag *hoax* shoots to dominance, pushing *Disbelief* forward in the text cloud. The comments are all theories of a government conspiracy. They think the video's a fake.

But then, the hashtag *hisnameishugo* emerges. It steadily climbs toward a peak as somewhere, somehow the boy's identity is revealed. The number of comments and posts grows from tens of thousands to millions. The video is becoming the most widely shared piece of content on the Internet.

The boy was from a small town in Colorado; he had been walking home from the bus stop when he fell ill; he was found dead an hour later by a neighbor—all the details come to light and the curve shifts in real time as the world expresses its feelings.

Different descriptors occupy the field of "pervasive sentiment" at different points until one word comes to represent the most widely felt emotion: *Empathy*. LightYears characterizes 33 percent of people's posts as empathic. The next closest sentiment is *Anger* at 24 percent. Then *Sadness*, *Disbelief*, and *Fear*.

I look at Hugo's face, then back at my text cloud. So people care? So what? The usual comfort I feel from the words on the screen eludes me. Instead, the room seems to darken. My stomach aches. I crawl toward my bed under the weight of an invisible pressure.

Maybe Bell was right. Maybe this thing I built actually has no value.

I text Janine: **U up?**

She replies: **Y.**

U OK? I ask.

Y. Sad. Did u see Hugo vid?

The worst. Meet tmrw? Bike the bridge? I write, buoyed slightly by the thought of seeing her. There's a long pause.

OK. Meet at Jane's at 10?

Y. C U then, I write. I bury myself under my sheets. My watch buzzes with the voicemail from my mom I'd forgotten to listen to. I press play.

"*Hola, cariño.* I spoke to your dad. I'm fine. Let's talk tomorrow. *Cuídate,* okay?" she pauses and then says, her voice trembling slightly, "*Te quiero,* Luisa." I can't remember the last time she said my name, or that she loved me.

"*Yo también, mama,*" I whisper to myself. And in this moment I do love her. I love her and want her to wrap me up and carry me away in her green dress.

CHAPTER 5

Holy fucking shit. I wake up and there's an e-mail from Joe.

Dear Luisa,

It is with great pleasure that I write to inform you that you have been chosen for the Avarshina Fellowship. Please do not share this news publicly (social media, etc.). Details will follow in the coming weeks.

Congratulations,
Joe

I am in shock. I am in literal disbelief. I read the e-mail over and over. Joy pulses through me in orange waves. I dash out into the hall-way looking for someone to tell. Janine is going to lose her mind. And then I freeze. My mother. The thought of her is like a boot in my gut.

I go downstairs anyway. The living room is empty and the TV's on. They're reporting cases in Mexico, France, China, Germany, and Japan and the current death toll is unknown.

The door to my dad's music room is closed again. I pause outside and listen. The piano booms through a series of slow, deep chords. They vibrate silver and caramel brown and they are so beautiful it almost hurts.

I exhale a deep breath and walk away. It will be my secret for now. Mine and Janine's. I will enjoy it for as long as I can.

I put the gloves and mask I got at Front Line in my pocket and text my dad saying that I'm going out. I hop on my bike. I squint at the daggers of sunlight bouncing off parked cars. I forgot my shades, but I'm too excited to go back.

The streets are less deserted than they were last night, but everyone is wearing some kind of protection—a mask, a scarf. They stare at me as I ride past barefaced. I stop and put on my mask.

I get to Jane's Carousel by the river just before ten. It's closed. No sign of Janine, so I walk around to the side. I peer through the glass at the horses. I envision them rising and falling as they whirl around, happy children on their backs, tugging at the reins. I conjure the mechanical organ's music—the walloping thump of the bass drum and the crash of cymbals. Boom! I jump back, startled by this imaginary sound.

Janine rides up in a mask. I have to remind myself not to give her a hug.

"You are not going to believe what I'm about to tell you." I can hardly contain myself. She stares hard at me. Her eyes are hollow. I feel a tug inside my belly. "Wait," I say. "What's going on with you?"

"I'm not feeling well," she says softly.

A bolt of red. "What do you mean?"

"You know what I mean," she replies. The tugging is more like a twisting now. I grip my handlebars. I study the skin around the sides of her mask, like it will tell me what's true.

"Wait, wait." That's the only word I can find.

"Let's just ride. Please," she whispers. She starts off and I follow.

I press my feet to the pedals and my mind spins with the whizzing of the wheels against the air. I gasp for breath in between bursts of red light. Is this really happening?

I try to form thoughts, to grab on to thoughts that will anchor my heart as it rises into my throat. But I just keep hearing the word *wait* and feeling like I'm going to float away.

We ride up the ramp onto the Brooklyn Bridge. It's a steady climb to the first granite tower. We've done it a thousand times. I push through, counting my strokes. I reach the crest and look back. Janine is barely halfway. I ride down to meet her.

"Stay back," she warns. I freeze. It's so confusing. The more I try to understand it, the more unreal it becomes.

"This can't be happening," I mumble as I tap my foot on the ground.

She notices. "Are you freaking out? I'm sorry."

"Jesus," I bark. "Don't worry about me." Saying that helps a little—whatever I may be feeling is nothing compared to what's going on with her.

"I shouldn't have come, but I had to see you," she says. I eye the river below. The swift current makes the bridge seem to sway. "And I had to bike the bridge one last time."

"Don't say 'last.'" My voice cracks with desperation and her eyes crinkle into a smile. A beam of silver light like sun breaking through clouds. I love her.

Then suddenly, she falls to the ground coughing. She rips off her mask. Her bike tips and my vision blurs red.

"Fuck," she says after a minute.

"We should go," I say, looking back at the river, hoping the current's rhythm will settle my churning stomach. "You need to rest."

She stands up slowly.

"You okay to ride?" I have no idea what I'll do if she isn't.

She flashes a wicked grin. "It's all downhill from here." She puts her mask back on, picks up her bike, and starts pedaling down the path. I pull the gloves out of my pocket. My hands are shaking, but I put them on and ride. Janine's long black hair flows behind her like a waving flag. I look down and count each time my knees straighten and bend.

We come off the bridge and turn onto Tillary Street.

"Let's go to the park," she calls from up ahead.

I pull up next to her. "I don't think that's a good idea."

"I know. But let's do it anyway. Unless . . . you shouldn't be around me."

I adjust my mask. "I'll be fine." I want this to be true more than I believe it is.

We ride to the park where we used to go as kids. We hop on a pair of swings. We pump our legs. Quickly we are flying above the bushes, glimpsing the Statue of Liberty in the distance. I'm still counting—each arc forward and back again as red, yellow, and brown swirl around me.

"When did it start?" I ask.

"Yesterday. I woke up and I just didn't feel right. You know when you're about to get sick and you have that thing in your throat? I started thinking about Clara and her coughing on me. I started to freak. So I went online to try and find out what the chances were I could've gotten it, you know, just from touching someone. And that just freaked me out more." She coughs. My stomach flips. "There were all these stories of people and how they got it and people who think they have it and I was just bugging out. And that Hugo kid. That just fucking killed me." She wipes her dripping nose on her sleeve. "I read that if you come into direct physical contact with someone who's infected, you have a ninety-five percent chance of getting it."

I squeeze the swing's chains, hard. "Where did you read that?"

"I don't know. I must've read a thousand posts and articles."

"Why didn't you tell me?"

"I guess I didn't want to scare you. By last night I started feeling really shitty and by this morning, I just knew."

"They don't know that much about it yet," I tell her, looking for a loophole, a way out. "Maybe you'll be fine. I saw a video," I say. "Some woman in California saying she had cured herself."

Janine lets her swing slow to a stop. "There are hundreds of people saying they have cures. None of it's real." She stands and braces against the chain. "I should get home. My parents don't know I'm gone." We avoid looking at each other.

"I'll ride with you," I mumble. I can't fathom saying good-bye yet. Or ever.

"Okay." Her voice pulls our years of friendship around us like a blanket.

We start to ride. There's a rattle underneath her breath. I whistle a steady note to drown it out.

"Wait, you were going to tell me something," she says.

I stop whistling and pump the brakes a little. "It hardly seems to matter now. But . . . I got it," I say. "The Fellowship."

"Oh my god."

"Yeah. I had to read the e-mail, like, ten times to believe it. I still don't believe it actually."

"I believe it."

"I really thought he hated me."

"You always think that about people. And you're always wrong." I smile. Maybe I *do* do that. "It makes me want to cry I'm so fucking happy for you," she says.

"You're the only person I couldn't wait to tell." A swell of silver as we come out of the park and onto Atlantic Avenue.

There's an NYPD Emergency Services truck parked by the curb. Two officers in protective suits stand in front of it. We turn to avoid them, but the second we do, one of them calls out.

"Hold it there!"

We slow to a stop. "Shit," I whisper.

"Dismount your bikes, now! You shouldn't be in the park," he yells.

"It's public property," Janine yells back as the officer approaches us.

He looks carefully at Janine's face. "Miss, are you sick?"

"No. I've got a wicked hangover. I was up all night doing blow and binge drinking with my boyfriend." Before the cop can say a word, Janine's body erupts in convulsive coughs. She pulls the mask off and drops it as she falls to her knees, vomiting.

I drop my bike to the ground. "Janine!"

The cop steps back and reaches for his walkie. Janine crumples into a pile of her own puke.

I look past her as the wind catches her mask and time slows down. I watch the thin paper shell skitter across the pavement. It seems to be taking everything I care about with it.

"You guys are wearing suits," I shout. "Help her!"

"We are not authorized to touch the specimen," the second cop says flatly from ten paces away.

"'The specimen?' What the fuck are you talking about? She's my friend." I kneel down, still at a distance.

Janine tries to climb to her feet, but she just slides back down. My stomach wrenches.

"Janine, it's me. You're okay. Just breathe."

The scream of an approaching siren.

My eyes meet hers. "What's happening?" she whispers to me. "I can't feel my feet."

"Just breathe," I say again. She looks up at me like a child. "Help is coming," I say, my own breath shallow as I press my hands against the pavement.

The ambulance arrives and two EMTs in full HAZMAT suits descend on us.

"Step back," one barks. They lift Janine onto a gurney. They shoot her up with something.

"What are you doing?" I yell.

Janine looks over at me. "Fall in love for me, okay? Fall in love and tell me all about it." Her eyes roll back in her head. Seconds later, she's inside the ambulance. I lunge toward the door.

"Sorry, no." The EMT blocks my path.

A second ambulance pulls up. "Where are you taking her?"

"Brooklyn Hospital Center. You'll be quarantined and observed," he replies.

"Me? I'm not sick."

"You will need to be evaluated. That's the protocol." He slams the doors in my face and they drive away.

The paramedics from the second ambulance jump out, grab me, and shove me inside.

"I'm not sick!" I protest. They say nothing.

I watch through the rear windows as the scene recedes. The shiny steel frames of our discarded bikes shine in the sun like scrap metal carcasses. I sit stone-faced, the initial flood of horror evaporating into an icy numbness. I close my eyes, count the tapping of my feet, and drift.

Next thing I know we're outside the hospital. A long line of cars and emergency vehicles snakes along the front of the building. I'm brought in on a gurney to the special ARNS triage area. My hands and forearms are scrubbed down by nurses in surgical gowns, masks, caps, and gloves. My mask and black gloves are replaced with a new set of clear latex gloves and a mint-green surgical mask and gown.

"Where's my friend?" I ask a passing nurse. "Her name is Janine, long dark hair. She was right ahead of me."

"Just relax," she replies through her mask.

"I'm perfectly relaxed. I just want to know where she is."

"Shhh, honey" is all she says.

I'm wheeled into a row of gurneys. I scan each face. My stomach churns and the room turns reddish. No sign of Janine.

I take out my phone. I look back at our texts from the night before. They're so ordinary. I keep scrolling back. Our whole friendship is right here. I place my hands down and feel the bed sheet. I look at my knees, my scar. **I love u**, I write. Send.

I check to make sure Joe's e-mail is still there, still real. I imagine that apartment again. Simple and spare. Bright. All mine. How will I convince my mother?

A cry from the next bed. I feel it like an electric shock across my chest. She's about my mom's age, with blond hair and amber eyes. She pulls a blanket off her torso. She's covered in blood. I look away. I tap the gurney railing with my foot and close my eyes.

"My IV," I hear her say. I glance back at her. A needle is dangling from her arm by a piece of tape. It's dripping blood.

"She's bleeding!" I yell to anyone who might hear me.

"It's the bag," the woman says. She nods toward a bag of blood hanging from a portable stand. She's not bleeding. It's a transfusion bag that is leaking. A nurse rushes over to take care of it as I turn my back. I disappear into blackness.

"Luisa?"

I startle awake. "Yes?" I mumble. A nurse named Starr is standing next to me. Several hours have passed.

"I'm here to ask some questions and get some stats, okay?" I nod. She attaches a device to my index finger. It beeps as I tell her that my grandfather died of lung cancer and my uncle has diabetes but I'm not sure what type. She puts a blood pressure cuff on my arm and a thermometer under my tongue. I look over at the next bed. It's empty now and the sheets are a clean, crisp white.

"Normal," she says, removing the cuff and checking my temp. She plants a small yellow flag on the end of my gurney.

"What's that for?" I ask.

"Low risk." She wheels me through a packed hallway. There are flags on all the other beds—some red, some yellow. Doctors with three-day beards and mascara caked around their eyes rush by yelling orders. But Starr takes her time getting me through. She brings me into a private room.

"You'll be isolated in here for the next six hours and if there are no symptoms, you'll be released," she says.

"What about my friend? Janine Stevens. She collapsed and they brought her here right before they took me. Could you check on her?"

"I'll try." She grabs the tablet from the compartment at the foot of the bed and begins typing.

"Do a lot of people have it in New York?" I ask.

"A lot of people will take any excuse to go to the emergency room," she answers without looking up.

"You've been doing this a long time?"

"Too long." She puts the tablet back. "I'm supposed to retire this year. But yes, New York has the most cases so far. You comfortable?" she asks. I nod. "Doctor will be around soon to check you."

"Do I need to be in this bed? I'm not sick."

"I know, baby. But right now we're keeping everyone in beds. It's how we keep track of you." She motions to the tablet.

I look down at my watch. No response from Janine. I focus on the treetops out the window. A gust of wind blows them from side to side. I can almost hear the whisper of the leaves. It reminds me of my father's smile.

Shit.

He has no idea where I am.

A doctor wearing a scrub mask, gown, cap, goggles, and gloves arrives. He wears a black mesh bag across his body.

He pulls out the tablet. "I'm Dr. Jamison." His bright eyes crinkle around the edges. "Any fever, cough, aches, runny nose? Anything like that?"

"No."

"And you were brought in with a friend who was ill?"

The word *friend* flashes brown and plants a lump in my throat. "Yes, but I haven't touched her since—"

"Since when?" he cuts me off.

"I don't know. Days ago at least? I definitely didn't touch her today or since she got sick."

"You're sure about that?" I press my feet against the rail so I can concentrate. The carousel, the bikes, the bridge, the park. I try to replay it all like it happened to someone else.

"I'm sure," I say. He types notes on the tablet.

"What happened to her? To my friend?" My voice is quieter than I expect. Maybe only part of me wants the answer.

"I can't tell you that." A tear escapes the edge of my eyelid. I wipe it away quickly and put my attention back on the rail. "I'm sorry. I am only assigned to triage for low risk. I would like to keep you for observation until tomorrow, but we don't have the space, so after six hours, if you're asymptomatic, we'll release you to your—" he looks back at the tablet. "Father."

"You called my father?"

"You're a minor. A parent has to be notified. After you're discharged, if you experience any flu-like symptoms, go to the nearest emergency room or call 911. It's best to wear protection at all times." He pulls an extra mask and pair of gloves from his bag. "Good luck, Miss." And he's gone.

I lie back and look at the clock.

Sabrina was two years older. She had a gravelly voice and a high pony-tail. Her eyes were ringed with black liner. Always. I inched past her on the bus. I wanted her to notice me. And was also scared she would. I sat down. She yelled my name and hurled a pair of goggles at my face. I caught them. Did she see me flinch? She turned back toward Kathryn McDonald, who smoked cigarettes and sometimes brought a flask of vodka to school.

The bus trudged up the Westside Highway. I closed my eyes and the hum of its tired engine mingled with the sound of my breath until it drowned out the chatter of the other girls' gossip. Would he come? The question asked itself again and again.

Through the wrought-iron doors of their school. Down the mahog-any halls, past the dreary oil paintings and vacant classrooms. The smell of chlorine grew with each step. I changed quickly into my suit and wrapped my long hair inside my cap. My legs were strong beneath me as I headed past the competition in their emerald green, a crowd of little grasshoppers.

Would he be there?

The stands were filling up. We took our place on the benches. I sat with earphones in my ears and watched the door, waiting for the 800-meter free. Sabrina swam a personal best that day. I remember the heaviness of her teenage body as she climbed out of the pool. It made me feel like a child.

I was up. I stripped off my warm-ups and stretched my arms overhead. I placed my feet on the blocks. My toes gripped the edge. Coach nodded at me and I bent forward. In that moment, I wasn't nervous. I wasn't anything. I was just ready.

And then there he was, my dad, upside down in my view, with sunglasses on, unsteady on his feet. He was drunk. The anger rising up in me, blinding my view with waves of purple. I looked back at the still lane stretching out in front of me. I closed my eyes and waited for the horn to sound and the water to wash away the sting.

A nurse comes in, tall and dark-haired with a tattoo of a heart on her temple.

"I'm Joanne," she says. "How are you feeling?"

"I'm fine," I answer. "Where's Starr?"

"She's gone. New shift."

"She was supposed to look for my friend."

She doesn't hear me or doesn't care. "Open your mouth," she says. She gazes at my throat with a penlight. She takes my temperature again. "You look fine," she pronounces. "Your father is waiting for you."

She pulls my gown off and throws it into a biohazard bin. She pats my knee and opens the door. Sounds from the hall bleed in— the tinny warbling of the PA, the moaning of the sick, the beeping machines keeping track of heartbeats and breathing for the dying.

"Take care, sweetie," she says and disappears into the noise.

I follow the exit signs to the lobby. My father is standing there, right in the center—a point of stillness amid chaos, a buoy in the middle of a swaying sea.

CHAPTER 6

"Janine," I start to say. He pulls me to his chest and wraps his arms around me. "They came and took her. They just took her and drove away." I look up at him. A swirl of different colors and a surge of energy up the center of my body.

I don't let myself cry because what if I can't ever stop?

"She couldn't feel her feet," I whisper.

My dad pulls down my mask and grabs my face. "Are you all right?" His voice is urgent. It focuses me. I feel the roughness of his hands against my cheeks, but panic leaps into my throat. He's not wearing a mask.

"Don't touch me." I pull away.

"Are you all right?" His voice trembles. "They wouldn't tell me on the phone."

"I don't know. I think so. They said I'm fine."

"They did?"

I nod. "They said I should go home."

His expression softens. "Okay, lamb. It's going to be okay."

I relax into his arm around my shoulder as we walk. His hand presses against the bar on the heavy revolving door. A *whoosh* as it moves. Force equals mass times acceleration. One of physics's simplest and most fundamental formulas, right there in action. The mass of my father's hand, its flesh, blood, and bone; the acceleration generated by an impulse in his brain that says *push*, carried out by motor neurons springing into action, by his weight shifting forward and connecting with the door. *Whoosh.* The mind creating an effect on the physical world.

Outside in the heat, I realize I'm still holding the extra mask and gloves Dr. Jamison gave me.

"Here," I say. My dad puts them on.

We walk two blocks to our car. I get in. Relief settles over me as we seal ourselves in and the world out. He starts the engine. The vents blast us with warm air that quickly turns cold.

The radio blares another news report. Military-controlled quarantines are being set up outside New York City and San Francisco to deal with the hospital overflow. They describe conditions as "grim." They say it won't be long before they run out of space.

I turn down the radio until it becomes a blur of background noise. I lean my head against the window.

"What's that?" my dad asks.

"What?" I reply.

"I thought you said something."

"No. I didn't." We pull out into an empty street. "You remember that story you used to tell us, that summer we spent at the beach?"

"'The Night Shadow'?"

"Yeah. 'The Night Shadow.'" I silently note the numbers on the buildings as they pass. "Tell it to me."

"A small boy and his father ride on horseback through the woods. The boy keeps insisting there's something chasing them, but the father tells him it's nothing. On and on they ride, the boy growing more and more upset. When they arrive home, the boy is dead. There was something there, but no one could see it except the child." He pauses. "What about it?"

"I don't know," I say. "I was just thinking about it. It always scared the shit out of me."

"You know, you shouldn't have gone out."

I close my eyes. "I know; I'm sorry. I didn't know she was sick."

"Look, it's my fault. Fifteen thousand people have died. I should've made it clear you were not to leave the house."

"Fifteen thousand? I thought it was three."

"It's up to fifteen now. Maybe more."

"Jesus." I open my eyes as we pass an enormous truck emblazoned with the Front Line logo. It's parked at an intersection and three lanky young dudes are passing out emergency supplies to a long line. Everyone's wearing masks.

"Promise me you won't go out again," my dad says sternly.

"I won't. Promise me you won't tell Mom."

"I won't." The sun bounces off the parked cars as we drive up Lafayette Avenue. The murmur of the radio fills in our silence.

EMILY ZIFF GRIFFIN

My mother. I hardly ever see her, but she never leaves my mind for long.

"His name is Dan," she said as we walked up Central Park West, the smell of the horse-drawn carriages like a tickle in the back of my throat. "He's kind, intelligent, vulnerable."

"What does 'vulnerable' mean?" I asked.

"He's not afraid to show his feelings." We turned the corner onto 81st Street on our way to the Planetarium. The wind kicked up a pile of autumn leaves and the massive jewel box that houses the scale model of our solar system came into view. My mom clasped my hand in hers. My brother was two steps behind. And there he was: Dan, with his coffee-colored hair and thick, round glasses. I instantly wanted him to like me.

"This is Luisa," my mother said, a nervous edge in her voice. "We call her Lu."

I smiled and put my right hand forward. "How do you do?"

"She's adorable," Dan said, looking at my mom like they were alone.

"And this is Ben." Ben's eyes were fixed on the hulking model of the sun rising eighty feet over our heads. He looked like he was hoping it might open up and swallow him.

"Hey Ben." Dan effortlessly matched Ben's cool exterior.

"Hey," Ben muttered. We walked up from the sun along the Cosmic Pathway. From the Big Bang, past the formation of the Milky Way, the sun and the planets, first life on earth, the dinosaurs, and on and on over thirteen billion years, to the miniscule blip that comprises the existence of humans—depicted as the thickness of one human hair. Millions of years with each step up the ramp and I had that feeling like after a

dream where everything—life, death, the biggest mysteries and questions of them all—seems to come into focus. It all made sense, and then it was gone again.

We measured our weight on scales calibrated to reflect the surface gravity of various planets. We watched a film about dark matter, the invisible stuff that makes up most of the known universe. We ate popcorn and ice cream in the cafeteria. And then we said good-bye to Dan and got on the subway.

We sat in an empty car, my mother's arms around us. "I like him," Ben said.

"I do too, very much," my mom replied, squeezing us close as the train rocked us to near sleep on the long ride home.

I saw Dan only once more. My father was away performing in a concert. I heard them downstairs after I was supposed to be asleep. In the morning, I saw my mom kissing him in the living room. Her legs were bare under an oversized T-shirt and her hair was wild like a lion's mane. Dan's eyes caught mine as I stood in the doorway, unnoticed by my mother. I turned and went back up to my room, embarrassed.

"I have something else to tell you," I say.

He shifts in his seat. "Okay?"

"I got an e-mail this morning. From that guy Joe. Bell wants me for the Fellowship." I look at him.

"Wow," he says. "Wow." I watch his Adam's apple twitch as he swallows. "What did you tell them?"

"I didn't tell them anything yet." He doesn't respond. "Hello?"

"Yeah, yes. Look, this is amazing, Lu. I am incredibly proud of you. I just, I'm not sure what to do."

"Because of Mom."

"For one thing, yes."

"Do you agree with her? Because it's honestly bullshit of you guys to let me put in all that work if you never had any intention of letting me do it."

"I had every intention of letting you do it." His words boom through the car in a burst of orange. A surprise. "I know what it means to be chosen for this. You're nearly seventeen. And I've seen plenty of seventeen-year-olds, not to mention I was one once. You're completely capable of being on your own. I know that. But your mother has a strong opinion about this."

"Why does she get a say about anything? She's the one who left. Doesn't that mean her opinion no longer counts?" Her scent pulses white off my seat belt. I dig my thumbnail into the handle on the door.

"She's your mother. Her opinion will never not count."

"She doesn't really feel like what a mother is supposed to be."

"I'm not sure any mother does, especially at your age. But she obviously cares about you very, very much."

"Dad, I know it's easier for you to think that, but you really have no idea."

"What's that supposed to mean?"

"Sorry to be blunt, but there was a long time when you weren't exactly paying attention. I actually thought it was your fault she was like that. I used to wish she'd just kick you out." I don't have the guts to say what it really was: that sometimes I wished he would drink himself to death.

"I used to wish that too. But then I might have tried to get clean at the wrong time for the wrong reasons. I might have failed and never tried again. I'm glad for every shitty moment of my life because all of that has allowed me to be here to live another day. That's not promised to any of us." I dig my nail in deeper, then look at the mark it's left behind. "But you're right," he continues. "It is my fault she's like that. That she became that way. And that breaks my fucking heart. Every day."

"I'm sorry," I say. "I'm being an asshole."

"You're being honest about how you feel. And you're being an asshole." His eyes crinkle in a smile. "As for your mom, she's angry at me, not you. Don't forget that."

"So what do we do? About the Fellowship?"

"I don't know. But we'll figure it out."

I stare out the window.

"And know that I'm on your side," he says.

It's nearly dusk when we arrive home. The streets are eerie and quiet and I can't get inside fast enough.

Ben comes tumbling down the stairs. "Dude, you okay?"

"Janine collapsed," I tell him. "They took us to the hospital."

"Shit. Is she all right?"

"No. She's not." I start climbing the stairs.

"Are you all right?"

I turn and look back at him. "I don't know. I really don't."

"Ben," my dad barks. "You need gloves and a mask."

"I've decided I'm immune."

"This isn't a joke," he says.

"I know, but—"

"Shut up, Ben!" I freeze. That sharp tone. That rush to anger. That was him all the time before he got sober. "I'm sorry," he says. "I didn't mean to snap. I'm just—I want to make sure you're both safe."

"Okay, fine," Ben mumbles. "I'll find something in the basement." He turns back to me. "What do you mean you don't know if you're all right?"

"I mean I think my best friend might be dead and so I don't know if I'm actually okay or what I am." I turn and continue up to my room.

I shut the door behind me and don't even bother to turn on the lights. I look down at my clothes. I rip them off and stuff them into an old backpack. I zip it tight and shove it into the closet.

I get into a hot shower. I concentrate on the act of getting clean. The soap that smells of jasmine. The shampoo that I've been using since sixth grade. I lean on what's familiar and push aside what isn't.

I get out, get dry, and climb into bed with my phone. A missed call from my mom. I open the e-mail from Joe. I click Reply and stare at the blank screen. *Thank you so much*, I write. *I'm excited by this honor.* I add a smiley face, then delete it. Send.

A reply appears instantly. From Bell. *Luisa, hello. As soon as this little global catastrophe is behind us, we'll get to work. Any questions? Yours, TS.* Roses raining down. Holy shit.

Reply: *Just one.* I hesitate. *Why did you choose me?*

A long pause. Regret sweeps over me with a clicking sound.

If you are searching for flattery, don't. I will not spend my time validating your existence. I will spend my time lighting the path to your highest potential. I chose you because I expect our work will serve each other's goals.

I tap my foot against the bed to quiet the hissing that rises with a lump in my throat. *Understood,* I reply. I wait, but nothing else comes.

I Google him. Over sixteen million hits. If I'm honest, it's not the first or second or third time I've looked him up. I click on Images. Almost every picture is him from the chest up, midspeech. In some he looks cold and diabolical, in others charming, like some kind of frat boy jeans model. Always, though, those blue eyes with their piercing gaze.

There's only one person I want to talk to. Only one person who will say, "Who gives a shit about your mom? This is about you." Only one person who will talk me out of worrying and tell me to shut the EF up and enjoy it.

I dial Janine. Please pick up, please, please. Four rings and her voice mail. I click off. I look at my last text to her. **I love u**. I say the words out loud and shut my screen to black.

That night I dream Janine and I are standing in front of a long, white tent. She's dressed in a white satin suit and her hair is tied back in a braid. She looks vibrant and gorgeous, like a bride. Her skin is so luminous I can practically see through it.

Everyone from school is lined up next to us. I'm holding a list of their names. George and Des from swim team step forward. Janine nods and I send them inside. Same with Annalise, Ben, hot

Alex, that kid Francis. Then Rose Gerson and Madison Dewy, the girls from Missy's party, step up. Janine shakes her head. I send them off the other way, teetering in their Jimmy Choos toward a dark, expanding void.

"Is this your wedding?" I ask Janine as Clara Adams appears.

"I've never been in love," she answers.

Clara coughs delicately into a handkerchief, leaving a bloodstain that matches her apple-red sweater.

"I'm sorry," she says. Her eyes are streaked with tears and iridescent makeup. I try to speak and suddenly I'm plummeting through darkness without anything to stop me.

I wake up with a jolt and I know: Janine's gone.

That invisible weight again pressing on my chest as I try to stand. I go downstairs. I find my dad in front of the TV in yesterday's clothes.

Over forty thousand dead.

Still, no one has found the infectious agent at the root. Quarantines and military hospitals are expanding to the outskirts of the major cities affected—New York, Boston, Miami, San Francisco, Los Angeles, Portland, Seattle, Chicago, Detroit, Austin, Columbus, Denver, and more. They're calling them "death camps."

The din of the television news anchors makes me gag with a sour taste. The living room crackles with popping sounds and flashing colors. This sensory chaos is grief.

"Not good, not good," my dad mutters to himself.

I grasp the back of the couch with both hands. "Hey," I say.

He looks up. His eyes are wild. "Hey. Lu."

"Have you slept?" I ask him.

"I fell asleep down here for a while. I tried Carol again. No answer."

I slump down at the kitchen table. "It doesn't matter," I tell him. I already know: Janine is dead. I don't need to hear it from her mother. I lean forward and press my cheek against the wood. My eyes trace the grooves of the grain. "I wish I could go for a swim," I say.

"You are not to leave, do you understand?" That sharp tone again.

"Okay," I mutter. My dad just stares at me. "I said okay."

"I keep thinking about what Carol and Tom are going through. If anything were to happen to you, I just—"

"I know," I interrupt. "But I'm fine. I am."

"Well." He softens. "You're not exactly fine." He's looking at me in that way, like he sees into my heart. "There's no way to prepare for this. I wish I could take away the pain and the fear." Wind rushing through trees. "I also know this will be one of the things that defines your entire life in ways you can't imagine."

If I don't die too.

"There has to be something we can do," I say. "There has to be a solution. Isn't there always a solution to every problem?"

"I guess. Yes. But solutions don't always look like we think they should. Often there's more than one potential answer. And one answer may open up other questions, or problems. Things aren't always simple."

"I just want to fix it," I say. "The whole thing."

"Me too."

"So what do we do? How do we fix it?"

"Well. I play the piano."

"I'm serious, Dad."

"So am I. That's my gift. That's what I have to offer. So I make music. Even if no one hears it but me. It changes things, I think. On some level."

"I don't think my gifts change anything," I say.

"I would say your gifts are still revealing themselves. One of them is that you care. That matters. That helps, even if you can't see how."

Right now I don't want to care. I just want to stop the world in its tracks and spin it in reverse.

I point my attention at the television, to the sound of the president's voice.

"Dr. Timmons at the CDC has just given me a briefing, as has General McCall. We're asking for everyone's cooperation while we get this situation under control," she says, speaking from an underground bunker. "Regarding the infectious agent and whether it's something we've seen before, or might be an act of chemical warfare, we are investigating all possibilities. We are working hard to contain the spread swiftly. That is our best and most immediate means of minimizing the loss of life."

The TV runs a banner underneath the president: ARNS DEATH TOLL CLIMBS RAPIDLY.

"Real swift," I say.

"We are seeing cases emerge in other countries and are working with our allies to share information and resources. Additional updates will be provided as more details become available. In the meantime, stay calm. Stay strong. God bless you, and God bless the United States of America."

The screen switches to a news anchor standing in a studio.

"That was President Cartwright speaking from an undisclosed secure location. Now we are taking a deeper look back at what has become known as the 'Hugo video.'" The anchor steps aside and a screen comes into view. Hugo's plaintive face is frozen in the center.

I shiver in a wave of red. "Have you seen this?" I ask.

"It's unbearable," my dad replies, transfixed as the video begins to play. I go into the kitchen.

My watch buzzes. My mom: **Please let me know you're OK**.

Fuck it. I tap Call.

"Hello," she answers.

"Hey, it's me. I'm calling you back." I put on the kettle.

"I've been worried," she says.

"I'm fine. We're all fine. It's all a little crazy, obviously."

"It's only going to get worse," she says flatly.

I watch the flame on the stove. "Why do you always assume the worst?"

"I don't *always* do anything. But they don't know what this thing is. It's going to get worse before it gets better, trust me." I bring my hands close to the flame. "I want you to take this seriously. If you stay in the house, you should be okay. But lock the doors. Keep the lights off. Don't go out."

What if it's already too late?

"Janine got sick," I tell her. "She went to the hospital."

Silence.

"Hello? Are you there?"

"That's terrible," she says.

"It's not her fault," I say.

"No. I didn't say it was."

My eyes are trained on that flame like it might solve the mystery of the whole universe. The heat starts to be too much. I pull my hands away.

"Do you have enough food?" I ask.

"Yes," she says. "You don't need to worry about me. I'll check on you tomorrow. I have to get to the lab now."

"You're going out?"

"I have to work. I have to try and help."

"Oh," I say. The kettle whistles.

"I'm sorry about Janine," she says.

"Me too." I pause. "Love you." But she's already hung up.

I make a cup of tea and go back into the living room.

My father looks up at me. He's weeping. "That video is just—it's the saddest thing I've ever seen. It's—how could they put that on the air? The boy's eyes—" He curls up on the couch and trails off into sobs.

The news drones on about the quarantines. People are dying covered in their own piss and shit because the doctors and nurses can't tend to them quickly enough.

I have to get upstairs, away from him, away from the TV.

I retreat to a chair in my room. Each sip of tea spreads warmth across my chest. Each sip brings me closer to normal.

I put on a recording of my dad playing the piano. The first quiet notes move into languid, cascading trills. I close my eyes and listen. It's uplifting, bright. Silver and orange. The pace builds and the colors bombard me. I recall how that Italian physicist described a wave as a disturbance, how he said a wave is not a thing; it's a change within a thing. I picture a beach. I conjure the feeling of sand under my feet. I bury my toes in it, like the roots of a tree.

Okay, I think. *Let them come.* One swell after another. I hold my breath. Apricot and coral, amber and tangerine, all mixing with the piano's rising and falling. I reach toward the colors, but there is nothing to touch. Just like we can't hold words, only the objects they point to, I can't grasp the waves with my hands.

I could plot them on a graph or describe them with mathematics—certain colors of light vibrate at certain frequencies—but they aren't quite real. They exist only inside my own experience. A fabrication of my mind. And they belong only to me.

The piece ends and I open my eyes. I feel unusually calm. I sit in the stillness and let out a long, slow breath.

Then I notice a new x.chat message glowing on my screen. A shiver when I see the sender's name: Theodore_Nam.

```
The thought that roots and wends its way
    around the tree of life
Will choke the throat of mortal men and
    thrust them into strife.
We watch the poison turn them blue then
    tear their minds apart
And spread itself like the dying star of
    your exploding heart.
```

What the hell is that supposed to mean? I copy and paste the text into Google. Nothing comes up.

Thank you? I reply.

You have to at least try, Nam writes.

I read through the message again. Then again. My eyes dart to a shelf of books along the wall. I scan the color of each spine without registering the titles.

I stop. I close my eyes and listen to the silence in my room. I look back at the screen and three words suddenly leap out: *Throat. Poison. Blue.* There's a Hindu myth about gods and demons churning the ocean to make the nectar of eternal life. But one of the things that come from their churning is a poison called halahala. The god Shiva drinks the poison. It's so powerful it begins killing everyone. Shiva's wife grabs his throat to prevent him from swallowing it and destroying the universe, which was said to reside in his belly. The poison turns his throat blue and ultimately he is saved.

Halahala, I write.

Was that so hard? Nam writes.

What do you want? I demand.

To chat, he replies.

About?

Are you afraid of ARNS?

I'm afraid of dying, yes, I answer.

What's the antidote to fear?

I stare at the screen. **Knowledge**, I write.

Correct.

And? What knowledge do you have? I wait for more, for something, anything. But Nam dissolves the chat and logs off. I Google Theodore Nam. The *Billings Gazette* in Montana says he was a fisherman who committed suicide on his 100th birthday. He left a note saying his wife and all his friends were dead. He couldn't stand to be alone anymore.

I go down to Ben's room. My whole body is vibrating with excitement.

He's jumping rope, a pair of weights at his feet. His breath is heavy. His wiry body glistens with sweat. He's strong and fit and in this moment I am certain he can protect me from anything. He glances at me without breaking his rhythm, without a word. His eyes are raw and red. His whole face is drooping like an old man's.

"What's up?" he mutters.

"You tell me."

The rope whips against the air. "Annalise is dead."

CHAPTER 7

"Oh my God." I sit down on the floor, my gut tight. "How do you know?"

"People just started texting me. Des, George. Everyone." He lets the rope drop. His breath slows and he sits on his bed. "I just can't believe it, you know? I mean, I don't believe it. I can't get it to sink in," he says.

"I know. Same with Janine. I can't actually fathom it. Like, what does it even mean? She's gone? Gone where?"

"I can't help feeling like, of all the people, of all the douchebag assholes we know, why her? Annalise was a good person; she cared about people. She was so special."

A cloud of peppermint drifts toward me. "She was," I agree. "She was great."

Teardrops land in quick succession on Ben's leg. He smothers them with his palm. "I'm sorry about Janine," he says. He wipes his cheeks on his shirt.

"Yeah."

We sit in the quiet. I watch the sunlight pouring through his window hitting particles of dust that float in the air. They look like the gold flecks inside a snow globe, like slow-motion glitter rain.

"Are you worried?" I ask softly. "Like, did you guys hook up the other night?"

He shakes his head. "She wanted to, but she was wasted, so I put her in a car and sent her home. Nothing happened."

I exhale.

When our mother moved out, Ben sat at the foot of my bed night after night. He would hold my feet and I would cry. He would promise me it would be okay.

I move next to him. I hold him steady as his body shakes like the earth releasing energy along a fault—big, messy, a relief.

He leans his head against mine and settles. "Let's talk in the morning?" he says quietly. "I just want to be alone now." I nod even though I want to sit on his bed and hold his feet until dawn. I bury a kiss in the mess of dark curls above his ear and go back to my room.

In physics, there's a law that states that the total energy of an isolated system remains constant over time—energy is neither created nor destroyed, but merely converted from one form to another. I try to imagine all the people who died before I was ever born, all the lives that had been so important to the people living them, gone, and in most cases, forgotten.

If I think of Annalise and Janine as forms of energy that were neither created nor destroyed, then where did they come from? And where are they now? What happens to the energy my father creates playing the piano? He says it changes things. How?

I fall asleep rereading Nam's poem. I dream of a deep blue ocean with waves so big they swallow the entire earth, pulling it up inside them like a child cocooned underneath her mother's skirt.

The next morning is perfect. I open the window and breathe it in. My tree waves its heavy, leafy boughs in the crisp air. A small brown bird alights on a branch, singing. The day of the Blackout Bombing was like this. Clear and cool. Smelling of possibility.

I listen as the bird's short, sharp notes ring out across the garden. Underneath them, I hear that hum, like the sound of the earth's motion. And then, another sound. It's muffled, but I hear it. My stomach rolls.

I slam the window shut and pull on a pair of shorts. I go out into the hallway. I hear it again. I move slowly toward the stairs. It gets louder and clearer. Time jumps forward and I'm standing in the doorway of my father's bathroom. My dad is sitting on the floor. He's coughing. I see red like a blaze of fire. The toilet is full of vomit. His mask lies on the floor next to him.

"Dad." The single syllable is distorted in my ear like I'm underwater. He raises his arm: Stay back.

Finally the cough calms and he sits up against the tub. I drop to my knees.

"Lu," he starts. His voice is gentle. "You can't be in here. It's not safe, lamb." I flash back to the hospital and his bare hand on the revolving door. This is my fault.

"I'm sorry," I blurt out. He starts to speak, but I don't let him. "We can't tell Mom." Colors envelop me. Strange tones fill my ears. I grab at the tiles on the floor. How will I manage this?

"Sweetheart," he says, looking all the way through my eyes straight into my breaking heart. He puts his mask back on.

I look away and trace the grout with my fingers. "We can't tell her. She'll never let us stay here with you. We need to try and find some kind of treatment. We have to figure out how to keep you alive until someone finds a cure. Ben!" I yell into the hall.

"What?" he yells back.

"Get up here." His heavy stomps on the stairs combine with the rhythm of my dad's breath. I tap my foot and clutch the doorframe as everything spins.

Ben walks in and finds us. "No," he murmurs. He steps back and seems to fall through time, becoming a little boy before our eyes.

My father starts to cry.

"We need to figure it out, just the three of us," I plead. I can't look at either of them.

"Lu. I've already called your mother. She's on her way."

"I don't believe this," Ben says under his breath.

"We have to do something," I insist.

"Please go downstairs. It's not safe for you to be near me."

I stand up and look back at my father. I am five years old again wanting to wear sandals in a snowstorm and he's looking at me like I'm just a silly kid. Maybe I won't be cold. Maybe I know something he doesn't.

I whip around and rocket down the stairs. Fourteen steps to the bottom. I need to think. I need to figure this out.

That woman in that video. Evans B. She said she knew something no one else did. I search FLN for Thorny Rose. *The page you are looking for cannot be found.* Fuck. I Google it. The video seems to have disappeared from the planet. But I find her picture. Evans Birkner from Redlands, California.

Her pearly teeth sparkle from the homepage of a ten-year-old biotech conference website. She was the keynote speaker. An expert on the regeneration of plant cells using a digital DNA replication technique she invented. It says she plays volleyball in her spare time and is "mother" to a dachshund named Jenny. Her photo is polished, professional. But behind her plastic smile, there's a fire in her eyes. God, I could swear I know her from somewhere.

I open a message to Bell. *My father is sick. Can you help me?* I pace around my room in a haze of red. I refresh my e-mail every three seconds.

Finally, a reply. *I'm trying to help everyone,* he writes.

Is that a no?

For now. I don't have the cure, yet.

I stare at the screen.

You'll have to solve your own problem.

Fuck you.

I open LightYears. I look at the analysis of the Hugo video. A bunch of curving lines, a bunch of words and percentages. Now I know Bell was right—it solves nothing. It does nothing. And yet, he chose me. Why?

I hear my father coughing through the closed door. I double over. My mother will be here soon.

I stop in the center of my room. The walls orbit my dizzy head. I plant my legs wide and close my eyes. I imagine my feet heavy in the sand.

Think.

There's only one other person to try. I text Kamal: **I need to talk to Phoebe**.

Seconds later, the trill of an incoming video call sends my heart into my throat. The number is blocked. I put on my glasses. My exhausted face appears in midair.

"Accept," I command, shaking the fear from my voice. My image shrinks into a thumbnail and Phoebe's perfect features and razor-sharp bangs come full-screen into my view.

"Hello," I say. I try not to sound like a kid.

"Hey Lu. What's going on?" Her tone is kind. I relax a little.

"Well, I'm not really even sure," I begin. "My father is sick."

"Oh wow," she says. "I'm sorry to hear that." Her face is close, her voice intimate. We are like schoolgirls whispering secrets. The taste of salt.

"I thought maybe there's something you know of, some way to help him. Somewhere that might have a treatment or something. Seriously anything. I don't want him to go to one of those camps."

I look at her and suddenly feel like a fool. Phoebe Lowe might seem all-powerful to my sixteen-year-old, Kamal-obsessed self, but in the big picture of the actual world, she's basically nobody.

"Well," she says slowly. "I don't think there's much I can do. I'm leaving for LA in a couple of hours."

"Wait, why?" How could she travel to Los Angeles while I stay home and watch my father die?

"They need help there, managing volunteers. And . . ." She stops herself.

"And what?" She pauses. Her eyes. More salt on my tongue.

"This remains between us, okay?"

"Okay," I respond.

"That Hugo video. We got a message from someone saying he sent it. He says he knows about ARNS and since I'm the one he sent it to, the Peers want me in LA while they try and figure out who he is."

"You got a message about the video?" Uneasiness rumbles through me.

She nods. "On x.chat. Totally untraceable."

My eyes sting with the punch of yellow light. My entire body erupts in chills. "Theodore Nam," I murmur.

Phoebe's eyes narrow. "What?"

"He sent me a message too. Last night. I got an x.chat message from Theodore Nam."

"What did it say?"

"It was a poem about a Hindu myth I randomly studied in fifth grade. When I told him I recognized the reference, he told me the cure for fear is knowledge."

"You should come with me," she says.

"To LA? Yeah, right."

"You're obviously involved in something or you wouldn't have gotten that message. We can keep you safe."

Safe from what exactly, besides ARNS?

"Look, do you actually want to sit around and watch your father get sicker and sicker and—" She stops herself. "Sorry. But seriously, do you? Want to come?"

"What would I even do there?"

"You would help us find Theodore Nam. Find out what he knows, if he even knows anything. You would do something besides sitting on your ass."

Logic goes to war with temptation. "I don't have the money for a ticket."

"We're driving. Flights are impossible, not to mention danger-ous. They'll probably close the airports soon."

"Who's 'we'?"

"Kamal and I."

Now I really want to go.

"What?" Phoebe asks when I say nothing.

"What if I get sick? What if I'm already sick?"

"You can take precautions. But we need to do what we can to make a difference."

"You make it sound simple."

"Maybe it is," she says. "Look, I have to go. We're leaving at eleven, so if you want us to pick you up, text Kamal. Either way, I'm sorry about your dad; I really am. But maybe don't let yourself be a victim?" She pulls a mask over her face and clicks off.

I look back at Evans Birkner's picture. I map the distance from Los Angeles to Redlands: seventy-three miles.

"What should I do?" I say aloud. Silence.

I collapse onto my bed. Milk-white pillows smother my ears. I stare up at the walls papered with photos—three-inch square pictures of the city, me, Janine, trips I've taken. My life story covering the walls like church mosaics.

I settle on a shot of Janine sitting on my stoop wearing plaid bellbottoms and a don't-fuck-with-me expression. I pull down the picture and stare at it. I want to call and tell her I was wrong the other night. Photographs are just as good as memories, maybe better.

"What should I do?" I ask again. My pulse ticks in the quiet. Then a single word, a whisper so soft I can't be sure I even hear it: "Go."

I bolt straight up.

"Ben! Luisa!" My mother's voice rings out from downstairs. Footsteps on the stairs and then she's standing in my doorway. She looks like an astronaut in her protective gear. A blast of white.

"Do you have symptoms?" she asks. Her breath sounds shallow. I shake my head. "Put these on." She tosses me a plastic pack. "Where is he?"

"Upstairs," I answer. She nods and pauses. Her eyes are glassy and wide.

"Do not leave this room. You'll put on the gown and everything in the pack and stay here. I'll get your father into the car and take him where they can help him. Then I'll come back and sanitize this house so we can stay here. It's safer here than my apartment."

"You can't—"

She cuts me off. "This is not up for discussion. *Y ya. Entiendes?*" She walks out.

I follow her into the hall. "I know you're freaked out, Mom, but—"

She whips around. "Stop." Ben comes out of his room. "When you have children of your own, if you are lucky enough to survive this and whatever else comes your way and you have babies of your own, you can talk to me about being freaked out. Right now, you put on the stuff in the fucking bag and you stay in your room."

"You can't take him to one of those camps. He'll be left to die in some corner."

"That's not my fault," she says, her voice cracking.

Yeah, I think. *It's mine.*

She breaks my gaze and goes upstairs.

I turn to Ben. "We can't let her do this."

"I don't think we have a choice, Lu."

My parents' muffled voices drift down from the landing above. "Are you okay to walk?" she asks. I back up to the wall and flatten my palms against it. I tap my feet against the floorboards.

Then, footsteps coming down.

My father moves toward me slowly, clutching the banister in his gloved hand. A blanket hangs from his shoulders. His face is obscured by a mask, but his eyes are searching and warm, like the beam of a flashlight.

They reach the bottom of the stairs. Waves of red and brown cloud my view. Heat swirls off my father's body. Sweat drips down his temple even as he shivers against the blanket.

He looks at Ben and then me. "I have to go," he whispers.

"No," I manage to say.

"Yes, lamb." He lifts the mask. His beautiful smile sends the sound of wind rustling trees through the empty spaces in my body. "I can beat this," he says. He's trying to convince us both.

I look down at my bare feet. My skin and bones press onto the hard wood of the hallway floor in the house where I have spent my whole life in some way preparing for this moment. *How did I ever feel safe?* I wonder.

"I love you both," he says. He looks at Ben who stands by the door to his room, not saying a word.

"See you soon, Dad. Okay?" I say. I need him to say yes. I need him to make it true that we'll see each other again. He nods.

I lean against the wall. My hands beg for texture as they slide down behind my back. "I love you," I say. His eyes close. His lips curl upward in a smile. He replaces his mask and turns to go. My mother follows behind him.

"I'll be back as soon as I can," she says. "Stay in your rooms, don't touch anything, and don't talk to anyone."

"Where are you taking him? Which one?" I call as they disappear down the stairs.

"New Jersey is closest," she replies. I stand motionless. The sound of the front door closing. Then quiet.

I turn to Ben. "I'm going to LA." The words make the decision for me as they fly out of my mouth. "I'm going with Phoebe and Kamal. They're driving in an hour."

"Um. Not funny?" he replies.

"Not joking." I head for my room.

"I know you have some sort of lame high school crush on him, but he's never gonna be into you and using Dad as an excuse to try and tag along on some suicidal road trip is pathetic," Ben calls.

I dig through my closet looking for my hiking boots. "This isn't about Kamal," I yell back. Ben appears in my doorway. "This is about Dad," I continue, "and the fact that Mom's currently taking him to some hellish place where he'll be left to rot on some mat on the floor until they get around to dragging his dead body away."

"Stop," he says. "I don't want to hear that."

"Well, you have to. Because that's what they're doing, out there, right now."

"I said stop."

"I need to do something. If we do nothing, he will die." I find the boots and put them on. I throw a lightweight vest, some underwear, and a change of clothes into a backpack.

"If you go out there, you'll both die," Ben says.

I freeze and look up at him. "I am not going to die." I move to the door. "But seriously, tell me, can you sit here in this house, with her, waiting, while Dad's out there somewhere all alone? If you tell me yes, then maybe I'll start to believe I can. But at this moment, there is no fucking way that's possible."

We stare at each other.

"Okay," he says, exhaling. "I get it. You should go."

"Okay," I say. I charge out of my room, half-hoping to feel his hand on my shoulder as he tells me I'm crazy, tells me he knows how to make this all go away. But that hand does not come.

I shoot down the stairs while texting Kamal: I'm coming with you. I unlatch the door to the basement.

I pull down the red Tahoe Gear two-person tent and the lightest weight sleeping bag I can find. I go to the food stores and grab a pile of Mountain House meal pouches and a few packs of water purification tablets. I take some bungee cords, a canteen, a flashlight, a headlamp, and enough new batteries to power both.

Halfway up the stairs I stop and turn back. I climb the stepladder to the top shelf of the camping cabinet. I find the smooth brown suede box. I open it and pull out my dad's old hunting knife by the rosewood handle. I gently press my fingers to the sharp blade. It's been sitting up here for years, its deadly edge never softening, its pure potential just waiting for someone to come along and use it. I pull the sheath from the box, slide the knife inside, and stuff it into my back pocket.

I go back up to my room and attach the tent bag to my backpack with the bungee cords and stuff the sleeping bag inside along with my laptop.

I'm ready.

I open the camera on my phone and turn the lens on myself. My eyes are puffy. My skin is lifeless. I fake a smile, then relax my face.

What will I look like as an old woman? Will my features be the same or will they be dulled by time like a piece of glass churned by the sea?

I snap a photo of myself and hit Print. I pull it still damp from the machine and tack it up on the wall. The contrast of my blond hair draws an invisible line between this image and all the other pictures, between the life I've lived up until now and my unwritten future staring back at me. "Go," I hear again. That whisper that's barely a sound.

I turn to leave, then stop at my dresser. We once spent the summer at the beach on Long Island where my father was given a house to work on a commission. At the end of those two months, our skin brown and hair streaked golden, we trudged with our bags half a mile from the house to the train station. My father stopped at the crossing while we waited, knelt down and put a quarter on the tracks. When the express came tearing past, the coin was crushed into a beautiful brushed metal disk. He drilled a hole in the top and strung it on a long silver chain.

I haven't worn it in years, but here it is, sitting in a dish next to my black wooden jewelry box and the turquoise glass dolphin my mother brought back from a conference in Miami. I put it on, grab my pack, and a second later I'm out in the hall. Ben's coming up the stairs carrying his own tent and backpack.

"You sure about this?" he asks.

"I don't have an answer to that," I tell him. "I just know I'm going."

"Well, I'm coming with you. But you have to listen to me and not do anything stupid. I'm your brother and I'm older and I know more and you can't forget that, okay?"

A smile spreads across my face. I exhale relief. "Okay."

"And you can't die," he says. "Neither of us can die."

"Neither of us can die," I repeat. We head down the stairs and out into the summer day, the temperature rising now as the sun climbs toward its peak. Kamal's SUV is waiting. My whole body buzzes with nervous energy as I open the door.

"'Sup," Ben says as we climb in.

Phoebe turns from the front seat. "Good to see you guys," she chirps. Her eyes are hidden behind gold Ray-Bans that reflect my masked face.

"Hey," I say. I catch Kamal's eyes in the rearview. The smell of pine envelops me and my eyes burn with the urge to blink. But I don't. I stay fixed on his amber irises. I silently ask them to hold me, to keep me safe.

We drive down the block and I break his gaze. The houses shuffle by like a deck of familiar cards. We pass the empty spot where our car had been.

In that moment, I want to turn back. All the way back, to when I didn't know enough to know some things don't work out how you want them to.

I woke early, before dawn, a sound weaving in and out of the air outside the tent. It was a howl, high and haunting. I slipped out quietly as the others slept. As the last embers of our fire lay choking in the pit, there it was again. The howl, the call—close and distant at once. I put on my flip-flops and headed off down the path. Its knotted roots felt lumpy under my thin rubber soles. The old pines were lit silver by the moon and the sky was spread out like a canvas for the wash of shimmering stars above. They were just starting to fade with the sun's approach.

I walked softly, a twelve-year-old visitor, not wanting to disturb this ancient place that wasn't mine. I heard it again, closer now. There in the clearing ahead I saw her. A mother and her three pups. Their gray coats were rich and full. Their eyes were shining bright.

I stopped and sat down. Dew against my legs. The pups tumbled down and scrambled back up onto their feet, over and over as their mother chased them in jest. I understood the danger, but I was at ease. I knew I did not need to be afraid.

The stars continued to vanish and all at once the spell of night was broken. The game was finished. The mother looked at me. I jumped to my feet. A flash of yellow. What if my instinct had betrayed me?

She began trotting toward me, trailed by her young. Before I could run, she was right there. Right in front of me. Her gait slowed to a stop and she lay down at my feet. The pups came up behind, nuzzled against her resting body, and began to nurse. The mother stretched her paws to cover my toes like a blanket. Her warm fur tickled my skin as I stood motionless. I thought maybe I was dreaming.

Then, as quick as anything, they leaped up and disappeared into the deep green forest. The sun rose and I watched the trees for a long time, hoping they'd come back. But they never did.

EMILY ZIFF GRIFFIN

CHAPTER 8

"We have reports from at least two dozen municipalities extending as far east as Massachusetts and as far west as Oregon detailing another disturbing trend in the wake of the ARNS outbreak." We sit quietly as a reporter's smooth baritone comes through the radio. "Small groups of armed men have taken to the streets in organized patrols, claiming to be guardians of local safety but, in a number of cases, harassing those they deem suspicious and robbing people of precious food and water. These groups are claiming to be protected under the U.S. Constitution's Second Amendment but are receiving pushback from certain members of state and local governments who are concerned for the safety of their constituents. More as this story develops."

"Fantastic," Kamal mutters. He turns down the volume as his driverless Tesla glides to a halt at a red light. I'm still wary of cars that drive by themselves, even if it's officially safer. People can earn forgiveness for their mistakes, but machines don't care if they hurt you.

A taxi pulls up next to us. The driver is shrouded in a heavy black gas mask. Is it the large eyeholes and muzzle-like mouthpiece that make him terrifying? Or is it what the mask implies—suffocation, poison, death? He turns toward me and I shudder. The light changes and we cruise onto the Brooklyn-Queens Expressway heading west.

"We need to tell Mom something," Ben says. "She's gonna lose her mind."

I draft a text and pass him my phone.

"Mom," he begins aloud.

My cheeks flush. "Really? You can't just read it in your head?"

"I need to hear it," he replies. "Mom. I know this will be hard to grasp, but Ben and I had to leave. We have to try and help Dad. We will stay safe and be home as soon as we can. *Confía en nosotros. Te queremos.*"

Kamal turns to us. "Translation on that last part?"

"Trust us. We love you," I reply. I picture her reading these words and having no idea where we are. I imagine her grasping for a clump of her gown, like a life raft. Even though our relationship is complicated, I know she'll be terrified that we're gone.

"Send it," Ben says. I nod and it's on its way. The car speeds along the road, nearly empty of traffic. Most people who are leaving have already left. Those without electric cars are conserving gas and everyone else is staying indoors, sick, or dead.

The radio drones on, too quiet to really hear. I look at Phoebe in the front seat. Her pale skin is visible in fragments behind her glasses and mask. Her red hair is tied up in a messy bun. Beautiful still, but more ordinary now. Or maybe I have more important things to worry about.

"How about some music?" Kamal asks.

"Yes!" Phoebe turns to me. "Lu, whaddya got?"

I steal a look at Kamal in the mirror—a chance to impress him, or embarrass myself.

"Yeah, what do you have?" Ben asks. "Katy Perry? Or are you straight-up Taylor Swift?"

"Oh my God, I fully heard you singing Taylor Swift in the shower, like, a week ago." A week ago, when everything was normal.

He leans forward and whispers to Phoebe. "That's not true."

I lean forward too. "It is one-hundred-percent true."

She laughs and Ben rolls his eyes, but I know he's blushing underneath his mask.

I scroll through my playlists. I stop at "Dad's Old School Reggae Jams." This was always our go-to because reggae is literally the only genre that my dad, Ben, and I can all tolerate. I tap Play on the opening track: Bob Marley's "Sun Is Shining."

The song's slow, easy beat seems to prop me up. Comfort washes over me. Kamal and I lock eyes in the mirror.

"Good choice," he says as his head moves with the rhythm.

I smile. I enjoy his approval, but it's more than that. As we watch each other in the mirror, I feel like the diver leaving the platform twenty or thirty feet above the pool. It's like my feet have traded the solidity of the board for the expansiveness of the air.

Inevitability takes over as gravity goes to work. Nothing will stop the collision, and in this moment I know: Something's going to happen with us.

We turn onto the Brooklyn Bridge. The song ends and Kamal's face blurs as the bridge's tall, gray-brown towers come to loom in front of us. I look up at the bike path and Janine's voice echoes: "It's all downhill from here."

My chest tightens like I'm finding out for the first time that she's sick, that she's most likely dead. A swirl of heavy brown light. I shut my eyes. I snap my seat belt away from my chest until it locks. Loss is like a wheel that keeps spinning you back to where you started.

"So. What's the plan here?" Ben's voice settles me. I open my eyes and focus on the shape of his hands in his lap.

"We'll drive until dark, then find a cheap hotel to crash," Phoebe replies. "Should take us three days to get to LA."

"And what happens in LA?"

"We go to The Pulse. The Peers there will have a plan for us," Phoebe says.

"Oh good," Ben snaps. "The Pulse. Where we get to pretend we're homeless trust fund kids. Except Lu and I don't have trust funds."

"Ben. I know you're dealing with a lot right now. So's everyone. But no one actually forced you to come on this trip." Phoebe manages to sound both soft and cutting.

He sighs. "Sorry. I'm just. Yeah." He looks over at me. "So who are the Peers exactly?"

"Front Line is a leaderless organization. The local chapters are self-governing and self-sustaining. The Peers rotate in a leadership role; they oversee according to the Code, but they don't govern. Technically there is no one person in charge."

"Sounds like AA," I mumble.

Ben narrows his eyes. I can see the compulsion to challenge her thrashing around in his chest like a caged bull.

I eye the water. We're over one hundred feet up, halfway between Brooklyn and Manhattan. I imagine the car smashing into the guardrail and being vaulted into the air. How many times would we spin before plunging into the river? Would our hearts stop? Would time slow down? Would it even exist at all?

Ben can't help himself. "Come on." His voice crackles. "That's ridiculous."

"It's not ridiculous at all," retorts Phoebe.

"Whatever."

"Look, what you think you know? You don't know. It's just what you've been fed by a totally vapid, materialistic, fear-based culture that values money over people. When people value human life most of all, amazing things are possible. And people can be led without leaders because greed goes out the window."

Ben squints again. "Yeah. Not buying it. People value money because it matters."

"It only matters because we choose to value it. We could easily choose to value something else instead."

"Well, we've chosen money." Case closed.

"Yeah and catastrophe is a powerful equalizer," Phoebe counters.

"What does that mean? Are you, like, glad about ARNS?" Ben shifts in his seat.

"Of course not. But it will lead to progress of some kind. It will change things, some things for the better. That's the undeniable nature of hardship, right?" I wait for Ben to say something more, but he's probably thinking what I am: that Phoebe's words sound like something our dad would say. He disappears into his phone.

"There's someone near LA who says she has a cure," I say tentatively. "She put up a video on your site. Then it got taken down, but—"

"You mean that Evan whatever-her-name-is?" Phoebe sneers.

"Evans. Yeah."

"She's apparently some bipolar nut who went off her meds and started posting a bunch of psycho shit about conspiracies. She's not the only one. They're all mentally ill or just media-hungry."

"Right." A hiss wraps around my head as the disappointment registers. "I guess that shouldn't be surprising. But she sounded . . . convincing somehow."

"Crazy people always sound convincing because they believe themselves."

We rocket through the Holland Tunnel into New Jersey. We pass gas stations with lines of cars winding out into the streets. I half expect to see my dad's car.

"Is there a medical camp near here?" I ask.

"No, further south," Phoebe replies. "Near Newark."

"Do you think they're there by now?" Ben asks quietly.

"Yeah," I say. My watch buzzes with a text. My mom: **I am begging you, please don't do this. Turn around and go home**. My finger hovers over Reply.

I could be infected. My father might die. Evans B. is nothing but a joke and the entire world is turning upside down. I glance at Phoebe, then Kamal, then Ben. Out the window, industrial smoke-stacks and electrical wires, steel bridges and sprawling truck depots all stand like sleeping giants in the late morning light. They can't protect me.

Normally my mother's words would build a nest inside me. They would make my own point of view invisible. But as I inhale, my thin paper mask suctioning against my face, I remember that there is no normal now. And I know that there is no going back.

I shut my messages without responding and settle my head against the window. I focus on the music again: "Rivers of Babylon." Its sad melody and simple chord progression are comfortable like an old sweatshirt. My eyes close and, without meaning to, I fall asleep.

Dear Luisa,

I am doing my ninth step in The Program, which is where we make amends to the people we have harmed through our drinking and drug use. I realize as I'm sitting here that this is not as hard a letter to write as I imagined it would be. Because I have spent years apologizing to you in my head. And now I have the chance to do it in a way that you can hold on to for the rest of your life.

I remember the moment you were born so clearly it still takes my breath away. I remember the sound of your first cries and your small hands reaching forward. I remember holding you wrapped in a blanket and looking right into your eyes—eyes that still look exactly the same. I looked down and told you, you are not my property. I told you, your life is yours, not mine, to live. I wanted you to be independent, to be strong, to be yourself. And you are all of those things and I am so proud of you.

But what I'm most sorry about is that you became those things sooner than you should have because the difficulty of living with an addict didn't give you a choice. In too many ways, you had to be strong. In too many ways, you had to do things and make sense of things on your own. It was my job to protect you. It was my job to make you feel safe and loved, not to let you live your own life at the age of four, or seven, or ten. I'm sorry for that.

I'm sorry for the times I yelled. For the times I scared you or made you doubt yourself. I'm sorry for being drunk at the swimming pool. I'm sorry for not letting you stay innocent and trusting for as long as you should have. I'm sorry I can't go back in time. I do not expect or demand your forgiveness, but I will of course welcome it, if and when you choose to give it.

I love you,
Dad

I wake up disoriented. Farmland extends in every direction. "Where are we?" I ask.

"Just outside California," Kamal answers.

"What?" My body seizes. How could I have slept for three days? I grab for information out the window.

"California, Pennsylvania." Kamal can barely contain himself. "I've been waiting for, like, two hours to say that. You slept hard."

"Yeah. I still feel exhausted."

"I'm starving," offers Ben.

Kamal turns back toward us. "You guys did bring food, right?"

"We were supposed to bring food?" Ben asks sarcastically. He and Kamal exchange stupid faces. "Also, I have to pee," Ben says.

Kamal rolls his eyes. "Tired, hungry, and have to pee. You guys are such whiners."

"Are we there yet?" I whine in my most whiney of whiney voices. Kamal catches my eye in the mirror. I look at Phoebe. She's staring out the window. It's not like her to be so quiet.

"But seriously though," Ben snaps. "I really have to pee."

"Okay, okay. I should try and charge the car too." Kamal pulls up the map on his phone. "This isn't a good place to stop. We're about to go through back-to-back tunnels and then we can look for a safe place, cool?" Ben and I nod.

Phoebe takes off her sunglasses as we come around a bend. Up ahead I spot the double-barreled opening of the Blue Mountain Tunnel. I catch the words on the sign as we pass from the bright light of afternoon into the orange glow of overhead fluorescents. Phoebe's eyes are red like maybe she was crying.

"Are you all right?" I ask her.

"Fine," she says. But she isn't.

We shoot through the tube like a rocket. I consider the weight of the mountain balanced perfectly on all sides. Layer upon layer of dense rock, pressed down over millions of years, was slowly carved away to make this empty shaft now covered with tiles and a stream of lights. And by some miracle, the mountain doesn't collapse.

It's not long before I see a speck of daylight up ahead. We are almost through. But as we draw nearer, a dark silhouette framed by a flashing red light appears in the middle of the road.

"Kamal," I blurt out, bracing myself as the car gently slows to a full stop in front of the obstruction.

"Shit," Ben says. I quickly count the men who are standing between us and safe passage out of the tunnel: nine. Six with assault rifles and three whose tightly packed muscles and narrow eyes make them look scary as hell.

"I would really like to look more white right now," murmurs Kamal between flashes of mustard-colored light.

"Quiet," Phoebe snaps. My pulse leaps into my ears as a thin, muscular guy with a short beard and large rifle approaches the driver's side door. Kamal puts down his window. We all hold our breath as the tip of the gun noses its way inside like a curious dog.

"What brings you folks out on this glorious summer's day?" His voice is gravelly. To me, his face reeks of sulfur.

"We're with Front Line," Phoebe says firmly.

He chuckles. "And what's your business in the great state of Pennsylvania?"

"I should be asking you that," Phoebe replies.

I flinch.

"Because I can guarantee," she continues, "that my resources are more vast and more dangerous than whatever you and your friends think you can accomplish with these guns. My organization knows precisely where we are. If something happens to us, something will happen to you. So you should probably just get out of our way and let us pass."

"Hey sister, there's no need to get yourself so riled up."

"I'm not your sister," Phoebe barks.

"And I don't like nasty girls," he says sharply. A dark vibe spreads through the car. My focus darts between the gun and his mouth. He isn't that much older than we are. He has circles under his eyes. There's a wheeze underneath his words, like he's hungry for air. I can hardly breathe through the smell of sulfur.

I don't know why exactly, but I don't look away. I don't hold my breath or tap my foot. I plant myself on that beach in my mind, dig my feet down into the wet sand, and let the sensations come. There is something I can see that no one else can. The more I look, the more I can see it: He doesn't want to hurt anyone. But if he were made to feel foolish, he might do it anyway.

"Thank you for your service." My voice rings out like a slap. Those words, the ones I've heard so many times at my dad's AA meetings after someone tells the story of their recovery or volunteers to make the coffee.

The bearded man takes a step to the side. He pulls the gun back and glares at me through my tinted window. Then he bends down and leans forward. I open the window and look straight at him. Sulfur. His face. Yellow light. My feet in the sand. I allow it all.

"Thank you," I say again. "You're here to help. I can see that."

His mouth quivers. "Well, all right," he says after a moment. He motions to the others to let us pass. They step back. Kamal puts the car into gear and we go. I take in a deep, full breath as we emerge back into daylight. My whole body is vibrating. It's the feeling of swimming a personal best or solving a complex equation. Only better.

Seconds later, another tunnel envelopes us again.

"Jesus fucking Christ," my brother exclaims, daring to look back over his shoulder.

"That was utterly insane." Kamal's English accent and the smell of pine tug on every cell inside me—their own form of gravity.

"Nice one, Lu," Phoebe says.

Kamal catches my eye in the mirror again. This time I look away.

We pass through the second tunnel and out into the rolling countryside of western Pennsylvania. I lean toward my open window. Warm, sticky air smothers my face.

"Since I shockingly didn't just piss my pants, I still need to stop," Ben says.

Kamal alters the car's GPS. "There's a gas station at the next exit."

The sky begins to darken. Thunder rumbles in the distance.

"How did you know what to say to him?" Kamal asks.

I shrug. "I don't know. I just did." I look at my phone.

"You hear back from Mom?" Ben asks.

"Yeah, I got a text. You?"

"Two texts and a voicemail. She's pissed."

"She can be pissed," I say. "I'm pissed too. About a lot of things. And I care more about helping Dad than her being mad."

"I'm with you," he says. "But shit, you guys. I seriously thought those dudes were gonna shoot us. I probably would've shot us. If I were them."

"He didn't want to shoot anyone," I say.

We pull into a deserted gas station. More thunder rolls across the horizon, then lightning. The car slowly cruises past the pumps. They're hung with handwritten signs that say, "No gas." Kamal pulls the car up to the electric charging post.

"I hope this thing works," he says.

"Power's still on and it takes credit cards," replies Ben. "It'll work." He goes over to a bush and pees.

I hop out. This place is bleak. The glass door of the convenience store is shattered. There's trash littered everywhere and the darkening sky casts everything in eerie, flat light. I feel for my dad's knife in my pocket and re-secure it as I follow Ben and Phoebe into the store. The shelves and cold cases are bare. A huge pile of scratched-off lottery tickets covers the floor.

"Check this out," Ben marvels. "How long do you think it would take to scratch off all these tickets?" I shrug and go back outside. My legs are stiff from so many hours in the car. It feels good to move.

"It's working," Kamal calls from the charging station. I give him a thumbs-up and trail Phoebe to the ladies' room. Locked.

"There's probably a key behind the counter," I say.

"Let's just go around back." She leads us to a woodsy overgrown area behind the store.

I kick up some empty milk cartons and crumpled bags of chips on the ground. A heavy feeling passes over me. The storm is getting closer. "Looks like someone was living back here."

Phoebe pulls down her shorts and squats over a pile of dead leaves.

Thunder booms again in the distance. "That rain's coming any minute." I say. But Phoebe's staring a million miles away. I study her eyes. I swallow the taste of salt and squat down to pee. "What's up with you? You seem kind of off. I mean, not that I really know you well enough to say that."

She finishes and stands up. My eyes dart to her underwear as she pulls her shorts on. Black lace. A blast of heat down my arms.

"I'm fine," she says. "Or more precisely, I don't want to talk about it." She undoes her hair tie and bends forward. Her long red tresses spill toward the ground. She combs them with her fingers.

I pull up my shorts as a small orange tabby appears from under a cardboard box. She's mewing. I kneel down to pet her. "Hey little one," I coo. "Are you hungry?" She buries her soft head in my hands. She's just a baby. Her sweetness almost makes me want to cry. But I don't cry.

Instead, I feel for my knife. Because in a red flash, I know he's there even before he is.

He's young, maybe mid-twenties. His face is hollow and unshaven. His clothes are tattered and dirty, like he's been living in the woods for days. He grabs Phoebe by the hair and yanks her upright, a broken bottle in his other hand.

He starts to speak, but his voice catches in his throat.

The cough.

"You have a car?" he rasps. Phoebe nods. Her eyes narrow and she whimpers as he pulls her hair tighter. None of us moves. The knife's handle is cool against my skin. Red and yellow swirl in front of me, but I know what I'm going to do. Because I know what he's going to do. In an instant, his hands are around her neck. Phoebe is gasping for air and I'm in motion.

I rip the blade from the sheath and plunge it straight into his back. It's so fast I'm not even sure I've done it. But he lets go of her and stumbles. He reaches toward his back, then turns to me.

Thunder again and my whole body quakes. His eyes widen. I see a whole life in his face now. The disappointments, the joys, the dreams and wants. And these, the final moments. The realization that it's over. I see heartbreak stream out of his eyes in one long, coffee-colored ribbon. He crumples to the ground.

"Ben!" I yell. Phoebe is panting, still gasping for air. Kamal and my brother come tearing around the side of the store. We all stand frozen as the man stops moving. The air is thick. The only sound is our breath and the cat meowing. I look down at the man's face, at the pool of blood forming on the ground beneath him. He's dead and the thought that follows is too bizarre to comprehend: I killed him.

CHAPTER 9

I am ice-cold in the warm air. Blues, blacks, horns, bells, tones, and the taste of red meat overwhelm me. My mouth waters with hunger so intense I almost don't recognize it. I begin to shake. My brother rushes over and puts his hands on my shoulders.

"Are you all right?" He seems to be shouting. I look at him. I can't speak or move. I feel like I'm floating above everything and don't have access to my limbs.

"What happened?" Kamal demands. I glance at Phoebe who stands hunched over, her hands on her knees.

"Luisa just saved my life," she says. A drop of rain hits my nose. I blink. Tap my foot. Another raindrop. The sounds and colors start to calm. I walk over to the man.

"He was coughing," I mumble. I pull up my mask. "I'm going to be sick."

"Fuck, Lu!" my brother yells. "Did you touch him?"

My stomach is churning. I spit onto the ground. I find a still point in the dirt. I breathe. I notice the kitten again. She has no idea what's just happened, what any of it might mean.

"She didn't touch him," Phoebe answers. "He tried to strangle me. She stabbed him."

We all stare at Phoebe. She is now at risk.

"We have to go home," Ben says. "This is insane."

"No. Not an option," Phoebe snaps.

"Dude, my sister just killed some infected zombie. Some infected zombie who almost choked you to death." The meaning of his words is hard for me to grasp. It's like he's speaking a language I only sort of know. I pull out my phone with shaking hands. I dial my dad.

It rings and the wind rushes through the trees behind us. That sound, an echo of his image in my head. I don't know what I'll do or say if he answers. I just want to hear him tell me it's all right.

"Who are you calling?" Ben asks.

My dad's voice mail picks up. I click off. "No one."

I bend down and let the cat sniff my hand. Her only concern is survival. Sitting on the ground as the thunder booms again, I realize mine is too.

"We can't go back," I say. "There's zero guarantee of safety there and our only hope of helping Dad is to keep going." Tears pool in Ben's eyes. His lips turn down. "It's okay," I tell him. "I'm okay."

"What we shouldn't do is stay out here any longer than we have to," Kamal says. Phoebe nods and starts walking. I follow next as the rain starts, then Kamal, then Ben. We move quickly to the car. Light drizzle gives way to sheets of cascading water. White-hot blasts of lightning explode across the horizon and thunder pounds overhead.

Everyone climbs into the car, but I hesitate. A gust of wind rattles the trees again. It's like a message without words. "Hang on," I say and run back.

I kneel down next to the dead man. "I'm sorry," I whisper. Then I pull the knife from his back in one swift movement. The rain hammers down and washes away the blood. I hustle back to the car.

Phoebe is cleansing her neck with a wipe. "Can I have one of those?" I ask as I take my seat. She passes one back and I run it up and down the blade.

"You took the knife?" Ben asks. "It's totally contaminated."

"Not anymore." I throw the wipe out the window, stuff the knife into my backpack, and we pull back onto the road.

"Let the record reflect," Ben announces, "that I think continuing this trip is the worst possible idea in the history of bad ideas."

"Noted," Phoebe replies. She throws her gloves and mask out the window and replaces them with a fresh set from her pack. She offers me a clean pair too. "Here's the thing, Ben," she says. "You can't worry about getting sick. You just have to put it out of your mind and keep moving forward."

"I'm actually not worried about getting sick," Ben responds. "I'm worried about some nut job like that guy or the guys in the tunnel blowing our brains out to get our car or our food or whatever. ARNS is honestly the least of our concerns."

"Can you all be quiet, please?" I snap.

"Of course," Phoebe replies.

"Do you want to talk about it?" my brother whispers. I shake my head no and find the horizon out the window.

"What happens when someone dies?" I asked. My father was sitting at the foot of my bed.

"Well, lamb," he said carefully. "They stop breathing."

"Then what?" I asked.

"Different people believe different things. Some say they go to heaven. Some say their spirit gets taken back up into the stars and planets and comes back down into a new person or animal just being born."

"Animal?" I asked.

"Some people believe that, yes."

"So, like, I could be a horse?"

"Possibly," he said. "It's like they go away but then come back as something or someone else."

"Can we see them when they come back?"

"Maybe. But we might not recognize them. I think they would look different and maybe be very far away." I looked down at the hundreds of tiny silver stars embroidered on my quilt.

"What do you think?" I asked.

"I think that death is not the end. That's the thing to remember. Even if we don't know what's next." He swept the hair off my forehead.

"When we die, let's be next to each other so we can stand up together and come back to earth together," I said.

He smiled at me. "That's a perfect plan."

My eyes slowly hinged closed. The weight of his hand on my head was like the steady pressure of a ship's wheel on the rudder, guiding my mind swiftly into sleep.

Hours pass along with the flat prairies of Western PA. Fast-food sign-posts dot the highway edge like giraffes on a savannah. Kamal and Ben fall asleep.

Phoebe leans over and reprograms the GPS. "Change of plans. We're gonna stop in Ohio," she says. "I have an aunt there. We're gonna stay the night with her."

"Okay," I reply. "That's nice. Right?" She doesn't answer.

My phone buzzes. A new x.chat message from Nam.

"Holy shit. I got another poem."

Phoebe whips around. "Let me see." I hand her the phone and she reads it aloud:

```
"From dust he bloomed, a fragile rose
    whose petals slowly fell
As the seed inside kept burning
    still, the mind at least was well
They tore their clothes and begged
    for help, a nightly vigil kept
But when he was gone, all hope was
    lost and they, like Jesus, wept."
```

She looks up at me. "Do you know what it means?"

"There's something familiar about it," I say. "But no, I don't know."

"You should respond. See if you can get him to tell you something more."

"How do I do that?" I ask, wishing I already knew.

"Well, last time you gave him the answer to his puzzle."

"Right."

"Don't do that. If you give him the answer, there's nowhere left to go."

"But he's sending me a message and it seems like the answer is the message. I have to solve the puzzle to know what the message is."

"Yes, but you can discern the meaning without telling him you've figured it out. Telling him the answer is just about showing him you're smart. He already knows you're smart. You need to be even smarter and coax him into revealing something more." This is what Kamal likes about her. She's persuasive. Or is she cunning?

"Say something like, 'I know where you are.'"

"But I don't," I say.

She laughs. "Don't be so literal." Her salty eyes sparkle in the setting sun.

"Okay," I say. I type the words: **I know where you are**. I read it over, trying to hear it through the ears of a phantom stranger. "No," I mutter to myself.

"What?" Phoebe asks.

"Nothing," I reply. I make a change. **I know who you are**. I hit send, then lean back and wait.

The sun is dropping fast when we arrive in Granville, Ohio. We wind up a hill lined by sweet old Victorians, their grassy lawns peppered with American flags and swing sets. Phoebe's aunt Georgette lives at the top, at the end of a cul-de-sac. Birdsong and still summer heat envelop us as we step out of the car. This place already feels like home.

I follow Phoebe up the stone-covered path, past beds of brightly colored azaleas as Georgette bursts through the door. She's got a silk scarf tied around her face and no gloves.

Two large huskies come bounding out behind her and the smell of something delicious cooking inside fills my nose. The dogs jump up, trying to lick my face.

"Kelly! Barb! Get down!" Georgette shouts. She grabs them by their collars and holds them back. Her wide, brown eyes meet mine. She tastes like honey and instantly, I wish she were my mom.

"Come in, come in," she offers warmly, turning to Phoebe. "Sweetheart, let me see you." Phoebe lifts her mask and, like dawn into day, she transforms into an awkward little girl. Her shoulders slope down, her eyes seem to beg.

"Hi G," she says softly.

A sob escapes Georgette's plum-colored lips. "It's been too long."

"I'm sorry for that," Phoebe says. They hold each other's gaze. A river of emotion passes between them and I'm reminded: Phoebe has a whole history I know nothing about.

"Well," Georgette says, brightening. "I need to meet your friends."

"I'm Kamal, Ms. Maxwell. It's a pleasure to meet you. Thank you for having us stay." His good English manners make me want to I don't even know what.

"I couldn't be happier you're here. And please call me G."

"I'm Ben," my brother adds. "This is my sister, Luisa."

G looks at me the way my dad does. "Oh baby," she says gently. "You need to lie down, don't you?"

"That would be nice," I say.

"I have two rooms, plus the basement. I leave it to you to decide who sleeps where."

"Lu can have my room," Phoebe says. "I'll take the basement."

G puts her hand on Phoebe's back as we head inside. I glance at my watch. Nothing from Nam.

G leads us down the hall. "Everything is clean," she says. Phoebe stops in the doorway of a small bedroom. She surveys the two twin beds with their pink rose-printed comforters. The walls are covered with drawings and photos. There's a drafting table surrounded by paints, pencils, and markers. The whole room is teeming with the life of a teenage girl.

"What?" I ask.

"Nothing." She goes into the room and sets down her bag. I follow and take a seat on the edge of one bed.

I look around. "Is this all your stuff?"

Her expression is distant. "It's my little sister's."

"Where is she?"

"You should rest," she says. "I'm gonna take my stuff downstairs and help G with dinner." She grabs her bag and walks out. I lie back and sink into the pillows. The opposite wall holds a charcoal portrait of G's dogs posed on the edge of a cliff. They look strong and proud, like two sentries standing guard over a distant realm—the protected having become the protectors.

Time dissolves and I lose myself. The next thing I know, it's nearly dark outside and someone is knocking on the door.

"Come in." I sound groggy.

The door creaks open and Kamal's head appears. "Dinner's ready."

I look around, then sit up. "Thank you."

"How do you feel?" he asks. "Did you sleep?"

"I'm okay. I'm not sure if I slept. I feel like I didn't."

"You will. You're in shock. You need to eat and rest. You'll sleep."

I avoid his gaze. "I just feel . . . I can't believe what I did."

"What you did was amazing."

"I killed someone. I mean, what the fuck? Those are words you never think you'll actually say, right? Those are words people on TV say." My legs tingle. A burst of pine, but he steadies me with his eyes.

"You saved someone. That guy was going to die anyway. And he would've killed all of us if given the chance. You saved our lives, my life." He pauses, just looking at me. "I'm feeling pretty grateful."

I smile and step toward the door. He blocks me. His body seems to cast a shadow on the entire room. We stand there in silence. I tap my foot. If there were no ARNS would we be kissing right now?

If there were no ARNS we wouldn't be standing here at all.

"We should go eat," I say.

"Yeah. We should."

Neither of us moves.

"Guys! Dinner!" Phoebe's voice from the hall. It's like a pinprick on the face of a balloon. We turn and go.

We sit down around G's oval-shaped table. A massive tray of

bubbling-hot lasagna rests in the center. My mouth actually waters.

G pours herself a glass of wine and offers the bottle around the table. "I know you're all underage, but I won't tell if you don't." She winks at me.

"This looks amazing," Ben marvels.

"I was lucky to have gotten groceries before everyone started to hoard food. I'm trying to make it last, but this is a special occasion." G looks at Phoebe, whose eyes are trying to disappear into her plate.

Kamal pauses, holding a spatula. "I hate to ask this, but is it safe to eat?"

"Well, it's been cooking in a four-hundred-degree oven for over an hour, so I would think so. And I don't believe I'm sick."

"Good enough." We lift our masks and dig in. It's a relief to see everyone's faces.

"This is absolutely delicious. Cheers." Kamal raises his glass. "To G." We all join him in the toast. The wine in my throat feels rough and comforting, like an old wool sweater. I sneak another look at my watch, still hoping for something from Nam.

"Have you seen any violence around here?" Ben asks.

"Not really, not yet. The town has been extremely sane. It's a college town, you know, so people are rational, liberal. A lot of Christians here. Real Christians, social justice, take-care-of-your-neighbor kind of Christians. There's a sense of community." G sips her wine. "But elsewhere . . . my neighbor's son has apparently joined one of those militias they're talking about on the news. It's terrifying. They're armed and they're scared. Doesn't get more dangerous than that."

"Yeah, we met a few of those folks on the way here," Ben mutters.

G glances at Phoebe, who's slowly chewing her food, eyes down. "I've got an electric fence around my property from when Kelly and Barb were pups. We raised show dogs back then. So as long as the electricity holds, I should be fine."

"You and?" I ask.

G smiles and her whole face lights up. "Me and Donald, my husband." Ben, Kamal, and I wait for her to say more. "Didn't Phoebe tell you about Donald?" We look at each other, shaking our heads.

"Oh." She takes a breath. "Donald died in Blackout. Along with his brother and his brother's wife. Phoebe's parents." I hear this like the dull thud of a pile driver. A brown filter spreads over everything.

"Excuse me." Phoebe stands and leaves the table.

"Phoebe—" G calls after her.

"I'm fine," she snaps and disappears into the hall.

G twists the stem of her wineglass between her fingers. "She was seventeen and wanted to finish high school in Boston, go to Harvard. So she stayed there, lived with a friend's family. Her sister, Juliette, came here to live with me." She stops and looks out the window at the moon rising over the tree line. "Until today, I hadn't seen her in five years. I never had children of my own."

"Where is Juliette?" I ask, half-afraid to hear the answer.

G turns to me. "She woke up in the night with a fever. And a cough, they said. Just finished freshman year at OSU and was supposed to come home for the summer. The school sent her to the hospital, but their quarantine was full—" She breaks off. She takes a long sip of her wine. I taste the sweetness of honey on my tongue.

"Once they saw she was sick, they wouldn't let me bring her home. They said she had to go there."

I grip the edge of the table. "Where?" I need to know. It's like the details of Juliette's story will tell me something about my dad.

"There's an empty Walmart outside Columbus. They've turned it into a hospital, if you can call it that. I don't know what to call it. It's . . . I begged them to let me take her home, but they threatened to have me arrested. She was taken up there this morning. And now I'm waiting for news." She tries to sound upbeat as she catches a tear with her napkin.

I want to tell her that I know how she feels, that my dad is in one of those places, that I'm scared to death. But I won't get the words out without crumbling. And I can't crumble. Instead, I polish off my glass of wine and pour another.

"You know, Donald was a man of faith. He never feared death," she continues. "I like to think that's why he was the one who died. He was ready on some level. I wasn't. I'm not."

"How long were you married?" asks Kamal. I look at him. What does he think about death, or marriage?

"Thirty years," she says. "Nearly. Would've been thirty years that June. I was able to fulfill my wedding vows—until death, we did not part. I'm very glad about that."

"You sound so strong," I blurt out.

"I've had time. There's a pain that never leaves. But there are other things, good things. I wouldn't have had these years with Juliette. The chance to feel like a mother for a while. That's been a gift."

I picture my own mother's face, her dark eyes and serious brow.

Then, like the glow of a firefly, the image disappears. I stand up. I grab my plate and stop. "Should we each clear our own?" I ask.

"Might as well," G replies. "But just leave everything in the sink. I'll take care of it tomorrow."

"I cannot allow you to wash dishes after making that fantastic meal," Kamal says. He puts his mask back on.

"Please," she says. "I need something to do to fill my time. Otherwise I'll just sit around and worry."

We pile the dishes in the sink and go into the living room. We get comfortable on the mismatched couches and chairs. The dogs settle at G's feet. They look alert. I feel safer with them there.

"Do you think Phoebe's all right?" Ben asks as G turns on the news.

"This is all a lot for her." G glances down the hall. "She cut us off completely when her parents died. I think it was easier for her to pretend we had all died. When I told her about Juliette, I really wasn't sure she'd come."

"I'll check on her," I say. I get up and head down the hall.

"Second door on the left," G calls.

I arrive at the basement door and open it slowly.

"Phoebe?" I call down.

"Yeah?" Her voice sounds distant. I go down and find her lying on a cot, looking at her tablet.

"Hey," I say. I try to sound unimposing.

"Hey. What's up?"

"We finished dinner."

"Great." Her eyes remain buried in her screen.

"It was good to eat food." I shift from one foot to the other.

Finally she sits up and looks at me. "So she told you the whole story, I guess?"

"I don't know if it's the whole story. She told us about your parents. And your sister. I'm so sorry."

"You didn't kill them." She shoots me a cold look, daring me to stay. I don't move. "Regrets are like, I don't know, they're like roaches," she says. "Even if you crush them under your foot, you can't be sure there aren't a million more behind the walls, you know? It makes it hard to sleep at night."

I flash again to my father's hand on the hospital door, to the time when I was five and told him I loved my mother more than I loved him, to when I never said anything about his letter of amends. I hear a clicking sound. I lean against the banister.

"I'm new to regret," I offer. "Or, I'm new to confronting the things I regret. I never thought I regretted anything until this. I guess I always assumed there would be time to fix things or change them. But death makes going back impossible."

"Yup," she says. "Did Nam respond?"

"Not yet."

"He will." She returns her gaze to her tablet and I awkwardly turn to leave. "Thomas Bell just released a video," she says. "You're up for his Fellowship, right?"

"Yeah." I turn back.

"What did you think? When you met him?"

"I thought he hated me," I reply.

"I didn't ask what he thought of you. I asked what you thought of him."

I smile. "I don't think I've actually asked myself that."

"Well, you should," she says.

"I thought he was a disconnected, arrogant weirdo," I say after a moment.

Phoebe laughs. "There you go."

"But I couldn't help liking him."

"Yeah. People seem to like him. Or hate him." She turns the tablet and I kneel down next to her.

"Not too close," she warns. I scoot back. She taps Play and an image of Bell fills the screen. He's in blue, like always, lit up against the night sky behind him. City lights twinkle in the distance. The picture is swaying slightly.

"Greetings from the Pacific Ocean," he begins. "I find it useful to step off steady ground regularly. To experience my foundation rocking underneath me. I do this to remind myself that in order to enjoy stability, I must create it. I must employ the thing we as humans are unique to possess—my rational mind. Without that, I am adrift."

I look over at Phoebe. Was she always so cool, so tough? Or did she become that way because her parents died?

"Without seeming too mysterious," Bell continues, "I say this because it speaks to the bigger problem we are facing. We feel out of control and we want stability to return. Our foundation is rocking and our government is not bringing us to safety. But I am one step closer to putting a stop to this disease."

"Shit," I whisper as hope rises in my chest and the smell of roses fills my head.

"I'm here to announce that the Avarshina Lab has identified the infectious agent at the root of ARNS. It is a type of previously unseen enterovirus, similar to polio, perhaps a derivative. We hope to know more soon. Until then, I ask you to find your own steady ground. Stay safe. Stay strong. Stay hopeful and know that I am doing all I can." And he's gone.

My heart is pounding. "That's good, isn't it?"

"I think so," Phoebe replies. "Can't stop it if they don't know what it is." She clicks the tablet off. "His voice is so weird, though. He sounds like a mouse."

I laugh. "Oh my God, yes!"

"Is that how he sounds in person?" she asks.

"Totally. And so quiet. Like, you can barely hear him."

"Well, at least he's brilliant," she says. "I watch him and I think, he's going to stop all this. He's actually going to do it."

I study her face for a moment. "Hey, can I tell you something?" I ask. "You can't tell anyone."

"Of course."

"They offered it to me. The Fellowship."

"No shit! That's amazing."

"It is, right?" I let myself feel that joy for a second. An orange glow. "I haven't really gotten to think about it. My best friend got sick right after I found out, then my dad. And my mom doesn't want me to go, so."

"You have to go."

"I know."

"You have to." The look in her eyes is like antigravity. It makes me feel like I could do anything, like I could levitate.

"Do you want to come back upstairs and hang out?" I ask.

She shakes her head.

"Okay. See you in the morning, then."

"Yeah," she says. I turn to go. "Hey, Lu?"

"Yeah?"

"You saved my life today. Twice. Thank you."

Another wave of orange. I smile. "Goodnight."

I come back up. The others are glued to FLN. "Bell's ID'ed the virus," Ben says.

"Yeah, I just saw it too." I sit down. The death toll is up to a quarter million and there's no sign of it slowing down.

"But this is not good," Kamal mutters.

"How's Phoebe?" G whispers to me.

"She's all right. Going to sleep, I think." I stand back up. "And so am I, actually."

"Sleep well, sweetheart," G says.

I stop by a wall of G's family photographs on the way back to my room. Time and space captured in a constellation of frames—one woman's personal universe.

There's one of G and a man. It must be Donald. They're standing at dusk, in that particular blue light the setting sun leaves behind. They're high on a cliff. Ocean waves rip a jagged curve along the shore beneath.

Their young faces look straight at the camera. They are real and ghostlike both, evaporating with the slow decay of the photograph itself. They are vulnerable—not afraid to show their feelings—that word transporting me back to the planetarium and my mother's secret lover.

I close my eyes and picture my mother's face that day as she intro-
duced us to Dan. Her expression was hopeful and open. Her skin
seemed to glow. I see her there, not as my mother but as a woman
with her own unmet desires. I miss her, the old her.

"I love that one," G says, appearing next to me. "We spent the
summers on Cape Cod when Donald was teaching in Boston. We
had a little cottage on a cliff. Phoebe and Juliette and their parents
would visit. Those days were among the happiest of my life." She
stares at the picture.

"I'm sorry about Donald, and about Juliette," I say. "And I hate
just saying 'I'm sorry' to everyone because it doesn't capture at all
what I mean, which is that it's awful beyond words and I wish you'd
never had to go through any of it."

"Thank you. I sense you know what it's like." She puts her hand
on my shoulder. I relax into her for just a second. My mouth fills
with that sweet honey taste. I tap my foot and swallow. "Nothing
prepares you for life except living," she says.

I nod. "Goodnight," I reply. "And thank you. For everything." I
walk swiftly back to the bedroom, to the cool, hidden safety of the
darkness.

CHAPTER 10

I wake to my phone vibrating on the bedside table. It's early, still dark. It takes me a second to recall where I am and why. I've got a new message from Nam. A rush of heat at the sight of his name.

Tell me, it says. **Who am I?** I don't have an answer. I hear Phoebe's words: "Don't be so literal." I move to the open window and breathe in the inky sky and sprawling green grass. I scan the edges of the yard. I catch a glimpse of G's electric fence.

You're me, I write.

Meaning? he replies.

First tell me something. Tell me about the video.

I made the video, he says.

Why? I ask.

To help.

Is it real?

Define real?

I smile. Good question. **Why are you hiding who you are?**

Your turn, he writes. **Explain what you meant by "I am you."**

I look back at the fence. It's like the gas mask—an instrument of safety that makes me feel less safe.

I meant that we seem to think alike. I like puzzles too. There's a long pause. I wish Phoebe were here.

Yes, he writes.

I take one last shot. **Why me?**

Because I gather you are interested in the way reality is constructed.

Constructed?

Yes.

My fingers hover over my screen. The brightening sky seems to be blotting out whatever ability I have to be clever. A hiss seeps in through the window. I don't know what else to say.

The chat dissolves. Fuck.

I sit in the stillness. I hone in on the birds outside until they drown out the imagined sound of failure. I Google Evans B. again. There's that photo of her on the conference website. I stare at it for a long time.

I wake up to the sun pouring in. My phone is still in my hand and Phoebe is sitting on the opposite bed, fully dressed.

"We have to go to Columbus," she announces.

"Okay," I mumble, immediately distracted by a text from my mother begging me to call. Nothing more from Nam.

"I want to see the camp, see what's really going on, get some images and video we can post." She looks out at the lawn. "And I need to see my sister." This is the last thing I want to do. I think back to the hospital in Brooklyn and the woman covered in blood, to Janine, to my dad. Yellow waves as my palms begin to sweat.

I sit up and plant my feet on the floor. "It's controlled by the military. They'll never let us in."

"I'll figure out a way."

I want to argue with her, but the look in her eyes tells me I will lose.

I turn to my phone. I scroll back through Nam's messages. Maybe in the daylight I'll see something I didn't in the dark.

"You get something from Nam?" Phoebe asks.

I look back at her. As I open my mouth to answer, a blue pulse and the feeling of an invisible rope around my neck. All that comes out is a cough.

"You all right?" she asks.

I swallow. "Yeah. Sorry. What did you say?"

"I was asking about Nam."

"Oh. Yeah, nothing," I lie. I'm not sure why.

We meet Kamal and Ben in the kitchen. The heavenly smell of toasting bread and coffee almost makes everything seem normal. Ben's wearing his Brooklyn Nets jersey. It makes me think of home and I decide to finally text my mom: **We're safe**. That's all I can manage.

G approaches Phoebe gently. "How are you doing, my sweet girl?"

"I'm okay," she replies. "I'm sorry about last night. I guess I underestimated how it would feel to see you."

"I'm just so glad you're here," G says.

"I've decided I need to see Juliette."

G bristles. "Darling. Of course you want that. But it's not a good idea. And they won't let you see her." G's voice trembles. "It's a quarantine. It's all soldiers and guns. They don't want anyone seeing what's really going on."

"Yeah, we can't go anywhere near that place," Ben adds.

Kamal nods. "I'm inclined to agree."

"Honestly, I wish you'd just stay here with me and forget California," G says. "I can keep you safe."

Phoebe turns to Ben. "What if Luisa were there? Would you go?" He softens, glancing at me.

"I might."

"Might?" I exclaim.

"Look, I would want to go, of course. I get it. But . . ."

"I have to go. I have to. You guys can wait in the car or whatever, but I have to try and see her." Her strong jaw and gleaming eyes, her crystalline voice—all carefully honed tools for getting what she wants. I'm powerless to argue. We all are.

We pack our bags back into Kamal's car and stand uncomfortably in the driveway. If I were Phoebe, I would stay forever. Or at least for a while.

"You sure you have everything?" G asks.

Phoebe smiles, rolling her eyes. "G, you've asked us that three times already."

"I know, I know. I just want you all to have everything you need. And I don't want you to go." She and Phoebe take each other in like deep breaths by the shore.

"I will come back," Phoebe promises. "When this is over, I will. You just keep yourself healthy. Stay healthy; stay inside. Know that I will be back." I watch them through a caramel-colored haze. G wipes tears from her eyes with the edges of her scarf and Phoebe gets into the car, taking refuge behind her sunglasses.

I open my door and stop. "I wish I could hug you," I tell G.

"Oh, me too, darling. You stay safe, Luisa."

"I will." I climb in and shut the door. I tap my foot on the floor. I have no use for sadness right now.

A moment later, we're off. The streets of Granville pass by— ample houses with front porches and screen doors, flowerbeds and wind chimes. The barbeque grills are covered and the jungle gyms, empty. Do the kids in this town dream of moving to big cities? Or are they content to run through the grass, to drink lemonade on porch swings in summer, build snowmen in winter?

We turn onto Main Street. We pass an ice cream parlor, a drug store, a little Mexican place called Cha-Cha's.

"Everything's closed," Ben notes, scanning the street out the window.

"It's the Fourth of July," Phoebe says. "And there's, you know, a pandemic."

"Shit, it's the Fourth," Ben says. "I guess no fireworks this year."

I press my hand against the window. "Dad loves fireworks."

We come to a stop sign at an intersection. A church stands on the corner, white and bright, like a small-town schoolhouse distinguished by a large rose window on the front. I've only ever been inside one church—the one near school where they hold graduation and student concerts. It always seems devoid of spiritual presence when we're in it, like we're just borrowing the building from God.

A man and woman stand outside, talking with a priest. I strain for a closer look as we move through the stop sign. The woman is holding a teddy bear and weeping. I turn toward the open road and try not to think about why she would be crying.

Up ahead there's a lone cop car parked in the middle of the street. Its lights flash silently.

The intersecting boulevard comes into view. A sprinkling of people line the street holding American flags. They're all dressed in red, white, and blue; all wearing face masks and gas masks and scarves tied around their heads.

Kamal takes manual control of the car and hits the breaks. "What the hell is this?" he asks.

"Fucking A," marvels Phoebe. "It's a parade." A marching band is coming down the street and, behind them, a float carrying a handful of people in Civil War costumes aiming their antique muskets into the air. Everyone covers their ears and a single round is fired toward the sky. The float glides on.

There's a smattering of kids sitting along the curb holding out plastic bags that glove-wearing parade-walkers fill with penny candy. The 4-H club. A handful of high school football team members in their uniforms. A teenage girl sits perched on the back of an electric-blue convertible wearing a crown and sash dubbing her the "Pork Princess." She waves like the Queen of England while her obese mother films her with her phone from the front seat. Everyone looks morose, yet stoic. Like this is their parade and their America and no one is taking that away from them.

"I don't know whether to be impressed or horrified," Kamal says.

"Impressed," I reply.

"Horrified," snaps Phoebe simultaneously. My eyes are drawn to one girl. She sits near but apart from a group of other kids. She's maybe nine or ten, wearing bubblegum-pink overalls, her auburn hair in two long braids. She looks down at the pavement. She ignores the candy being tossed in her direction. Her shoulders shake. Tears drip down her cheeks. Maybe a parent gone, or a sibling.

Twenty feet of space and a car door between us, but in some way we are as close as any two people can be. We are united by the surreal pain of existing in a life that is still familiar but indelibly altered by loss.

"We should go," Phoebe says quietly. She's looking at the crying girl too.

Kamal nods and we turn around. We ride silently for several miles. The landscape turns to farmland.

We pass a Red Cross relief outpost in the middle of a field. "So lame," mumbles Phoebe. "They've got all those people lined up and I guarantee you all they've got is a pile of blankets and some pamphlets about washing your hands during flu season. They don't know what people actually need."

"At least they're trying," Ben replies. "I don't see Front Line anywhere out here."

"That's because this is the middle of nowhere. Go to any big city in the country and Front Line is everywhere, getting the most help to the most people."

"So people who don't live in cities are just out of luck?"

"God, Ben. Are you always so combative? And so literal? It's not realistic to help everyone. You have to focus on the most efficient solution, which is to help the highest concentrations of people."

"I know," Ben replies with a smirk. "I just like giving you a hard time." Phoebe's shoulders soften. I sense this energy between them like a drop in barometric pressure. Does everyone feel that, or just me?

Ben picks up his phone. "China is saying they've got a handle on a vaccine."

Again hope swells inside me. "Is it for real?"

Ben keeps scrolling. "CDC is saying no. But who knows. It's all about drug companies and money, so who the fuck knows. But if China cures this thing before we do? Embarrassing!"

Kamal laughs. "Oof."

"I know, I know. I'm an asshole." He looks over at me. "But it's kinda true."

"True that you are an asshole, yes," Kamal adds, smiling back at my brother. This moment startles me. It's like I'd forgotten they are such good friends, and like they had too.

We come around a wide bend in the road. A train whistles in the distance. I reach for the flattened quarter hanging around my neck. I think of my dad. His face. The wind in the trees. The sound of his smile. I look at Ben as the whistle moans in the distance. I feel small, like an ant carrying its hope for survival across the vastness of a city sidewalk.

"You heard from Mom?" Ben asks quietly.

"I texted her we're safe." He nods and his gaze drifts out the window. I follow it. Beyond the passing fields, there's a black cloud of smoke rising up into the clear blue sky. As we speed toward it, a smell weaves its way into the car. It's like burnt meat, metal, and rubber with a sweetness underneath it all. It's the kind of smell you never, ever forget.

"Jesus," mutters Kamal. He covers his face with his hands.

"It smells like Blackout," Ben says.

Phoebe flinches. "They're burning bodies," she murmurs.

I gag. Heat spreads down my arms and legs. Waves of brown, yellow, purple.

"That is so fucked," Ben says. "I seriously might puke."

We get closer and closer to the smoke rising. I imagine dead bodies being cast into a burning pit. The smell makes me want to evaporate into the ether. I try to plant my feet in the imaginary sand. I try to let the colors come, to tell myself they can't hurt me, but they just get worse. I start to panic. I look back through the rear window. Flash after flash and I can barely see the road. I want to get out. I want to go home. I want to make it all stop.

"You okay?" Ben asks. I turn and focus on his face, on his dark curls. I reach my hand across the seat, carefully so Phoebe and Kamal won't see. He grasps it. I close my eyes, tap my foot, and count down from a hundred in my head. I breathe through my mouth.

Slowly the colors calm.

I feel foolish. And freakish. What is wrong with me? Why can't I control this shit, or just accept it?

The Walmart sign appears up ahead, blurry behind a screen of hot air that seems to waver like a sheet of rippling water.

"That it?" Ben asks. Phoebe nods. The traffic slows. The car is silent. The parking lot is walled by razor wire, broken in only one spot: a military-operated checkpoint. There's a string of vehicles

EMILY ZIFF GRIFFIN

maybe twelve deep waiting to drive through. Ambulances, military jeeps, supply trucks, and us, the only ordinary car.

"No way they let us in here," Ben exclaims as we stop behind a truck.

"Have a little confidence," Phoebe replies. "Actually, Kamal, let's switch seats."

She and Kamal jump out and quickly switch sides. Phoebe settles herself into the driver's seat and takes down her ponytail. Her hair fans out around her face like the feathers of a firebird. Her shampoo smells of lavender.

"Kamal, when we get through I want you to go in and get some photos and videos. People need to see this. Are you up for that?"

He nods and we make the turn into the checkpoint.

"Do you have some sort of plan?" Ben asks.

Phoebe pulls off her mask and opens her window. "I always have a plan," she says.

I look out. Half a dozen soldiers in desert fatigues and gas masks stand stationed around lanes marked by tall piles of sandbags. Large gates run across the middle.

A soldier steps up to the window, his assault rifle cradled in one hand. His name is stitched onto his uniform: Connors. His strong, nimble frame reminds me of Ben's.

"This is a restricted area. Are you ill or transporting an infected person?" His voice is muffled slightly by the mask.

"I'm here to see my sister. She was brought here," Phoebe says. Her tone is fragile and seductive at once.

"I'm sorry, ma'am. No access without authorization."

"Please," she says evenly, emotion dancing across her face. "She's my only sister. Our parents died in Blackout and we were separated. I haven't seen her in five years," she pauses. "I need to tell her I'm sorry for leaving her behind." The soldier stares deeply as she communicates between words. "I need to tell her," she says again. "It's my last chance."

"I wish I could help you, ma'am, I do." His voice is shaking slightly. I lean forward. As I look past the transparent plastic screen of his mask, I realize that he's probably only a year or two older than I am—just out of high school and standing there, holding a weapon that could annihilate two dozen people in seconds.

"You *can* help me," Phoebe implores.

"My brother died in Blackout," he says. "That's why I decided to serve."

"So you know," Phoebe replies, drawing him further toward her with her eyes. "This is my last chance."

Connors looks behind him. "I'm sorry, ma'am. I have orders. You'll need to reverse direction at the turnout and exit on the other side of this barrier." He motions ahead. Phoebe remains still. Her stare is so intense we don't notice the commotion at first.

Then suddenly, we all turn.

A group of marines has surrounded a flatbed truck stopped in the exit lane. Their rifles are drawn and they're yelling.

"Connors," one of them calls, his gun trained on the truck.

Connors turns.

Another marine climbs into the back and pulls up a tarp. Two men are hiding underneath. "There a problem over there, Connors?"

"No sir," Connors yells, turning back to Phoebe. My stomach

rolls at the sight of the men. They are draped in bed sheets, barely able to stand when the marines order them to their feet. "Proceed to the next checkpoint. You'll be given the safety protocol. Say you are Red Cross volunteers." Connors pulls four VISITOR ID badges from a pack around his waist and hands them through the window. "Be in and out quickly. Don't touch anyone." Phoebe grabs the badges and shifts the car into drive. Connors motions for the gate to be opened.

"Thank you," Phoebe says. "Your brother would be so proud of you."

He ducks his head and waves us on as a military convoy comes tearing up the opposite lane. Two figures in HAZMAT suits lead the sick men out of the truck. Connors jogs over to assist them. We drive forward.

"I cannot believe you pulled that off!" Ben exclaims.

"I can," Kamal says. Before I can worry too much about the way he's looking at her, I notice piles of toys, bikes, clothes, boxes of cereal, and canned food—the stuff of normal life that once filled the store, now ripped out and baking in the sun next to a line of army jeeps and stretchers. I snap a photo with my phone.

We stop at the next checkpoint. An aid worker in head-to-toe protective gear approaches the window. "IDs?" she demands. Phoebe hands over the badges. "How long?"

"Excuse me?" Phoebe replies.

"How long will you be here?" The woman's voice is hoarse and impatient.

"Not long," Phoebe answers. "We're picking up supplies for the Red Cross."

"Park there on the left." She hands back the badges and points to an empty spot a ways down. We pull ahead into it.

Phoebe looks at Kamal. "You ready?"

He nods. "Let's do it."

She looks back at me and Ben. "We'll be quick."

"Yeah," Ben grumbles. Kamal and Phoebe get out.

I look over at the entrance to the store. "I'm going with you," I call.

Ben's voice comes down like a hammer: "No way."

I turn to him. "I want to see what's going on in there."

"Twenty minutes ago you were holding my hand, freaking out." At least he has the mercy to say this quietly enough that Kamal and Phoebe don't hear.

"I know, but I'm good now. I can do this." I need to test myself. I need to prove that I'm moving forward, not backward. "I want to see where Dad is."

"We don't know where Dad is," Ben barks. "He's definitely not in there."

I grab one of the visitor's badges and step out of the car. Ben scrambles out behind me.

"This is a place that's currently being referred to as a death camp," he yells. "Death. Get it? It's bad enough we're even in this parking lot. Not to mention your thing. Your *condition*." He says it like he isn't sure it's real. "I forbid you from going in there."

"You forbid me?" A flash of violet. I breathe deep.

"Yeah. I forbid you one hundred percent."

"She's not a child," Kamal snaps sharply.

Ben stares daggers at him. "Yes she is."

Phoebe steps between them. "Stop making a scene," she warns. "I don't want to get shot by a marine."

Ben's eyes burrow into her. "This is your fault." His voice wobbles. "It's ridiculous that we are even here. Your dying sister is not our problem. Your lame crusader mission is not our problem."

Phoebe steps back. "Asshole," she says. She pins on her badge and walks away. Kamal and I turn to follow her.

"You do this and I'll call Mom," Ben shouts.

"Go ahead," I yell back. "What's she gonna do from a thousand miles away?" I leave my brother standing by the car and catch up to Phoebe. "I'm sorry he said that. He's being a dick."

"It's fine," she says coolly.

"He's just scared."

"I'm gonna go ahead." She quickens her pace.

"Hey," I call after her. "Good luck." She smiles and turns, putting her mask back on and pulling her hair into a tight bun. The little girl I saw at G's is hidden away again.

"You sure you want to go in there?" Kamal asks.

"Yes." We walk toward the entrance. "He's just like my mother," I say. "Trying to control me, but he's the one who's scared."

"He doesn't want to see you hurt. I can't disagree with him there."

My face flushes with a burst of orange.

"What did he mean, 'your condition'?" Kamal asks.

"Nothing. Just something from when I was a kid," I tell him. "I don't have it anymore."

We pass deliberately through the Walmart doors. We're herded through an x-ray machine, then led to a bank of portable sinks. They tell us to wash our hands and forearms with antibacterial soap. It smells of cherry candy and feels cool on my skin. We're draped in green gowns. Our hands are sheathed in latex gloves, the wrist openings sealed against our skin with white tape. Our heads are crowned with shower caps and our faces are swallowed by fresh masks.

The inside of the store has been gutted, save for the cash registers—a perfect line of cheerful, numbered corrals. They look like the starting gates at a racetrack.

I glance beyond and there are rows and rows of beds. More than I can count or could've imagined. My heart seems to plummet into my legs. My stomach begins to twist and my head spins in a swirl of red and brown. I lose my footing and fall against Kamal.

He catches my gloved hands in his. "Whoa," he whispers.

I clamp my eyes shut. I conjure sand beneath my feet and the rhythmic sound of the ocean booming.

I open my eyes and look back at all the people. My stomach swirls and the colors tint my vision, but I hold my gaze steady. "It's just waves," I mutter to myself.

Kamal squeezes my hands. "Hey, hey. You all right?"

"Yeah. I just . . . I got a little dizzy. I'm fine."

"You sure?"

I nod. He takes my hand and we begin to walk. My legs buzz and his smell mixes with the nauseating odor of piss and shit. The place feels like an airplane cabin during turbulence. People's whispers are punctuated by the sounds of coughing, vomiting, and the beeping of machines.

EMILY ZIFF GRIFFIN

We move through rows of beds, body after body. Some are frozen in death; others are lifeless even as they continue to breathe. I see everything through a haze of scarlet and tree-bark brown. I strap on my watch over my gown, open the camera, and start recording.

We pass a sleeping child clutching a stuffed giraffe. We pass a woman whose face is obscured by her long hair caked to her cheeks with sweat.

A heavyset woman calls out "Sarah!" as we walk by. She looks at me like she knows me. She reaches out her arm. "Water, please!" she begs before burrowing under the thin white blanket that barely covers her large body. She shivers and so do I.

A loud crash as a nurse upends a tray of instruments. The clatter of metal on the floor halts the colors. I stop the camera and kneel down to help the nurse. Her eyes are swollen and ringed with circles.

"I haven't slept. I can't keep my hands steady," she explains as we pile her supplies back on the tray. I stand up and grab Kamal's hand. I start filming again.

I lock eyes with a man roughly my father's age. He lies under a white sheet, one shoulder peeking out. His cheeks are hollow and he looks up at me like he's asking for something. I look away, then back.

I wonder if somewhere in New Jersey there's a girl avoiding my dying father's eyes.

I gasp for breath as the swirling hues return. Kamal's hand presses against mine. Our fingers weave together like braided rope.

"This is worse than I thought," I whisper. He nods, carefully snapping a photo when no one is looking. We keep going.

We come upon a tent made from strung-up bed sheets. A

cardboard sign above the opening reads CHAPEL scrawled in black marker. Kamal drifts toward it, leading us inside. Several short rows of folding chairs face a trio of upended plastic garbage cans covered with burning candles.

I take a breath. The sensations ease up. Inside here, it's like being in the pool. There's a calm, reverent feeling. Three women sit shrouded in protective gear facing the flickering candles. Their heads are bowed in prayer. A fourth sits off to the side reading a Bible. She looks up at me. Her eyes sparkle in the light.

Kamal sits down and lowers his chin to his chest. He closes his eyes and begins whispering words I can't discern. I stop the camera and move closer. I take the seat next to his. He's speaking Arabic. I don't understand the words, but the harsh edges of the sounds mix with the softness of their rhythm. They transmit meaning the way music does, through feeling and intention.

I am lulled by his prayer. The sadness in his voice floods my body as the strength underneath it lifts me up. I gaze at the woman reading the Bible.

Is her God kind or punishing?

When Kamal finishes I put my hand on his knee.

"We should go," I whisper. He opens his eyes and nods. We stand up.

The woman with the Bible moves swiftly toward us. "Here," she murmurs, handing me the book. "Here."

"I can't," I whisper, handing it back.

"I'm not sick. It hasn't been touched by anyone infected," she assures me.

"No, it isn't that," I say. "I'm not religious."

Her eyes dance in the candlelight.

"Religion and spirit are two very different things," she says. "You have a spirit. Therefore the Bible is your story. Read it like a childhood favorite and God will find his way to you."

I want to believe her, but I don't. I've observed forces and dimensions we can't fathom represented on the page by math. I know there is more to reality than just our everyday experience. I am evidence of that. But saying the word *God* like it's a real thing makes me feel like an idiot. Holding a Bible makes me feel like a phony.

"Okay," I say, just wanting to go.

Kamal and I leave through the hanging sheets. We shuffle back through the sea of beds and arrive at the exit station. We dump our protective clothes into a bin. They give us yet another set of gloves and masks. I pause, holding the Bible over the heap of refuse, ready to drop it.

"Keep it moving," a voice calls from behind. Next thing I know, we're back on the hot pavement outside. The book is still in my hands.

Kamal glances at my watch. "You get anything?"

"I feel like my hands were shaking the whole time. Whatever I shot probably looks like shit."

"Yeah." He opens the photos on his phone.

"But I'm glad I went in," I add.

"You're not afraid of anything, are you?"

"Actually, I'm afraid of everything."

"Liar."

I smile and he stops walking.

"What?"

"I'm just thinking," he says.

"What are you thinking?"

He pulls up his mask. "I don't know. It's not the right time, I guess." His focus on me is steady, like the sun in a cloudless sky. I pull up my mask and meet his eyes, allowing the pulses of orange and silver that come. "We should go," he says, replacing his mask.

My fingers clutch the Bible as we walk, a buoy in unfamiliar water.

CHAPTER 11

Ben's sitting in the car when we get back. His eyes are red and narrow. His jaw is tight.

"You're still pissed?" I growl. Kamal and I climb in. Ben avoids my gaze and he says nothing. Phoebe arrives a minute later.

"Let's go," she says brusquely and disappears behind her sunglasses. Kamal puts the car into gear. The engine's soundlessness amplifies the tension smothering us all.

I look out the back window as we creep toward the checkpoint. The Walmart is like a murky lake—still and calm on the surface, roiling with putrid decay inside. My throat tightens.

We exit slowly through the barricades and I glimpse Connors manning his post. I want to call to him to get in the car with us. I want to save him even if he doesn't think he needs saving. Or maybe I just want my brother to not be angry at me.

We trade this bleak strip of suburban sprawl for the cow pastures and prairies of rural Ohio. The still-rising tower of black smoke anchors the view to the north. I stare at it through sepia tones until it fades into the distance.

I check my watch. No messages.

"Did you find her?" I ask Phoebe.

She blinks slowly. "I did."

"How is she?"

She smacks her lips and looks out at the wide-open swath of grass holding up an electric summer sky. "Did you get any pictures?" she asks.

"Yeah. I'll send you what I got," I tell her.

I look at the video I shot. Faces shuffle by in a shaky frame, but the camera lingers where I stopped walking: on the man with hollow cheeks and a pleading stare.

The footage continues past the point where I looked away. The man mouths something, looking straight into the lens.

I run it back a few seconds and watch again. I watch his lips.

It looks like, "I'm sorry." A clicking sound and a chill up my spine. I turn it off.

Kamal reaches for the GPS and puts the car into Selfdrive.

"How far are we?" Ben asks.

"A day and a half, little less. Depends how much we stop."

"We shouldn't stop at all," I say. "Unless we have to."

I look at Ben and try to think of something I can say to soften his mood. I'm searching for something funny, a story I can tell, but nothing funny comes to mind.

We pass a clapboard farmhouse with a tractor out front. An old barn and grain silo stand off to the side. Behind them, rows of corn that stretch toward the horizon. Nature is the rule maker here. Survival depends on willingness, hard work, and the miraculous, unpredictable generosity of the earth itself. I want my life to be like that. I want my love for my father and my willingness to do anything to save him to make a miracle occur.

The haunting howl of the train whistle breaks my reverie. X-shaped signs on railroad-crossing posts loom ahead of us. Red-and-white barrier bars reach high toward the open sky.

My eyes are pulled past them to the squiggly whisper of two moving figures up ahead. They are barely visible behind a wall of hot air refracting the light.

The whistle again, only louder now. It pulls my focus to the right. The snaking train comes charging across the plain.

The bells ring.

I shoot back to the crossing. The red lights are flashing. The bars make their smooth descent into place. The two figures are getting closer, now on our side of the tracks. We cruise toward them. Then our speed gently slows.

A clear look at their faces and a burst of yellow like a punch.

"Turn around!" I exclaim.

"What?" The car stops ten or so feet behind the tracks and the train comes ripping past with a jolt.

The two figures, a man and woman, are now on either side of the car. Their skin is pink with sunburn and their plain clothes are smudged with dirt.

"Seriously, turn around," I insist. Kamal fumbles with the

controls. I squint through the haze of banana-colored light making it difficult to see.

The man whips a gun from behind his back. He points it straight at Kamal's head.

"Open the window," he yells, his voice muffled by the thundering train.

I dig my nails into the seat. I glance at the woman standing by Phoebe's door. She's holding a knife. I remember my own knife, only inches from my hands inside my backpack. But this man, he has a gun.

Kamal brings the window down.

"I'm going to need each of you to step out of the car, slowly. No fucking around," the man says.

"We shouldn't be here," murmurs Ben. "I fucking knew it." Kamal puts his hands up and the man opens his door. The woman opens Phoebe's and then Ben's. My stomach drops into my knees. Practically blind, I feel for my pack. We might survive without the car, but we won't make it without food and water. My door opens with a sound like a soda top popping.

"Let's go, get out," the man with the gun says. But his voice wavers. It has a metallic taste.

I climb out, slowly, holding my backpack.

It's just waves, I think.

I glance at the train chugging past. Its rhythm dulls the color in my view just enough that when I look back at the man, I can see his eyes clearly. Uneasiness seeps from his pores along with his sweat. The guys in the tunnel were all about the feeling of power. But this man is desperate and afraid. Which means he's truly dangerous.

"Get in," the man calls to the woman with the knife, his gaze never leaving mine.

Our eyes exchange the light bouncing off each other's faces. Warmth starts to build in my chest. It quickly becomes a blazing heat that radiates out. It seems to envelope him. Sweat drips down his temples.

The last of the train's cars passes. The clacking and grating of the wheels fades into the distance and it's as if he and I are the only two people on the planet. His hand starts to shake. Tears begin to fall from his eyes. All the while, his gun is pointing at my heart.

My own eyes well as he begins to weep. Then, the swell of invisible heat holding us together recedes. He lowers the gun and wipes his face with the back of his hand. He looks quickly at Kamal, then scrambles into the driver's seat, slams the door, and peels out.

The four of us stand there watching our car get smaller and smaller.

"What the fuck?" Phoebe exclaims. "You just, like, looked at that guy and he started crying." She glances down at her hands. "I'm shaking."

"People talk about their lives flashing before their eyes and I always thought that was utter bullshit, but it just happened." Kamal's voice sounds wild. "I was standing there like, we are all about to die and I saw my whole life like one of those flipbooks."

I crumple to the ground.

"Shit." Kamal kneels down to face me. "You all right?"

"I feel weak," I say.

"Let's get out of the road, okay?" He helps me up and leads me over to the grass. I sit back down.

"You're hungry. And thirsty," Ben says, his tone still cold. "And we've just been carjacked at gunpoint. I knew this whole trip was a mistake."

"Take some deep breaths," Kamal says, ignoring him. I lift my mask and take in the fresh air, wondering if Ben is right. What if we are going to get ourselves killed out here?

Kamal picks up my pack. "Nice move grabbing this." He opens it and fishes out a nutrition bar. "Are you able to walk?" He hands me the bar. "Because we need to keep moving." I nod and slowly stand.

He turns to Phoebe. "Can Front Line send us another car or something?"

She looks at her watch. "No service." The rest of us check ours.

I look back at the railroad crossing. "We can follow the tracks," I say. "When we reach the nearest rail yard we'll either have service or we can jump a train."

The three of them stare at me.

"What?"

Kamal laughs. "You're like some kind of apocalypse Jedi." I smile and put my mask back on.

We start walking along the silvery curving lines that stretch out into forever as the sun dips behind a cloud, covering us in shade.

Ben hangs back a few yards as we find a rhythm. I keep checking my watch: no service.

"I'm sorry for what I said back there," Ben says suddenly. "About your sister not being our problem."

Phoebe turns. "Thank you. I know this is all hard for you too."

Ben nods and we keep walking. "What was it like? To see her?" he asks.

"Hard," she replies. "And now I have this image of her in my head. It's all I can see."

"But didn't you have that anyway? Weren't you already imagining something awful?" He's talking about himself. I can tell.

"Yeah, but what I saw is real. I know it's real now."

"Does that make it worse?" His interest is genuine, and I share it. I have a picture in my head. Our father is lying paralyzed on a cot in New Jersey, shivering, scared, and entirely alone. Would I feel better or worse if I could see him?

"It's awful," she answers. "I don't know if it's worse."

"Was she able to talk?" I ask.

"I don't really want to talk about this actually," she replies sharply.

We walk on without speaking. It's late afternoon when we reach the rail yard. Massive diesel engines buzz as they refuel. A lone worker walks alongside one of the trains making notes on a clipboard. We watch him. He's just a guy at work. If we didn't know what was happening, this would look like just another ordinary day.

"Stay here," Phoebe says. She charges toward him, stuffing her mask and gloves into the back pocket of her denim shorts.

We find some shade and watch her delicate fingers pull her bangs aside. Her jewel-like eyes catch the light. Her bra strap falls from her shoulder and lands on the smooth, milky skin of her upper arm. She smiles like, "Oops."

The worker's eyes fall on the pink band of elastic. He cocks his head to the side as she talks. He's going to tell her whatever she wants to know.

I look over at Ben and Kamal watching her. I forget for a second that I exist.

A minute later Phoebe heads back toward us. The worker watches her go. She moves like she can feel his eyes on her—chest high, hips rolling from side to side. I wonder how she learned to be the way she is. How did she become a woman and not just a girl?

"The train on the fourth track over there is going to California," she tells us. "It leaves in about an hour and arrives in LA the day after tomorrow."

"Amazing," Kamal gushes. We sneak around the hulking masses of steel and find the westbound train. We walk down until we come to an open boxcar.

"This looks good," Phoebe says.

Kamal hesitates. "So we just jump in there or?"

I throw my backpack inside. "I guess so."

Phoebe climbs in first, then Kamal, then me. The humid air inside envelops us in deep shade and the smell of stale coffee. Ben remains standing on the graveled cement.

"What's up?" I ask.

"I didn't say good-bye," he answers. I search his face, boyish like our dad's. His eyes are glassy. "I need to see him again."

"You will. When this is all over and we go home, you'll see him. And you won't have to say good-bye."

"C'mon, Lu. We both know that's not how this is gonna go."

"I don't know that."

"Well, I do. And look, I get it. We came on this trip because we wanted to do something and we were desperate. But at this point, we're just being delusional. You saw that place. It's filled with people just like Dad. I'm sorry, but they're all going to die, every last one of them. I need to say good-bye, if it's not already too late. I have to try. I can't live with myself if I don't."

I look down at the scar on my knee. I think of my father, how he would hold me when I fell. I want to see him too. I want to be next to him on the couch, to hear him playing piano through the closed door.

"I have to go back," he says.

But that's not the life that's waiting for us back home.

"And I have to stay," I tell him. "I'm not ready to give up."

We stare hard at each other, tethered by the intangible bond that exists only between siblings. It's a bond that begins before birth and in that sense before time, before space, before matter.

"I'm not a child," I say evenly, peppermint washing over me.

"I know," he says. His eyes brim with tears. "I know." He turns to Kamal and Phoebe. "You guys have to take care of her. Keep her safe."

"Of course," Kamal murmurs.

"'Cause we made a deal not to die." He smiles. Silver light flickers across my eyes. God, I love Ben.

He looks up at Phoebe. "One of these trains going to New York?"

"That one," she says, pointing to the train on the farthest track. "He said that one leaves tonight, going east."

Ben nods and looks back at me. I grab my bag and pull out a Mountain House meal pack and a nutrition bar.

"Here, take these. And some water." I hand him my canteen. He takes a long sip. He's careful to keep his lips from touching the rim. He passes it back.

I press my hands against the cool steel of the train floor to stave off the sadness that's starting to swirl in me. "*Te quiero, hermanito,*" I say.

"*Yo también, hermanita.*" My eyes follow him across the yard until he disappears into the darkness of an empty car. I lean back against the wall and take a drink.

"How much water is there?" Kamal asks.

"It's almost full."

"Okay, so we're not going to die from dehydration. Probably."

"Did I say I was sharing it with you?" I smile and take another glorious sip. Then I pass it to Kamal, who does the same and passes it to Phoebe.

"About half gone now," he says. "Let's not drink more until we absolutely have to." I nod. "What about eats?"

I open my bag. "I've got mac and cheese, cherry pie, lentil stew, and six bars, which are each a full day of calories."

"Cherry pie, please," Kamal replies immediately.

Phoebe takes the lentils and I go with the mac and cheese. I pull up my mask and take a bite. "Oh, holy shit, that's disgusting!" I spit it out the door of the car.

Phoebe breathes through her mouth, "Mine tastes literally like dirty socks."

"Mine's delicious," Kamal chirps with a devilish, grinning mouthful of syrupy red pie goop.

"Jerk," I tease.

He pauses, eyes bright.

"Gentleman," he corrects, breaking off a piece of pie. I take it, then look away. I try not to smile too wide.

We sit and wait for the train to move. The cicadas outside work up a racket and the air cools as the sun goes down.

"Too bad about Ben," Phoebe says after a while. "I was just starting not to loathe him."

"Yeah, he can be an asshole." I check my phone for the one-hundredth time. "And he can be the best."

"But it's better he's going back," she adds. I look across the yard to the empty car where Ben is sitting. He's going home to our house, to my tree in the garden, his room, his bed, a kitchen full of food, and our parents. Or, our mom.

"I hope I'm not making a mistake," I mumble.

"You're not," Phoebe says. The train lurches, then glides smoothly forward. I leap to the doorway and Ben appears from the shadows of his car.

"Be safe," I whisper. We stand looking at each other until we lose sight. I sit back down next to Kamal.

"He'll be fine," Kamal says. I nod.

Phoebe tucks herself into a cool, dark corner and shuts her eyes. The smell of diesel and hot metal melts into waves of honeysuckle and bergamot, grass and hay. The breeze cools my skin. The click-clack rocks us with the easy rhythm of a mother's hand. I close my eyes for a minute and let it trick me into forgetting where we are and why.

When I look up, Kamal is sitting at the edge of the car with his feet dangling out the door. This makes me nervous.

"Be careful," I tell him.

He keeps his eyes on the rolling landscape outside. "I haven't heard from my parents in ten days," he says.

"Where are they?"

"They went to our place in Bermuda two weeks ago. I talked to them once after they got there. Then all this started and they haven't called. They don't answer the phone or e-mail or texts."

"Is there someone else there you can maybe reach?"

"Tried our neighbors; no answer. Our club told me they hadn't been in for a week. The thing is," he continues slowly, "I'm not sure I care that much." He turns toward me. "I mean, I would obviously be sad if something's happened. If they're dead. But in a lot of ways, if they died, my life wouldn't actually be that different. Awful to say. But I think it's the truth."

"Maybe it's just impossible to feel it in the abstract, until it's real."

"Maybe," he replies quietly, looking back outside.

"I keep wishing it were my mom, not my dad," I confess. "And then I feel like the worst person alive."

Kamal pulls his mask up onto his head and looks at me.

I pull mine up and meet his eyes. This act of rebellion is like diving into the Red Hook pool in the middle of the night—freeing, and dangerous enough to make it worth doing. I inch closer to him so I can smell his smell underneath the fragrant air. I tell myself to remember every last detail of this moment so I can share it with Janine.

And my heart breaks a little more.

"What were you praying about in the chapel?" I ask.

"I was praying for an end to this. I was praying for all the sick. *As'alu Allah al 'azim rabbil 'arshil azim an yashifika*, which means 'I ask Allah, the Mighty, the Lord of the Mighty Throne, to cure you.'"

"That's beautiful."

"But I was thinking especially of your dad."

I let the train rock me toward him just a little closer. My legs dangle next to his and I grip the floor with one hand to steady the sensation of falling.

"Even though, in Islam, you aren't supposed to pray for non-believers." I look out at the setting sun's golden beams flashing across the sky. They mix with silver sparks of my own creation as we chug across the plains.

"'*As'alu Allah . . . ,*'" I begin, then stop. Kamal says the whole prayer again. "One more time," I ask. I commit it to memory.

"You're meant to say it seven times," he says. And so we do. Seven times, together.

I don't expect a miracle, but the act of speaking words that have been said by millions of others for over a thousand years, of asking for the thing I want most, connects me to something beyond myself. It lets me take action when I don't know what else to do. If it's possible for a prayer to be answered, then maybe mine will be. If it's not, then I'm no worse off than before.

"Thank you for that," I say.

He nods. I get lost for a second in the arcing lines of his shoulders curving down across his broad chest, meeting at his narrow hips.

"Why did you come on this trip?" I ask suddenly.

"Phoebe," he replies.

I pull my legs up into the train and glance over at her. She looks gentle and harmless asleep. Like a tiger.

"She's so focused and furious about the things she cares about," he explains. "It's good to be around someone like that."

"Right," I manage to say.

"I guess I was afraid that if I didn't go with her, I would end up in my parents' ridiculous apartment drinking myself into oblivion, then passing out and drowning in the hot tub, or something equally pathetic." He pauses. "I was basically just afraid of being alone."

I think back to the moment I first saw Phoebe, her eyes sparkling like a cat's and her red hair shimmering like waves of fire. How powerful she seemed. How small I felt next to her.

"But you know we're just friends, right? We've always just been friends," he says.

A smile creeps across my face. "Good," I say.

His smell is getting stronger by the second.

"Good?"

And his eyes glimmer in the twilight.

"Yeah. Good." A flash of red light explodes across our faces. For a split second I think it's just me who saw it, that it's a signal someone sick is close. But then I hear the boom and I realize: It's fireworks.

"No way," I marvel. Another one bursts wide across the sky, then another.

"Happy Independence," Kamal says.

I laugh. "Thank God we got away from the scourge of English tyranny."

We sit and watch. We don't speak. I think of my family and the years when Ben and I were little, how we would sit on the beach eating buckets of fresh clams and watermelon, waiting for the fireworks to start. How we'd snuggle under blankets when the salt air grew brisk and fall asleep in the car on the way home. Memory is a kind of time travel, but it eventually demands we accept that there is no going back.

"Why did you come?" he asks. "Do you really think you can save him?"

"I'm afraid that if I say no, that's what will happen. But the truth is I'm not sure. I'm trying not to think about what will happen if I can't."

Kamal places his gloved hand down next to me, palm up. An invitation. My thoughts race. A flash of orange and a wave of pine. I put my own hand on top of his. Our fingers interlace. The bright, exploding lights fade away and the stars take their place.

The train rocks us.

"I feel almost safe," he says after a while. "And maybe . . . does it sound weird to say I feel, like, more alive than usual?"

"It sounds the opposite of weird," I reply. "I know exactly what you mean." The chilly air swirls around us and we sit like that. Rocking, holding hands, looking out into the crisp night.

And then I decide to tell him.

"So I have this thing," I begin. "It's what my brother was talking about before."

"Okay. . . ."

"It's not like something horrible." Part of me wants to pull my hand away from his. But I don't.

Maybe I even grasp a little tighter.

"It's just a condition. Where I feel my emotions differently from normal people. I feel them with different senses, like I see and smell and taste them." I'm afraid to look at him. "Sorry. I'm not used to explaining it to people. So it's hard for me to describe."

"Keep trying." His voice is gentle, curious.

"Well, like, right now, I'm nervous. So I'm seeing little bursts of yellow light. And pink from the cold. And I can smell you."

He sniffs his own armpit and laughs. "I guess I do kind of stink."

"Not like that," I say. "When I'm feeling a lot, of whatever kind of feelings, people sometimes make me smell or taste or hear things. With you, I get the smell of pine trees."

"Pine trees. Like Christmas?"

"Yeah."

"I quite like that actually. I love Christmas trees."

"Me too."

"I'm glad it's not something disgusting. I mean, does anyone ever smell like dog shit or something?"

"Not so far."

He looks at me. "What about Phoebe?"

"She tastes like salt."

"Huh."

Silence.

My free hand slides over the lip of the door frame. I move it back and forth over the edge. What is he thinking?

"It's really kind of cool," he says finally.

I exhale relief. "You think?"

"Yeah."

"I've always hated it. I've always thought I had to try and override it. Keep it in check. I always thought it made me weak. And weird. But since all this started, I don't know. It's like I'm starting to understand it better and it's actually not so bad."

"Is that what happened with the guy who stole the car? Did he give you some sort of feeling?"

"I'm still not sure what that was about. I did feel a warm sensation between us. Like I could feel his fear in my own body somehow. What I've started to notice, like with him and the guy at the gas station, the guys in the tunnel, is that I seem to know by sensing something inside them what they really want, and what they might be about to do."

"So you *are* a Jedi."

We both laugh.

"Obviously."

"Can you tell what I want?" he asks, turning serious.

We lock eyes. Colors scream in all directions. My legs seem to crumble underneath me.

It's just waves.

"I think so," I say softly.

His hand tugs on mine and, without words, we move to the corner of the car and lie down facing each other. We put our masks back on, but there are only inches between us. With each inhale, we move closer together. We exhale and separate. The rumble of the train shakes the floor underneath us.

Kamal was right: We are more alive than usual.

At some point, I let my eyes close and I drift into a dream.

I'm at the top of the Empire State Building with the woman who gave me the Bible. We're looking north over Manhattan. It's dusk. The city sparkles like diamonds against a lavender sky. The wind blows through my hair, long and dark like it was when I was a child.

"Can you feel it?" she asks. "The wind? That's God's hand, washing you clean." I look down and see she's very pregnant. A second later she goes into labor, but it's nothing like it is in the movies. She closes her eyes. She concentrates. Seconds later, a perfect little baby boy with dark curly hair pops out from underneath her dress. His face is blissful, serene. His eyes are closed and he doesn't cry.

The woman turns to me, beaming. "Look at him. Just look!" She puts the baby in my arms. I hold him nervously, his plump red lips making soft sucking sounds. "Let's call him Lazarus," she says.

I nod yes.

"Lazarus," I say, looking down at his sweet face. And then his eyelids flutter open, revealing blank spaces of skin where his eyes should be. I jump back and wake up terrified, grasping to remember where I am.

The train has stopped dead in the middle of a field.

"Lazarus," I whisper to myself. Kamal and Phoebe are both asleep. I look at my watch: 11:35 p.m. "Lazarus." I scramble to my pack and take out the Bible. I move toward a pool of moonlight by the door and impatiently page through the chapters until I find it: the story of the Raising of Lazarus in the Book of John.

In the story, Jesus goes to visit the tomb of his recently deceased friend Lazarus. The villagers, including Lazarus's two sisters, are upset that Jesus didn't come sooner and save this man whom they all loved.

Jesus tells them that if they believe he is the Son of God, Lazarus will rise again. Then he goes to the tomb, tells the Jews to move the stone that blocks the entrance, and calls to Lazarus to come out. He does. The dead man, risen from the dead.

I studied the Bible as literature in school, but there is one line from this story, one important line I had forgotten. And now, as I sit on the floor of the boxcar, awake in the fresh air, I find it, printed in condensed, soft black letters on the middle of a whisper-thin page.

Jesus sees the villagers crying. He is deeply moved and the Bible says, "Jesus wept." I pull up Nam's last poem on my phone:

```
From dust he bloomed, a fragile rose
    whose petals slowly fell
As the seed inside kept burning
    still, the mind at least was well
They tore their clothes and begged
    for help, a nightly vigil kept
But when he was gone, all hope was
    lost and they, like Jesus, wept.
```

The poem is about the resurrection of Lazarus. Now I see the thread that ties this message to the first one, and both messages to ARNS. They are about somehow stopping death. ARNS has put the entire world on a mission to stay alive, to cheat death. We're just like the Gods in ancient India and the Jews in Bethany. We are looking for the magic potion or even the divine miracle that will save us. Maybe Nam holds the key to it. I open x.chat.

Halahala. Lazarus. I get it. I want to know what you know, I write. I have one bar of service, but the message goes through.

He responds instantly. **What is it that you "get?"**

That the poems are about stopping death. So stopping ARNS. And I think you know how. I tap Send, but my signal drops out. I move closer to the door and stick my phone outside. The air is still and cool, pulsing with the sound of crickets. The full moon has risen high and the land is bathed in its shimmering glow. One bar of signal now, but the message won't go out. I climb down from the car.

My feet sink into the dewy earth. I look out across the field. There's a small house about forty yards away flanked by woods. Its warmly lit windows are a beacon. They remind me of everything I long for—food, a warm bed with sheets that feel cold when you get into them, an old movie on TV, family in the next room. I move toward the house, watching my phone. Ten paces become twenty become thirty and finally, one more bar. The message sends.

I think you know how, Nam responds within seconds. I stand staring at the words, held by the windless air.

Tell me, I implore. Waiting for his reply feels like trying to catch a handful of falling snow, like I will never be able to grasp enough before it all disappears. **Tell me how,** I write.

If I told you, you wouldn't believe me, he writes. I shake my phone like the answers I want will come loose through force.

But there is a way to stop it? I ask.

A long pause. I hold my breath.

There is.

My eyes close. The dank, mossy ground under my feet, the radiance of the moon all around, and the idea, however vague, that there may be a way to save my father. I begin typing, asking for more, but Nam dissolves the chat.

"Fuck!" I cry out at top volume. My voice echoes across the plain. In reply comes a strange sound. It's a bone-rattling yowl. It's as lonely as a locomotive whistle, as loud as a siren. It's a sound I've heard only once before.

I look out toward the treeline and see her, dipping in and out behind the tall pines that guard the edge of the forest. A wolf. Her silver coat sends a wave of heat over my skin, like a blanket I can't see.

She howls again. I step toward her like I stepped toward the ocean waves tumbling over my kissing parents when I was small. I take another step. She slows her movement. Her dancing gait eases into a panting stance. Her eyes sizzle like bolts of lightning and my pulse booms. But somehow, I am not afraid.

I am you, I think, the words I'd written to Nam springing up. "I am you," I say softly as heat builds behind my ribs. She howls again. Her head lifts toward the stars, then circles down and around in a bow.

I'm walking toward her. My mouth opens to call to her, but the air on my vocal cords is stifled by a different sound: An engine releasing its brakes with a heavy wheeze.

The train starts to move.

I look away and look back. The wolf bounds swiftly toward the black woods.

I launch forward, terror my driver as I imagine being left behind. My lungs pump in rhythm with the engine. Each of us picks up speed.

Kamal's frame appears in the open doorway of our car.

"You can make it!" he calls, kneeling down and extending his arm. My body burns with effort. I am running side by side with the train. There is no room for fear. I'm just digging for whatever it is that lets me swim faster than I have before. For that thing that will let me run fast enough to grab Kamal's hand and jump.

I reach toward him and my screaming legs rocket my body into the car. I land in a heap on the floor. I can practically feel the bruises forming. But I'm in. I'm okay. Kamal exhales a whistle and leans back on his hands. Phoebe is up and kneeling. I try and catch my breath.

"I'm sorry," I say, still panting.

"Are you fucking kidding me?" Phoebe snaps. "What if you'd been left out there?"

"I know. I'm sorry. I had to tell Nam about Lazarus, but there was no service and then—" I stop. I picture the face of the wolf. It sets off a longing in me. The train sounds its whistle. I look out at the land and grab for the flattened coin around my neck. My view darkens with shades of brown. I want to go home. I want to see my dad.

CHAPTER 12

"It's all right," whispers Kamal as my eyes fill with tears. "Can you tell us what happened, slowly, from the start?"

"What do you mean 'tell Nam about Lazarus'?" Phoebe asks.

I calm the swell of brown haze by sitting with my back straight against the hard wall of the car.

"I had a dream about that woman from the chapel," I begin. "She had a baby named Lazarus. That made me remember Lazarus in the Bible and I realized that's what Nam's second poem is about. Which means both poems are about stopping death. But I had no service, so I had to get off the train to try and send him a message. I told him I think he knows how to stop ARNS."

Phoebe's eyes shimmer like calm surf under a heavy moon. "Did he respond?"

I nod.

"And?" She repositions her legs underneath her.

"He said that I do. That *I* know."

"Wait, that you know or that he knows?"

"Me. That I know how to stop it." The train's wheels screech as we come around a wide bend. "That's all he would say."

"Sorry, who is Nam and what are his poems?" Kamal interrupts.

"Lu's been getting messages from the same guy who sent the Hugo video." Phoebe turns back to me. "Do you know what he means? That you know?"

"No. But I want to believe him."

"So do I," she says.

"No shit," Kamal adds. "Can I see the poems?"

I hand him my phone.

He looks up after a minute. "These make absolutely no sense to me."

"They're both references to ancient stories. Lazarus in the Bible and a Hindu creation myth."

He laughs. "I should've paid more attention in school. But you don't know what he meant about stopping ARNS?"

"I wish I did."

He looks back at my phone. "You have a signal here. We should look at some news while we can."

Four hundred thousand dead, we learn. People are afraid to go to work. Food supplies are dwindling further. Government and municipal services are being scaled back as resources and manpower are stretched thin. They're calling it "early-stage deterioration."

"That's like what happens to someone's grandmother with Alzheimer's," I say. I sound like Ben. "Let me see my phone," I say. I write Ben a message asking how he is. He writes back: **Hungry**. That means he's okay.

"So how long before late-stage deterioration?" Kamal looks to Phoebe.

"No way to know," she replies.

"What about Bell?" I'm thinking about him standing on that boat at night, making promises. "He found the virus. Shouldn't he have something else to offer by now?"

"That was only two days ago," Kamal says.

"Jesus. Right," I mumble. "It feels like weeks."

I stare out at the flat, open prairies of what the map tells me is northern Kansas. The clouds hang so low it seems they could fall out of the sky. There are no buildings, no telephone poles, no trace of human presence. Like the sun, like the oceans, this land does not need us. It will soak in the rain. It will freeze over in winter, then thaw again in spring. Like an orphaned child, it will manage to survive on its own. But unlike me, it won't know the difference.

I open a text to my dad. **Don't give up**, I write. Send.

"So Lu, what is it that you know but don't know you know?" Phoebe asks.

I glance at Kamal, then look away. "I don't know."

"Yes you do," he says in that certain way. The way Janine would've. With a smile I can hear behind his mask. With a gentle tone that dares me to be myself because he knows who I am and believes in me.

I feel my cheeks flush. I look down at my hands in their latex sheaths. They could belong to anyone, so nondescript. No jewelry, no polish. It's my senses that tell me they belong to me. That I can feel them is what makes them mine.

"If you begin with a belief that the world is flat," I say, "you'll never be able to conceive of it as a sphere. Your brain will just stop there, deciding that it knows. It will never allow you to consider an alternate perception."

"There's a term for that," Kamal offers. "I forget what it is. But my dad does crossword puzzles. He's like the crossword puzzle champion of the world. I remember him saying that when you answer a crossword puzzle clue incorrectly, it becomes exponentially harder to find the right answer. Your brain is like, 'I've already figured this out, I solved it, let's move on.' Doesn't matter that it was wrong."

"It's called cognitive dissonance," I say a little more softly than I mean to.

Silence as I worry I've embarrassed him by knowing the term he couldn't remember.

"God," he says, staring at me.

"What?" I reply with an edge that surprises me. Maybe I'm not actually willing to feel shame for knowing things.

"I love that you're so smart," he says.

A crazy burst of orange as a grin explodes behind my mask. I tap my foot.

"I feel like this riddle or whatever it is, this question, it's like that," I say. "It's like we're looking at something in two dimensions that actually exists in three."

Kamal picks up the Bible from beside my pack and thumbs through it.

"He said I wouldn't believe him if he told me. So we somehow need to go back to a point where the world is neither flat nor round, where there are no limitations. Where the unbelievable is what's true."

"So, like a miracle," Kamal says.

"Maybe. Yes."

"It must have something to do with the poems," Phoebe says. "Why else would he send you the poems if they didn't hold a key?"

I look down at my phone again. I Google Thomas Bell. The page starts to load and my battery dies.

"I need to think about it," I say.

We sit for hours and hours, not talking, rocked to the edge of sleep by the rhythm of wheels against track. The sun rides past its peak and the land becomes mountainous and rugged. The grass blurs into pebbled earth and the train slows to another stop. I feel safe in our little car, like if we could just stay here like this forever, we'd be fine.

"Colorado?" I ask.

"Think so," replies Kamal.

I get up and move to the door. I breathe in.

"Careful. We could start up any minute," he warns.

I grab the edge of the open frame. I take another breath.

There's a noise in the distance. It's like the muffled sound of barking dogs. "Did you hear that?" I ask.

"What?" Kamal asks.

It's like a growl.

"You don't hear that?" I demand.

"I hear it," Phoebe says.

Kamal focuses. The growl shifts into a shrill hollering. "Sounds like coyotes," he says.

"I think it's a woman yelling," I reply. It's getting louder.

"That's what coyotes sound like."

"That's a human voice," I insist and within seconds, they appear.

There are three of them, two women and a man. Next to them, two stocky Rottweilers tug against metal collars.

Kamal leaps up. My stomach twists in a flash of red light. I move away from the door. One of the women is sick.

"Howdy," says the man. His voice is somber and rich. His bald head is completely covered in one of those insane tribal tattoos. All three of them are pierced and tatted and clad from head to toe in silver-studded leather. They're like refugees from a future that took place in the past.

"Mind if we join you?" says the plumper of the women as she hoists her buxom frame into the car. Without waiting for an answer, she pulls two large rucksacks in behind her.

"Doesn't seem like you're giving us much of a choice," replies Phoebe as she rises to her feet alongside Kamal.

"Guess that's true," says the woman. Her smile is both warm and menacing. "Francesca, but call me Freddie." She sticks out her hand to shake. We don't move. "This is Cami and Darleen," she adds, pointing at the dogs. They jump up and settle at her feet. The man climbs aboard behind them.

"I'm her brother, Ron. My girl here's Jordana," he says, lifting the visibly ill woman onto the train. "We heading west," Ron says. He unrolls a sleeping bag and helps Jordana sit down. None of them is wearing masks or gloves.

"That's great, but she's obviously sick and we're not and we'd like to keep it that way. So how about you find another car?" Phoebe snaps.

Ron looks up at her with a confused face. "Other doors're locked," he replies plainly.

I think of my camping knife.

Freddie speaks up. "Look, we don't want no trouble neither, 'kay? This is a big car. You take this half and we take that one." She heads to the far end of the car. She whistles to the dogs and they follow.

Kamal whispers in my ear, "Should we be scared?"

I gaze at these strangers through clear eyes. No waves. I shake my head.

"Okay, that'll work," Kamal says.

"Are you insane?" Phoebe hisses.

"It's okay," I say.

Ron gently pulls the sleeping bag out from under Jordana and carries it over to Freddie. Jordana climbs to her feet. She takes a step, then collapses to the floor.

"Shit," I gasp.

Ron moves to help her. "Whoa there, baby. What happened?" he asks calmly, bringing her eyes to his.

"I can't feel my feet," Jordana replies. Janine's exact words. I shudder. My mind spins red.

Kamal steps up and reaches for Jordana's ankles. Ron wraps his arms under her shoulders. They carry her over to the sleeping bag and lay her down.

"Thank you," Ron says.

Kamal glances at his gloved hands. He steps over to the door, strips off the gloves, and throws them off the train.

"I'm sorry, but this is crazy," Phoebe barks. "You can't just come in here like this. This is our car. You're not even wearing any protection." One of the dogs jumps up, growling. Freddie grabs her collar and settles her down with a sharp whistle.

"Oh, it's yours?" Ron says. His face twitches like this might be the fight he's been waiting a while to get into. But still, my senses are calm. He's not going to hurt us, I don't think. "Maybe it's our car," he continues. "Maybe I made a reservation."

"Okay, whatever," Phoebe replies. I look quickly at Jordana. Her shallow breath has become a wheeze. Her eyes are hollow like all the others I've seen. My stomach starts to churn, but I keep my focus on her.

"How long have you been sick?" I ask. Ron eyes me carefully.

"Five days," Jordana rasps.

Ron picks up her hand with his. "We're going to California for a treatment," he says.

"You're not worried about becoming infected?" Kamal asks.

"We're immune," replies Freddie. "We been with her this whole time and we've got no problems."

"They don't know if anyone is immune," Phoebe says snidely. Ron stares at her like he doesn't speak the same language.

"Well, we're not getting sick," he says.

"What kind of treatment?" I ask.

"The Paqos in the desert got a cure," answers Freddie. "It's not on the news 'cause the drug makers want their own shot at all that money when they make a pill, but the Paqos know how to take it out."

"What's a Paqo?" Kamal asks.

"Mystic. Medicine man. They go all the way back to the Inca Indians." Ron's voice is so full. It's like being inside a piano when someone strikes a low note.

"Have you heard of a woman named Evans Birkner?" I ask.

"Sounds familiar," Ron says.

"I told you, she's not for real," Phoebe interrupts.

I ignore her. "She's from someplace called Redlands. Says she cured herself. I'm going to find her when we get to California."

"Sounds familiar," Ron says. I lean against the wall, staring at him, wishing he'd say more.

The train starts moving.

"Here we go!" Freddie hollers with a smile. She pours a dish of water for the dogs. Kamal, Phoebe, and I stare with longing. She drags a heavy-looking paper bag from her rucksack. "Good news is," she says, "I got beer."

She pulls two six packs of Bud Light cans from the bag and rolls one over to each of us. I wrap my gloved hands around mine. The sound of cans popping open one after the other and the first sip. So blissfully normal.

We pull up our masks and drink. The alcohol spreads out through my body like spilled marbles on a wood floor. I relax, cell by cell, molecule by molecule. Bone, muscle, organ, blood—every inch of me releasing.

We sit drinking beers. The sun's dappled rays flutter in on the breeze and an easy buzz settles over us. We go from two sets of three to a group of six.

I reach into my pack. "I've got these," I offer, tossing the six meal bars to the center of the car. Everyone grabs one and Freddie rolls each of us a second beer. I hesitate, holding it.

From the moment I discovered it in ninth grade, alcohol has helped me dull my feelings. It's taken the edge off those overwhelming sensations that have kept me on the outside of everyone else's experience. But now I realize, I don't want that anymore. I want to feel things. I want to feel everything.

"No thanks," I say and roll the can back. Freddie shrugs and puts the beer back in her bag.

Ron wipes Jordana's brow with a cloth.

"My father is sick too," I blurt out.

"Sorry to hear that, girl," he says.

"I wish he had someone like you by his side."

"Where's your mama?" Freddie asks.

A flash of purple rises up like a weed. "She took him to a camp," I say flatly.

"You from back east?"

"New York," replies Kamal.

"I've never been there," Ron says. "Just seen it on TV."

"Where are you from?" Phoebe asks. Her buzz softens her smugness only slightly.

"Atlanta," Freddie says. "We hitched a ride in a van with some folks, but when 'Dana got sick, they booted us. We've been on foot since."

"Only doing 'bout five miles a day 'cause she's been weak. Yesterday when her leg started acting up, I knew we had to catch out."

"'Catch out'?" Kamal asks.

"Hop a train," Freddie whispers.

Ron gets lost in the view for a moment.

"But she's a tough trooper and she gonna make it. Believe that," he says. Looking deep into Ron's face, I do believe it. And I want it to be true.

More hours pass, dusk rolls in. I'm hungry. I watch the moon rise against the sky. A pack of wild horses runs across the jagged, rocky hills in the distance. I remember one morning in Maine walking with my father at dawn, stumbling on a moose grazing. Gnarled barbs crowned his head. His sleek, high haunches and grunting breath—he was magnificent and my father began to cry.

At five years old, I needed him to explain to me that sometimes people cry when they see something beautiful. He said it reminds us we are part of something bigger. I pretended to understand. Now I watch those horses run and I feel that beauty, that connection. It's hard to breathe.

"That your Bible there?" Freddie asks, eyeing the book where Kamal left it.

"Yes," I tell her. "But someone gave it to me. I'm not a Christian."

"Ahh," she says like she doesn't quite believe me.

"Are you?" I ask. "Christian?"

She shakes her head, mouth full of beer.

"Do you believe in God?" I ask.

"I believe in a kind of God, but it ain't no bearded white guy in the sky." She laughs.

"That story is old," Ron says. "Christ and those tales, that's not how this world is gonna grow forward. Right?" He looks dead at me.

"I have no idea," I reply.

Ron stares through me, head cocked, smiling. "Your father a man of God?"

"He believes in something. He calls it a higher power. But it's not a bearded white guy in the sky either." I smile at Freddie.

Ron studies me. "Where y'all headed?" he asks after a moment.

"LA," replies Kamal.

"I'm with Front Line," Phoebe says like she's speaking to a child.

"Oh right on," Freddie exclaims, raising her near-empty can. "Saved my dogs during Hurricane Sarah. Good people." Phoebe softens a little more.

Ron turns back to me. "What about you, wolf girl? What do you believe in?"

A chill runs up my spine. "What did you call me?"

"Wolf girl. You got that wolf vibe. Nobody ever told you that?"

I just stare at him.

"But that brain gets in the way too."

A gust of wind rushes through the car, chasing his words like the swirling tail of a Chinese dragon. Jordana starts to cough. Ron puts his hand on her chest. He pats her until it quiets.

My stomach twists. Kamal, Phoebe, and I pull our masks back on.

"How did you two meet?" I ask.

"I was working in a coffee spot called—"

"Joni's," Jordana interrupts.

"Shhh," Ron says. "You need to rest, little bird."

"No, I'm telling it," she says, smiling. She props herself up to sit. "He was working at Joni's, making coffee for shit tips. My mama had just passed and I was looking for a job. I'd go in there every day and get a hot tea and a piece of cornbread. That was my little piece of joy. Every morning."

"I'd always give her a large cup when she ordered a small," Ron adds.

"And we'd get to talking on days when it was slow and he had time." She leans against him, softening into his body. He takes her hand. A cough threatens to explode, but it settles. "One day I told him I hadn't ever left Georgia. Spent my whole life there, never once gone anywhere."

"And I told her, 'We gonna change that.'"

"Next morning when I came in for my breakfast, he had one of those big camping backpacks stashed behind the counter. He told me to go home and get anything that mattered to me. Said we were getting on a train that night. I got my parents' wedding rings and a week's worth of clothes. Left everything else, even my mama's ashes." Her voice crackles in the moonlight.

"We never been apart since," Ron says. "Every minute the past three years, we spent it all together. No 'hers' and 'mine,' just ours."

Jordana lets out a sigh like she's lying down by the pool on vacation. Her face is relaxed, content.

"Our great adventure," she says, looking at Ron. I feel their love well up in my own heart.

"You're lucky," I say. I think of Janine and what she will never experience. I think of how my parents were once. "To know love."

"Love is what we're here to do," she says.

Ron lies down next to her and begins whispering in her ear.

"We're never gonna stop. We're gonna ride every inch of this land, see every setting sun. We're gonna stay up all night, get in all the trouble we can find. We're gonna fly through the morning, one train to the next. See oceans, see rivers. Swim in clear waters. Run through fields, down hills, across mountains and back again. We're gonna have each day and the next, just us. We're gonna laugh at nothing and cry at something and feel rain and snow on our faces. We've got all the time in the world."

He keeps muttering on and on like that, building images for her word by word, like if he stops talking she'll stop breathing.

I can almost see the pictures reflected in Jordana's eyes. It's like I'm watching a silent film playing across her corneas. I think of my mother's research and the basketball player dunking the ball, how we feel the same thing watching.

Freddie is humming, rocking gently with the movement of the train. Kamal sits in one corner, his knees hugged into his chest. Phoebe sits in another. I am nearest to the door. We are like the points of a star, each riveted to Jordana and Ron by a set of invisible cords.

I suddenly feel the need to stand. Ron stops talking. Everyone looks toward me as I grab the edge of the wall to steady myself. Jordana and I lock eyes. It's like she's asking a question and I'm answering, all without words or gestures.

I don't feel time; I don't feel space. Just the sensation of being tangled together with Jordana like a mess of gold chains at the bottom of a jewelry box. Then, that warmth again, radiating from behind my ribs. And a thought: Nam's messages. Is this what he's talking about? Is this the moment where the impossible will be revealed as the very real? Can I save her?

I feel like a fistful of sand is slipping through my fingers and I'm trying to grab the final grain.

She breaks my gaze and turns to Ron. "I'm sorry," she says to him. "I love you, but I'm not like you."

Then something courses through her. A wave, like the air itself was displaced by an undulating form. Did anyone else see it?

A flicker of light passes across her eyes, then disappears. The dogs sit up and bark.

"No," I call loudly.

But that's it. Jordana is gone.

We all remain frozen, staring at her body.

I look down at her hand clutched in Ron's. He places his other hand on her forehead, then slowly bends forward and kisses her lips. He exhales a big breath and looks up at Freddie. "Wow," he says quietly. Tears roll down his cheeks. He doesn't wipe them away. He just sits there holding her hand.

"Her time to go," Freddie says. Tears fall from her eyes as she and her brother stare at each other. There it is, that invisible tether between siblings. I think of Ben and how in the hardest moments of my life, he's always been there.

"I'm so sorry," Phoebe offers. Ron nods, then returns his focus to Jordana's face.

I turn my attention to sound. *Click-clack, click-clack.* The train. I think of the engine pulling the first car. The first car feels the weight of the second and pulls it forward. Down the length of the train, each car moves in sequence. Each car creates its own momentum, then pulls the car behind it, and the train travels forward as one.

Our presence here, our weight, has an imperceptible but very real impact. We make a difference to the cause and effect of the train's motion. We matter even in this moment of feeling powerless. And we've become part of one another's story.

I sit back down and look out at the passing land. The night passes slowly. I drift in and out of sleep, always aware that we are sharing this confined space with Jordana's lifeless body. She is here but not; in this world and maybe also some other one.

Whenever I wake, I see Ron, also up. His eyes don't seem to leave Jordana. He'll look at her and laugh, then become more serious. It's like they're still talking to each other.

"It's you and me," I hear him whisper. "For the rest of ever." The rest of ever. I look at Kamal. He's up too—listening, watching. I think of my father's words to me when I asked what he believed: Death is not the end.

CHAPTER 13

Amber rays fire up from below the horizon, heralding the sun's arrival. The landscape shifts from the burnt orange–tinged mesas of the southwest to the pale khaki, cacti-dotted sand of the California desert.

We are getting close.

The temperature rises steadily as the light deepens, rendering everything in a matte, washed-out haze of dusty, golden gloom.

"What are you going to do with her?" Phoebe asks suddenly, her tone worn down to kindness. Ron looks up as though he hasn't considered the issue. He looks to Freddie and back to Phoebe.

"We'll lay her to rest, then we'll keep going," he says.

"Get back on the path," Freddie adds.

"Back to Atlanta?"

Freddie smiles. "Back to somewhere. Home is wherever we are."

Ron looks happy to be reminded of that.

The sun continues to climb. Time passes. I glance down at the Bible. It's still sitting on the floor of the car. I've always liked the idea of a Catholic confessional, a place to let my darkest thoughts and actions be seen by someone who knows things I don't.

I want to tell Ron about what happened with the guy who stole our car, what happened with the wolf in the field, what happened as Jordana slipped away. I feel like he might have a way of understanding it. Maybe it would even sound normal to him. But I don't have the words to begin.

"We lived in Boston." Phoebe's voice cuts sharply into the quiet—a songbird breaking the silence of the night. She pulls her mask up onto her head, her beautiful, salty face compressed in the flat light of the shade. "I was a junior and my uncle was visiting for my mom's birthday. They were going to the museum for a show of paintings by Gerhard Richter. A German artist," she adds, looking at Ron.

"We left the house together. Mom, Dad, and my uncle got on the train. My sister, Juliette, and I had school, so we walked north across Copley Square, past the library and the Marathon Bombing Memorial. I always played a secret game with myself where I would try not to look at the memorial. Not because it was so upsetting, although of course it was. But it had just become one of those superstitions you have as a kid where you convince yourself something means one thing or another and you stick to it."

She pushes her bangs aside and I notice I'm holding my breath. I exhale slowly, as if somehow controlling my breathing will help Phoebe tell her story.

"Anyway," she continues, "we walked across the green and up

the two long blocks to school. My mom and I had had an argument the day before. About me wearing eye makeup to school. So I left the house with none on and then went straight to the bathroom on the third floor before first period. I pulled out my eyeliner and poof, the lights went out. I assumed it was a fuse or something and there was plenty of light from the window facing the courtyard.

"I pulled one eyelid closed and began gliding the soft gray pencil across it. I remember the sound of the old radiator gurgling. I took out my mascara, rolled the brush up the length of my lashes, and spread out the clumps with my fingernail. Then *BOOM*. There was a sound like fireworks. *That's weird*, I thought. But I kept going with the mascara, doing the other side and checking myself in the mirror." Phoebe pauses, looking out the door. Her expression is cool and composed. The rest of us sit completely still.

"There was another boom and then some noise out in the hall, like a murmur. Then a roar. I came out of the bathroom. The halls were dark and full of people. Out a classroom window you could see the smoke. Everyone was screaming, crying, pushing past each other, reaching to hold each other. But I just stood there. I just stood there with my makeup on, feeling like the floor was dropping out from under me. It was only four stops from Copley to the museum. Just a ten-minute ride. If it hadn't been winter they would've walked. But it was long enough for them to be at the wrong place at the wrong time. Long enough for me to never see them again."

I watch Phoebe through a lens of cocoa-colored light. Tears tumble from my eyes and my mouth parches. I glance at Kamal as she shifts her seat and seems to gather herself.

"A few weeks later when things started getting back to normal, I went to the museum and I looked at those German paintings. Each one was different from the next. Portraits, landscapes, abstractions. But there was one that made me stay for a long time looking at it. It was called "Betty" and it was a picture of the artist's daughter. Her face was turned away though; it was just the back of her head.

"There was just something about it. Maybe that it was a father's view of his daughter. Or the idea that I couldn't see her face. I sat in front of that painting and cried until they turned the lights off and told me I had to leave. And then I was done. I decided that everything that came before was like a separate life and it was over. I was gonna be the girl in the painting, looking forward, not back."

"And that's when you stopped talking to G?" I ask.

"Yup. The whole thing was like the Marathon Memorial. I just pretended it wasn't there. I told myself that when you lose everything, you can do anything. And that meant I was free." She stops talking. Her eyes meet ours like a swimmer's bubbling up from underwater. "I've never actually said all that out loud before." She looks at Ron. "And I'm just so sorry for your loss."

"I give thanks to you, beautiful sister," Ron replies, rubbing tears from his leathery cheeks.

Kamal pulls his mask up onto his head and wipes his face with his T-shirt. "I'm glad you said all that out loud."

"Me too," I echo.

"And me," adds Freddie.

"I know how you feel," Phoebe says, still looking at Ron. "Except I don't. Because you seem sad, but you don't seem angry. You don't

EMILY ZIFF GRIFFIN

seem to feel like your entire world just imploded, like you're stuck in some lifeless void where everything you care about has been taken from you. I don't understand why you don't feel that way."

"You felt better being angry?" he asks.

"I didn't have a choice."

Ron smiles. "You always got a choice. 'Dana's dead; she's not gone. What do I have to be angry about?"

"I'm not religious," Phoebe says. "I don't believe in life after death."

"I don't believe in death after life," Ron counters. "That's not religion; it's reality. Clear as any science."

"Science?" I smirk. "There's no science to support life after death."

"Well, that, wolf girl, depends on who you ask." We stare at each other. I want to know what he knows. I want to believe what he believes. I want him to help me, to save me, to save all of us. "They want you to be afraid to die, so they can control you," Ron says.

He sounds like Evans and my body shudders with recognition. I hear a deep droning sound. A rush of different colors pours over me and that heat rises behind my heart. Suddenly I understand what Evans meant in that video, what Ron is saying now.

"The world is not flat," I murmur.

Everyone stares at me.

"What if someone made ARNS?" I say quietly. "Like, engineered it. Engineered it to create panic and fear in order to take control?"

Phoebe looks intrigued. "To take control of—"

"Everything," I say.

"Believe that!" Ron exclaims.

"So, like terrorism?" Kamal says.

"Yes, but with a bigger plan than just the initial destruction. Blackout was about killing people and crippling the economy. The event and its immediate aftermath were the whole thing. This is about preparing us for something else."

"How do you know that?" Now Phoebe's looking skeptical. So's Kamal.

When Albert Einstein was my exact age, sixteen, he began to think about someone chasing a beam traveling at the speed of light. Before he'd even learned the physics that would make it possible, he knew there was a phenomenon of perception—relativity—that needed to be reconciled mathematically. He was like the boy in "The Night Shadow." He was like the wolf that knows when it's time to venture into the field, and when it's time to retreat into the woods. He just freaking knew it.

"I don't know, but I know," I say firmly. "There's more to this, I'm telling you. ARNS is about power and control." I turn and glance out the door. Telephone poles, palm trees, roads, and buildings. Civilization. "Maybe it's Nam. Or the government. A foreign government. Maybe it's all three."

Everyone follows my gaze to the landscape outside.

"We're almost there," Kamal says.

Phoebe's watch trills. Phone service. But my battery's still dead.

"I have a video from Nam," she exclaims. Kamal and I scramble to see her screen.

It fills with thick swirls of black and gray smoke, obscuring everything behind it as the camera creeps through space and then settles. Through the haze, flitting flashes of fire emerge, along with a rhythmic sound. *Thunk*, pause. *Thunk*, pause. The smoke clears a bit, revealing a large pit. It's maybe the size of a small house's footprint. In it, a fire blazes and through the flames we see: the bodies of the dead.

"Oh God," Kamal whispers.

The *thunk* sound becomes wed to the image of lifeless human remains being hurled into the pit, landing on the pyre, then being swallowed by flames. Their clothes and hospital gowns erupt on contact. Their hair sizzles and dissolves instantly, rendering their burning heads bald as their bodies crumple slowly into a heap of blackened limbs.

We turn away gagging as Phoebe drops the phone and runs to the door. She vomits off the side of the train.

"Shit," I mutter. I grab my head in my hands and shut my eyes. I try desperately to conjure the sensation of my feet in cool sand as my stomach twists violently and colored flashes pummel me. In this moment, I just want it all to stop.

"What is that?" Ron asks.

"A picture of hell," Kamal answers quietly as Phoebe sits back down. "You all right?" he asks. She nods. "It's one thing to be told that's what's going on, but to see it. It's—beyond comprehension." Kamal's breath is short. "The disrespect is—Cremation is forbidden in Islam. Muslims will be outraged."

"Everyone will be outraged," I add.

"If you're right, Lu," Kamal continues, "then it's obviously Nam.

He made the videos, which he sent to Phoebe so Front Line would put them in front of people and create panic."

"Very possibly. But not necessarily," I reply. "He said he made the Hugo video to help."

"Why should we believe anything he says?"

"Why would he send Lu messages to help her figure it out if he were the one behind it all?" Phoebe asks. "Yes, the information creates fear and panic, but without that you have an uninformed public with an underestimation of the threat and the danger, which makes the threat and danger bigger. It goes both ways."

Ron bellows with laughter.

"What's funny?" Phoebe snaps.

"You all like to think," he says.

"Yes, that's how you solve problems," she retorts.

Ron chuckles to himself. I glance outside.

"What's that?" I ask looking at what appears to be a dried-out riverbed.

"The LA River," Phoebe replies.

"Where's the water?" I ask.

"Global warming."

On the far side of the pale silt ravine, an empty freeway snakes by. We glide past a tall mess of sunbaked brush and the asphalt disappears and reappears in spurts. We cross a small bridge. The smell from a eucalyptus tree fills my lungs and makes it easier to breathe.

The train slows and we come parallel with our destination: Front Line's massive tent city known simply as The Pulse. It stretches out forever, encased by a tall fence topped with razor wire. It might be a commune, but not just anyone is allowed in.

I catch only glimpses: a rainbow of different colored tents; a man riding by on a horse, balancing a wooden bucket on his head; shirtless men and bikini-clad women working in a garden bed the size of a square city block, fresh tomatoes climbing high on vines; a pigpen; rows of chicken coops; smoke rising from a berth of grilling stations. The smell of roasting meat makes my mouth water.

Like with Freddie and Ron, it's hard to tell if this place is a vision of the future or a vestige from the past.

Within minutes The Pulse is behind us, replaced by a network of crossing tracks, signal switches, and railroad equipment. This is it; we're here. The train comes to rest, a final burst of steam escaping as the brakes engage. Relief.

I gather my pack. I put the Bible back inside and stand up. I look at Ron.

Starr. Georgette. Ron and Freddie. Another good-bye. Another connection that's meant everything for a brief time and will now be washed away like a sandcastle at high tide.

I kneel down next to Jordana. Her face has turned pale blue. I swallow the hint of chocolate the color leaves on my tongue. I feel a spark; maybe it's that warmth again. It rises up and out of my body and pours itself over hers, warming her cold limbs, bathing her still vessel in light that cannot be seen with ordinary eyes.

"Wolf girl," Ron says, breaking the exchange. My spine lengthens and I turn toward him. He hands me a crumpled piece of paper with an address scrawled across it in black marker: 1418 N. SPRING STREET.

"May you find what you're looking for," he says. "May you see into the dark." His gaze unnerves me. I put the paper into my pocket.

"Thank you," I say. I look to Freddie. "Thank you and good luck to you. To both of you." I throw my pack down out of the train and jump out behind it.

CHAPTER 14

Kamal and Phoebe follow as I head straight along the shimmering rails. The tall, faceless buildings of downtown loom behind us and The Pulse calls us forward. I feel strong. I feel ready, for what I have no idea.

"Merz is waiting for us," Phoebe says. "With food."

"Best possible news," Kamal exclaims.

Phoebe catches up to me. "What was on that piece of paper?"

A burst of blue. "Nothing. Just a drawing of Freddie's dogs," I lie. "Can I use your phone to text Ben?"

She hands it to me.

"Did you send Merz the video?"

"Not yet," she says. "I guess I should."

"You're not sure?"

"I do think people need to know what's going on. It's why I fought for releasing Hugo. But I don't know. There's more to think about now." Her sudden uncertainty rings out like an alarm. It's so unlike her and in that instant I start to wonder: Maybe she's keeping a secret of her own.

A clear picture of The Pulse comes into view as we follow the tracks around a curve. The smell of roasting meat returns and my stomach growls.

"Have you been here before?" I ask Phoebe.

"Yeah, I came for the protests after Blackout."

"What was it like?"

"It was thrilling. And scary. I owe this place and this movement a lot. They gave me purpose when I felt like my whole life had been burned to the ground." Her phone buzzes. "Ben says he's a block from your house."

I smile.

We approach the gate. It's like the one at the Brooklyn Navy Yard, only with even more security. We are patted down from head to toe and given fresh masks and gloves. A medic takes our temperatures and examines us for any sign of infection. I stare beyond his penlight into his steel-colored eyes. *Hurry up so we can eat.*

We pass the physical and are sent down a winding path, past the chicken coops and pigpens.

"So who lives here, really?" Kamal asks.

"Scientists, lawyers, business leaders, coders, artists, scholars of all kinds. Serious people. They have shelter, healthcare, education, everything," Phoebe replies. Kamal kind of grunts. "Does that surprise you?"

He shrugs. "I guess I imagined everyone was just sitting around smoking weed all day growing vegetables."

"Yeah, no. This is what the whole world could look like if we wanted it to."

We arrive at a makeshift hut made out of old tires and chain-link fencing. Inside, the smell of the rubber sticks in my nose. Sage burns into wide, smoky tendrils, obscuring the bright-eyed, short-haired head of the young man there to greet us.

"Welcome!" he exclaims cheerfully, waving away the smoke. "Your parcels are numbers fifty-two, three, and four." He passes us each a basic one-person tent and self-inflating sleeping mat.

I pass the tent back. "I have my own."

"Okeydokey. I'll be texting each of you a map and the Code of Conduct. Read through it; tells you how we run. Each parcel has a fast-charger for phones, tablets, what have you. And here's some head-lamps and canteens for water. Jules will take you down," he adds, point-ing back outside to a six-seater bicycle rickshaw that's waiting for us.

We head back out and climb onto the rickshaw.

"Good morning," Jules chirps. Her thick, dark-skinned legs flex with effort as she pedals us straight into a throbbing surrealist hipster explosion of life. "Where we heading?"

"Meal Center," Phoebe replies.

Jules nods. "Excellent." She builds up speed, expertly navigating the narrow passages that cut through the various tents, lean-tos, and fire pits.

"So how does this work with ARNS and people living so closely together?" Kamal asks.

"We've had a couple of cases," Jules replies over her shoulder. "But we have the Code. And there was a modification created by the Peers in case of infectious disease. So it's pretty straightforward in terms of protocol. The few cases we've had have been contained quickly. Zero-tolerance policy basically; immediate expulsion."

I look down at my phone, curious about the Code, but no battery, still. "So they just kick out sick people?" I ask.

"There's a Front Line medical camp a mile away. Anyone with symptoms would be taken there for treatment. So yes, there are no infected people allowed inside The Pulse."

I survey the massive expanse as we ride through row after row of tents extending in every direction. "It's incredible you have this much space."

"It was slated to be a football arena, for a new team," Phoebe explains. "But the deal fell through and the land got tied up in arbitration. The investors agreed to lease it to Front Line for practically nothing until the case is resolved. It won't be for forever, but it's pretty amazing for now." I nod. It is amazing and I can see why Phoebe wanted to be a part of it.

The Meal Center is just a cafeteria under a tent: long rows of mismatched tables and folding chairs, industrial-size chafing dishes, water coolers. We stand before trays of green summer vegetables, plump roasted chickens dripping with fresh garlic and herbs, thick slabs of juicy pink watermelon, baskets of golden cornbread slathered in gobs of butter. My knees literally weaken.

"Look at that," marvels Kamal.

"All of it grown right here." A familiar voice. I turn to see Merz standing behind us. His cocky stance and searing eyes are more attractive than I remember. "Help yourself," he says.

I step forward and pile an empty plate with mounds of everything. We take seats around a table in the corner and devour our food. We barely stop to breathe.

"We haven't seen the news today," I say once my plate is clean and stomach full.

"Well, China and its vaccine are full of shit," Merz replies. "Bell leaked a video last night saying his team is making progress. He may be full of shit too." He turns to Phoebe. "Where are we with Nam?"

I look at Phoebe. The video was sent to her and it's up to her to decide what to do with it.

"I got another video," she says after a long pause. Kamal and I shift in our seats.

"Can I see it?" Merz demands.

Phoebe's brow is tight and her eyes flit around nervously. She hands him her phone.

The sound is enough to make my stomach turn. When it's finally over, Merz is quiet. A breeze rustles the bushes outside the tent. Birds whistle their songs, oblivious.

"We need to show this to the Peers," he says finally. "We need to call a meeting." He looks at his watch. "The Cove at eight." Phoebe nods and Merz gets up and walks away. My eyes trail him involuntarily. His swagger seems to leave a stream of brooding energy behind him, like a speedboat's wake.

"Should I have told him about the poems?" I ask.

Phoebe follows Merz with her gaze. "Let's wait until the meeting," she replies.

"If what I said on the train is true, then spreading that video is only going to make people more afraid. It's exactly what whoever created this thing wants."

"First of all, we don't know that anyone created ARNS. Second of all, it's not up to us to decide what should be done with the video. That's not how Front Line works," she says.

"I think putting it out there is dangerous," I tell her.

"You should say that at the meeting."

We walk back across the expansive grounds. Ben must be home by now. I'm afraid to find out what happened when he walked through our front door. Our angry mother. The details of our father wasting away, alone on some filthy cot. Maybe something worse.

Instead I think about how I will find Evans Birkner. I think about that video from Bell. I want to see it. I want to hear of his progress, whether it's real or exaggerated. And I want to see his face. Because he still signifies the bright possibility of my future, maybe even more so now that I exist in a present defined by mounting loss.

We follow the busy paths carved through the mess of tents and lean-tos made from plastic milk jugs, random bits of wood and corrugated steel, garbage bags and tin foil, old tarps and parachutes. There are roofs of thatched palm fronds and tree branches, doors made of broken mirrors and pinecones, walls papered with newspaper. Nothing has been wasted. There's something comforting about that. It makes me feel like we don't really need much to survive.

We find our parcels: three vacant eight-foot square plots of open dirt marked and numbered with spray paint. There's a box on the ground with a thick cord that runs out from the bottom and disappears into the ground. I immediately plug in my phone.

I look at Phoebe and Kamal staring blankly at their rolled up tents. "You've never been camping before?"

"I stayed in a tent when we went on safari in South Africa," Kamal replies. "But it had a queen-size bed, electricity, and bowls of fresh fruit in it, so I'm thinking that wasn't quite camping?"

I smile.

"It's been a few years," Phoebe adds.

I unfurl my tent and line up the stakes. I use the Bible to hammer them into the ground.

"It appears you have been camping at least once or twice," Kamal observes.

"Yeah. We used to go as a family." Family. As the word forms in my mouth it's like an invisible hand reaches into my chest and grabs every ounce of breath. I gasp for air. I'm suddenly dizzy with a swarm of flashing hues and images.

The four of us around the fire on Mount Katahdin.

My mother holding me against her chest under a silver-starred sky.

Running with my brother through the forest blanketed in pine.

My father driving tent stakes into the earth.

It's like a dream bent through a kaleidoscope of different colors. I shut my eyes and feel for the ground with my hands. I grab fistfuls of warm dirt. I imagine my feet in the sand. I bring up the sound of ocean waves crashing. One. Two. Three. Four.

The visions slowly recede. I open my eyes. I look up at the cloudless sky. And I know.

My father is dead.

I scramble to my feet. "I have to call my mom."

I pull my phone from the fast-charger and stumble down the path toward the large fence that separates The Pulse from the rest of the world.

If the entirety of human existence can be represented by the width of a single strand of hair, the walk to the fence is as long as the Atlantic is wide. Time stretches like taffy as the phone rings in my ear—it's like the warbled drone of a heartbeat in slow motion.

I put on my glasses and my mother's face appears floating in front of me, the gray lattice of the fence bleeding through the projected image.

"Luisa, *cariño*." Her voice cracks into sobs before she can say another word. "Where are you? Are you okay?"

"Mom. Yes, I'm okay. I'm not sick. I'm safe." She gulps for air and my eyes open wider as though that will bring more of her to me.

She gathers herself. "Lu, *mi vida*," she says.

"Yes, I'm here," I answer evenly, waiting for her to tell me what I already know.

She sighs. A pause. She looks at me. Her mouth quivers, and then she says simply, "He's gone."

I look past the fence to the train tracks, the empty freeway, the unfamiliar mountains behind it—all of it bathed in the soft brown light of my sadness, like an old photo. It strikes me in that moment: I am so far from home.

"Lu?" Her voice is warm and her face relaxed like it was when I was small.

"I'm here," I say. "When?"

"An hour ago. We tried to call you."

"My battery was dead," I mumble. "Where was he? Was he alone?" My voice falters.

"He was here. He was at home," she says softly. "He was with me. And Ben." I exhale a breath I didn't know I was holding. "He waited for Ben." She smiles through tears.

"But you took him to the camp."

"I never made it there. I realized he needed to be home. He needed me. And . . . I loved him." Silver flashes across my mind along with Jordana's words: *Love is what we're here to do.* "I'm sorry," she says.

"It's okay," I tell her. "It's not your fault."

"No, Lu. I'm sorry. For all of it, for everything. I should never have left you."

"This is my fault," I say. "It's my fault." Yellow now. Yellow and that hiss that tells me I fucked up.

"No, sweetheart."

"Yes. I went out with Janine and she was sick and they took us to the hospital and Dad had to come and get me there, and he touched the door. That's how this happened. So you should know that this is my fault and you can go ahead and blame me." I go nearer to the fence. I wrap my fingers through the chain-link.

My mother's silence fills me with shame.

I lock eyes with her.

"This is not your fault," she says. "We don't know how this happened. We can't know. But it's nothing you did or didn't do. The only thing you have to think about is that your father loved you. That you brought him joy every single day and you made his life meaningful. He asked me to tell you that. He needed to make sure you know that."

Tears come and the world melts into the color of the earth itself.

"This is not your fault," she says again as I cry.

"Are you . . . you're not sick?" I ask, the sadness ebbing against fear.

"I'm not sick. But I need you to come home. Please, please come home."

"I will. Is Ben with you? I want to see him."

"Yes, he's here." She calls to him and steps out of view.

"Hey," Ben says, taking her place.

"You got your good-bye," I whisper.

"Yup. I don't know if he heard me."

"I'm sure he heard you." I swallow. "What was it like? Being there?"

"Hard." His voice wavers. "But it was the right thing, to come back."

I look down at the ground. "Did he wonder where I was?"

"He was pretty out of it. But I told him you had gone to try and save him. I swear I think he smiled when I said that." I manage to smile too. "And he left this for you." He carries the phone over to the kitchen counter and trains the lens on a piece of music paper. Written across it in my father's neat, all-cap hand: LU, MAKE SOMETHING OF YOURSELF.

I snap a screenshot of the note.

"What does that mean?" I ask. "He never cared about me being an achiever."

"Like I said, he was really out of it."

I close my eyes, imagine planting my feet in the sand, and try to picture him writing those words.

"I never told him I forgave him," I say, looking back at Ben. "When he gave me his letter of amends. I just never said anything about it. I always thought there would be time. I thought when we were adults we would sit down and talk about everything like our childhoods were movies we'd all gone to see."

My eyes are begging my brother for something my father isn't there to give—a release from my shame.

"He knew you forgave him, Lu." He pauses. "Do you want to see him? I could take the phone up there."

"Okay," I say even though most of me doesn't want to. My breath is shallow as I watch Ben's POV tromp up the two flights of stairs, past everything that is most familiar to me in the world. I hold the fence tighter.

The creak of the door to my father's room as Ben opens it. He steps inside, then hovers at a distance.

"I can't go too close," he says. "But that's him." His voice cracks and I half laugh: Of course we are compelled to state the obvious. That's the only way to stay attached to the reality we know.

My father's eyes are closed. His cheeks, yes, they are hollow. But even through the haze of brown that blankets my view, his skin seems luminous. His lips seem to be turned up, the hint of happiness. He looks strangely beautiful to me.

"I'm sorry," I whisper to my dad. "And I forgive you."

I stand there, half waiting for him to wake up and say something.

Suddenly, I need to move. "I have to go," I say more loudly.

Ben flips the camera around. "Come home, all right?"

"I will. Tell Mom I love her."

I click off and turn in a circle, looking at everything. The palm trees, so impossibly tall, sway like slow dancers. The mountains' jagged peaks stare down. The sun blazes.

I hear my father's voice in my head. Or is it the wind blowing across the dusty asphalt?

Death is not the end.

I scroll through my texts looking for the photo of the four of us after Ben's graduation. Our bright eyes, our joy. My parents splitting up was like a stone landing on a windshield, an asterisk of splintered glass spreading out in all directions. It made my sense of safety fragile.

My father dying is like a sledgehammer. There is no safety now. There is no net.

I start walking. The fence, the mountains framed by tracks and highway, the sun, sky, and trees. To someone else, everything would appear just as it did five minutes ago. But to me it all looks different—brighter and more alive. It's in higher definition now.

Without meaning to, I find myself at the front gates of The Pulse.

I walk out and keep going.

I head toward the tall buildings on the horizon. With each step, I replay our last moments together. The fear and sadness in his eyes as we said good-bye. Not knowing what to say, wanting to say everything at once. What regrets flooded his mind at the end? What things did he wish he'd done differently?

Sensations and tears come so hard that I stop short, immobilized. My legs feel as though they are welded to the pavement.

A thunderous voice rages purple from deep inside me. "Show me something!" I scream. I'm calling to God or my dad or the Universe or whatever it is that might exist beyond me. I'm talking to whatever it is that might understand something I don't.

"Show me something!" I yell again. I wait, looking skyward, turning in all directions. I'm looking for a sign.

Nothing. Just a breeze.

"Show me!"

What comes in response is not what I expect. It climbs up from the bottom of my lungs with the fury and thrust of a rocket's blast. It explodes from my mouth, knocking me to the ground.

A cough. The cough.

The one I have watched consume so many has now chosen me. My stomach twists like a towel being wrung and light the color of blood flashes across my eyes.

I begin to panic. This can't be happening.

But it is.

My throat is aching. My nose is filling up with fluid. My limbs are suddenly stiff, my whole body chilled.

I hear Jules's words from her sunny perch on the rickshaw: Zero-tolerance. Immediate expulsion. I can't go back to The Pulse.

I pick a direction and start to walk, slowly. I'm shivering and my mind is cut loose from reality like a boat from its mooring.

How do you begin to conceive of your own death?

I trudge along for what feels like miles. My head is pounding, my body feels like it weighs a thousand pounds. But something is driving me forward. Maybe it's knowing I can't go back. Maybe it's that if I stop moving, my fear will swallow me. Maybe it's something altogether deeper, something beyond logic or physical capability.

The Pulse's desolate surroundings eventually transition to wide commercial streets. Storefronts and restaurants. A bank. Most everything is closed and all the signs are in Chinese.

I stop outside a dumpling house. The windows are lacquered black and painted with red-eyed, golden dragons that shimmer in the afternoon light.

I turn away from them and pull out my phone. I look at the map. I'm on a stretch of Broadway in Chinatown. To the north stands Dodger Stadium. The dried-up river's to the east. As I keep scanning for some familiar landmark, some idea of where to go, I notice Spring Street and I remember: the piece of paper Ron gave me.

I pull it from my pocket, enter the address into my phone, and start walking again.

The occasional car roars past. Along one deserted stretch of industrial buildings, I hear the muffled sound of techno music and imagine a rave going on inside. Hundreds of sweaty bodies and neon lights. I suppose dancing is one way to greet the end of the world.

When I make it to 1418 N. Spring Street, a large warehouse on an empty street, I can barely stand. A carved wooden sign hangs squarely on the front. Just three letters announce the name of this mysterious place: Lux—the Latin word for "light."

My cough erupts and I double over. My gloved hand slams against the door to keep me from falling. I pull it back: my germs.

The cough calms. I stare at the door, unsure if it will open, unsure what I will find on the other side. I think of Ron, that mysterious man who knew something about me, something I don't even have words for. He gave me the address. He told me to come. That means I have to go in. And so I do.

CHAPTER 15

Inside, the dwindling sunlight beams through a wall of windows that face an interior courtyard blooming with flowers. Cool air blankets my sweaty skin and white walls remind me of my mother's smell. I look down at the tiles beneath my feet. A moment later, I am lying in a heap. The chilled ceramic presses against my feverish face. My eyes close and I drift.

Next thing I know, I feel a presence beside me. I look up. It's nearly dark outside. A woman is standing over me. She is unmasked, but her features are obscured by shadow. No gloves. I glimpse the skin of her cheek in a shard of evening light. It's smooth and clear like polished marble. She appears neither young nor old, and as I look closer I realize I've seen her before.

"You're here," she says like she's been expecting me. She turns toward the light. Her eyes glitter and her voice reeks of wood-fire.

It's Evans Birkner.

I drag myself to a sitting position. "I think I'm infected," I say. Shame spreads across my cheeks with a hiss. It's like any other personal failure—a lost swim meet, a wrong answer on a test. I've been beaten.

She offers her hand to pull me up. I hesitate and she grabs my wrists, pulling off my gloves. A jolt of energy passes from her body to mine. An electric shock, maybe. Suddenly, I'm standing.

She steps close and gently removes my mask.

"Evans," I say, woozy. "Can you help me?"

She smiles. "Come." Her warm, smoky voice surrounds me like a cloak. She leads me down the long corridor, past the windows, toward a large white door. I hear the distant, muffled sound of singing. My whole body begins to hum.

The door opens and we step into a dimly lit room. My eyes land on the faces right in front of me, each of them lit golden by candles that everyone seems to be holding. Different ages, ethnicities. I struggle to imagine what they all have in common.

I look forward and the room seems to expand, revealing rows and rows of people. No one is wearing a mask.

At the center of the space, a choir stands singing at full voice. There are no instruments. The wall of sound knocks me back a step like a shove. It's like a hand on my chest commanding my body to hold firm against the music's force.

The room stands and sways as one, their candles flickering. In front of them, laid out on a bed of flowers lies a woman dressed in white.

"*I am in the darkness,*
I am in the light.

See me if you can,

Everywhere I am," they sing.

The melody is rousing, beautiful. The harmony reverberates against my bones and floods my vision with colors—silver, oranges, pinks. I don't resist it. I let it wrap me in joy and warmth and safety. I let it become my mother's green dress.

I think of my last moments with Janine. I remember Jordana slipping away. I see my father lying in his bed, so still. I see the man behind the gas station and the life leaving his body. All this death pushed me into darkness, and now the music is pulling me back into light.

The melody reaches a crescendo with everyone chanting "Rise up! Rise up! Rise up!" Their energy floods my veins like fresh oxygen—every cell vibrating like a tuning fork. And with the final note of resonant sound, everyone blows their candles out.

We stand still in the darkened room. The smell of melted wax and smoke drifts upward. The absence of voices has its own tone and there's a fragile perfection in the quiet, like the feeling of being effortlessly balanced on one leg.

A single spotlight beams down on the woman in white. My focus narrowed toward her, I recognize the delicate features of her face and her long, almond-colored hair. I realize the woman is Jordana.

I gasp for breath as Evans places her hand on my shoulder. She pulls me forward and leads me up through the center aisle. Everyone puts down their candles and turns toward us, raising their arms, hands spread wide, palms facing out. Their eyes are on me. A murmur passes through the crowd as yellow waves ripple through me.

"What are they doing?" I whisper.

"They are extending their hearts to you," Evans answers. "They are recognizing the divinity within you."

We reach the center, where Jordana lies. We stop. I look down at her serene face. Her head is wreathed with marigolds. Her skin is pale blue, bloodless with no makeup to hide it. She, like my father, is radiant. I hear Ron's words—she's dead; she's not gone.

"Greet them," Evans says, bringing my attention back to the hundreds of people standing before us.

"I'm sick," I say. "I need your help."

"Greet them," she says again.

I gaze down and see Ron and Freddie in the front. Their expressions are expectant and trusting, like they're waiting for the answer to a simple question.

I tentatively raise my hands, mirroring their strange gesture.

The room gasps. Everyone bows their heads.

I lower my arms and step back, becoming more and more uneasy. A bald, olive-skinned man comes forward with a chair. He sets it off to the side and beckons me to sit.

Evans closes her eyes and breathes in with the whistle of a boiling kettle. "Can you feel it?" A smattering of yeses.

More insistent: "Can you feel it?!"

The crowd responds in kind.

Her hands hover over Jordana's body. "We celebrate this work of art, one of God's perfect symphonies." Her oaky timbre smokes like fire. I grip the edge of my chair. "We have lost the instrument. But the symphony's resonance, its tone and melody, its emotion, intelligence, and wit—all its qualities and attributes continue to exist, even when the violin has crumbled into dust. This soul's sweet music will be played again."

More yeses flutter through the room. I think of my dad. Of his music. Of the beauty and meaning that he created. I think of how he loved me, how he saw me. Waves of tones and colors course through me. I plant my feet in the imaginary sand and feel the waves. I feel them and I begin to weep.

Evans brings her hands to rest on her own chest, one on top of the other. Her eyes hinge shut. "Let us turn within," she calls to the room. I close my eyes reluctantly—for a moment I'm afraid of the dark. But it's a relief to look at nothing.

"Deep breath in," she instructs. My nose completely blocked, I breathe in through my mouth like I would before a dive.

"And let it out." We all exhale. Everything settles inside me. "Again," she calls. We inhale, becoming one giant lung. I feel like I am floating in a pool.

"You must choose," she calls, almost songlike. "Is it light or darkness?"

Now my head begins to spin.

"Let it out."

We release.

"And again!" she calls. I pull another deep breath through my mouth. "Is it faith or doubt? Is it life or death?"

Then, as the entire room exhales, I fall to the floor. Pitch black.

I come to seconds later surrounded by concerned faces—Ron, Freddie, Evans, the bald man, and others. I'm confused. I'm embarrassed.

"I'm sorry," I mutter. "What happened?"

Evans kneels next to me. "It's okay. You're all right." Her tone is hushed.

"You fainted. The deep breathing," Ron says. "It can do that."

"This is just as they told us it would be," whispers the bald man, looking excitedly at Evans.

"Shhh," she snaps.

"What?" I mumble, the uneasiness continuing to mount.

"Help her sit," Evans says. "Let's get you some water." She motions to a young man, who runs off down the aisle. "You're all right now," she assures me, stroking my head and looking down at my bare leg, at the scar on my knee.

The man returns with a paper cup. "Here. Drink," Evans says. She tips the cup to my mouth and the sleeve of her white shirt slides up. She has a tattoo on her forearm. A tattoo of a wolf. I jump back, choking on the water.

I scramble to my feet and step away from the crush of people. "Who are you?" I demand, staring at Evans. My heart is revving like a jet in a torrent of yellow.

"I am Evans Birkner," she answers plainly. "You already know that."

Our eyes drill into each other's.

"Why are you looking at me like that? All of you?" I whip in circles. A high-pitched tone pierces my ears. Blue pours in, covering the yellow. Paranoia. My body shivers with chills. The fever. "Does this have something to do with Nam?" I bark. "With Theodore Nam?" I am nearly shouting.

"Please, be calm," Evans says, as even and gentle as a child. "I do not know anyone by that name. All I know is that we are here to welcome you. We are here to shine a light on you. We are here to help you fulfill your destiny."

"I need the cure," I say. "You said you have a cure."

"You already know what you have to do," she says.

"Tell me," I plead.

"She's not ready," Ron says softly.

"Yes I am. I'm ready," I insist, having no idea what they're talking about. My head throbs.

"We'll meet again when it's time," Evans says. "You should go now."

I search each of their faces. "Please," I beg.

"You should go," she says again.

I turn and move slowly down the aisle, past the worshippers, who raise their hands up to face me.

"Stop that," I snap.

I reach the door. "Death no more!" cries a voice. I stop and spin back on my heels. A deranged-looking man with long dreadlocks and a beard stands in the center of the aisle. He fiddles with the tunic he wears. "Death no more," he says again. He glances down and begins muttering to himself. I turn away and hurry toward the exit.

"Choose the light," calls the bald man as I burst through the door of the sanctuary. I don't look back again and by the time I reach the front door of the building, I'm running.

Strangely, the faster I run, the more energy I have.

I tear through the empty streets back toward The Pulse. I pass the building with the techno music still pumping, louder now. I look up at the second floor and see that the sound is pouring from an empty window. A beautiful, dark-skinned man wearing a shiny, kelly-green jacket sits leaning out, smoking a joint. His eyelids are painted to match and they shimmer in the streetlight as he calls down to me.

"Whatchoo looking for, baby doll?"

Safety is the word that flashes across my mind. I am desperate for some semblance of it. I don't respond to the man in green, I just keep running.

I turn back onto Broadway, back along the stretch of closed shops. The dumpling place with its fearsome dragons and next to it, a store selling Chinese trinkets and clothes. I stop in my tracks as a woman throws open the metal grate out front.

"Hello," I blurt out, panting.

She looks at me nervously, then hurries inside. She flips the sign on the door: OPEN.

I'm soaked with sweat when I get near the gates of The Pulse. My head churns. I stop to catch my breath and look at my watch. Six texts from Kamal asking where I am. I write and tell him I'm on my way back.

I look toward the checkpoint. I'll have to pass another physical to get back in. And I'll have to be careful about not touching anyone or anything once I do.

The Peacekeeper on duty scans my name into their system. She sends me forward to the medic area, where a man in scrubs approaches with a thermometer.

"It's gonna be off the charts," I say, smiling.

"Oh yeah?" he asks.

"I just went for a long run. It must be eighty degrees out there." I think of Phoebe as I casually fan myself with my damp T-shirt, giving him a glimpse at my bra.

"You shouldn't be out there alone, especially at night," he says.

"I know."

He presses his stethoscope against my chest. "So you're a runner?"

"Swimmer mostly," I say. "But we're kinda far from the beach." Another smile.

"I'm a runner," he says. He holds up the instrument's metal disk. "Definitely elevated." He puts the thermometer in my mouth and looks into my ears. "You look a little congested." He removes the beeping stick from under my tongue.

"I was running along the riverbed," I tell him. "I'm super allergic to the tree pollen."

"Me too," he says. "Whoa. 101.8."

"Told you," I say. I open my eyes a little wider. I breathe a little slower.

He stares at me.

I conjure an image of every cell in my body standing at attention like soldiers on a line, projecting the appearance of health.

"Put these on," he says, handing me a set of gloves and a mask. "And drink some water. Like, a lot of water."

"That's my plan," I say. I put on the protection quickly and my smile fades the moment my lips are shielded from sight.

I wind through the tight paths of The Pulse like a warrior returning from battle. I am desperate for the sight of a familiar face. I want all those sensations. Pine, salt, peppermint. I want the sound of my father's smile shaking the leaves against their branches.

My father. A wave of recognition: he's gone. I'd let myself forget.

I find my way back to our parcels. I half expect Kamal and Phoebe to still be sitting in the dirt, the tents and stakes spread out on the ground. Instead I find the tents assembled and empty.

I collapse into mine. Everything aches. I lie still and watch my breath—the up and down, the in and out. It's automatic if I let it be. But I can influence it. I can slow it down. I can hold it.

I alternate between letting it flow naturally and controlling it. The game allows my mind to wander. Do I choose light or darkness, faith or doubt, life or death? How many breaths do I have left in this lifetime?

I am near sleep when I hear Kamal and Phoebe coming down the path. I crawl to the door of the tent and climb out.

They freeze when they see me.

"Hey," I say.

"Oh shit," whispers Phoebe. Kamal drops down to the ground where I sit.

"Stay back," I warn him. "I'm not feeling well."

He looks at me so completely, so deeply, I imagine he can see all the way through to whatever microscopic spark of light inside me makes me who I am.

"I'm really glad to see you," I say.

"I don't think I've ever been more glad of anything." His voice is quiet and direct like we are the last two humans left on earth. "Where did you go?" he asks.

I swallow, holding his gaze. "I went to call my mom." I pause. A heavy cough erupts from my chest, then calms. "My dad is gone," I say. Tears pool along my lashes, a sepia filter over everything. "Then I started walking. I didn't know where. I just wanted to be alone. That piece of paper Ron gave me." I glance at Phoebe, about to admit I lied to her. "It was an address. So I started walking there. And I started feeling sick. But I was afraid to come back, so I kept going and—Ron and Freddie were there. And that woman from the video, Evans B. They were having, like, a funeral for Jordana."

"Sounds like a dream," Phoebe says.

"It was like a dream. They were all so weird. I thought Evans was going to help me, but they said something about how I wasn't ready."

"What does that mean?" Phoebe asks.

"I don't know."

Kamal pulls off his mask.

"What are you doing?" Phoebe snaps.

"I can't breathe with that thing on. And right now I need to breathe," he says.

I look at Kamal. Silver flashes across my eyes. Heat rises inside me and his smell is everywhere. I feel like the physical shell that contains me might suddenly pop like a balloon. I feel like the rest of me might rush forward like a river, drowning me, Kamal, and everything that surrounds us. *This is love*, I think. *This is actual love.*

"We need to take care of you," he says. "What do you need?"

I look at Phoebe and back at him. "I need to do what I came here to do, which is figure out how to stop this thing. Nam says I know how, so I need to figure out how."

"They released the video," Phoebe blurts out. "I fought them on it, but they didn't listen."

"People will be freaking out about it, no doubt," Kamal says.

I feel a glimmer of strength. "Let's see," I say. I pull my laptop out of my pack and log into my server. I put the link to the video into the search bar of LightYears. I watch as the opinions and emotions of the world crystallize in the form of curves rising and falling along a grid. Feelings of outrage flare up. Disbelief.

The word *Horror* shoots to the top of the comment keyword ranking function, along with *Inhumane, Monsters,* and *Blasphemy.*

Then the sentiment turns against the president for sanctioning the indiscriminate burning of bodies. The hashtag *impeachher* spikes.

The number of comments and posts explodes into the millions. They are loaded with expressions of grief, sadness, and shared pain.

"What's happening?" Kamal asks.

"It's going viral," I answer. These three words stick in my mouth like a car lurching over an unseen speed bump. I look at Kamal. "That's it."

I click on *Pervasive Sentiment. Empathy* is again charting as the dominant emotion. Just like with Hugo.

I think for a minute, just watching the data amass. I imagine the video spreading, just like ARNS is spreading. Clicks and shares, clicks and shares.

I do a search for the geographic trajectory of the virus's outbreak. I'm looking for a map showing where specifically across the globe the disease has spread from one day to the next. It's easy to find.

I convert the data from the map into a graph covering the three days that followed the release of the Hugo video. Six percent of new cases were in New York City. Nine percent occurred in New Delhi, and on and on around the world.

Then I look at the geographical data from my LightYears analysis of the Hugo video. I convert that into the same type of graph, showing me percentages of *Empathy* responses based on location.

I lay one graph on top of the other and like a lock's tumbler falling into place, they line up exactly.

A calm settles over me.

"A perfect match," I say quietly, looking up at Phoebe and Kamal.

They stare back blankly.

"It's the videos. The videos are making people sick, specifically people who are the most empathic."

Kamal's mouth gapes open. "Um, what?"

"Where are you getting that?" Phoebe snaps.

"The places where the dominant feeling about Hugo was empathy are the places where the infection spiked. The patterns are identical. I don't know exactly how, but ARNS must somehow be triggered in the brain by certain neurons firing in response to the videos."

A flash of white. My mother. I think of her research again, of what she told me about why we love watching sports.

Maybe that is how it works.

"It could be like an autoimmune thing," I say. "Where there's a virus that's only activated by a specific neurological response. Something to do with mirror neurons maybe."

"I am suddenly feeling fairly stupid here," Kamal says. "Pretty freaked out, vaguely hopeful, and fairly stupid. What's a mirror neuron?"

"They're what my mom studies for a living. They're the part of our brains that makes us more or less empathic and emotional. People with high concentrations of mirror neurons—their feelings, especially their feelings of empathy, are stronger. I'm thinking the videos somehow activate the virus in those people."

"That's insane," Kamal says.

"It's fairly insane. But you can see it in the data. The places where people were most empathic about Hugo are the places where the infection rate went up. No way that's a coincidence."

Kamal glances at Phoebe, then back at me.

"The new video should have the same effect," I say.

I close my eyes and travel back to the sanctuary at Lux. The boom of the voices in the room. Everyone unmasked, shoulder to shoulder. No one ill or worried about getting sick.

Light or darkness, faith or doubt, life or death? A choice.

Maybe it's just a choice.

I'm hit with a torrent of warm, rich colors, strange tingling sensations, and that heat still rising up from my belly.

Choose the light. I think.

I bring to mind a vision of the ARNS virus, a multisided little ball. To me, it's red. I picture millions of these poppy-colored orbs coursing in waves through the lymphatic vessels connecting my brain to my immune system.

The sound is suddenly deafening. It's like a thousand screaming baby pigs. I put myself in the path of this blood-red squealing surge.

It's coming at me so fast, it's going to consume me completely.

Part of me knows that I can just open my eyes and stop it. But if I do, I will be right where I started. I will be sick. I will be scared. I will be nowhere.

I imagine my arms raised to defend myself. Bolts of yellow and that hissing sound meld with the red and I begin to experience the sensation of drowning.

I am gasping for air as a red swell crests above me, about to drop. I feel my lungs shrink and my eyes go wide. This is it. I feel the same disbelief I saw on the man's face behind the gas station, my knife wedged deep in his back.

I brace for the ultimate moment of destruction, of dissolution.

And then, my own voice: "It's just waves."

Again, louder. "It's just waves." I look up, expecting to be swallowed in red. But the squealing spheres have stopped in midair.

Everything goes quiet.

"It's just waves," I hear myself yelling as I float inside the otherwise soundless suspension of my own body.

I am like a deep-sea diver, weightless in the silent abyss.

The wave above breaks apart. The red balls come to hover all around me. Then, one by one, they rise back up and disappear.

Soon, they are all gone.

I breathe in, then out, then in again. I feel a sense of being lifted. It's like the first sip of morning coffee or the calm high after a long swim. It's like the way a bad mood can turn around with a good laugh. Relief spreads through me. I sit motionless and time seems to stop. Is it a minute, or an hour that passes?

Eventually I open my eyes. Kamal and Phoebe are sitting there. The night sky hangs above us. The air is clear and fresh like after a storm.

As clearly as I've ever known anything, I know in this moment: I am going to be fine.

"What just happened?" Kamal asks. "Where'd you go?"

I smile. "I'm not sure I can answer that, exactly. But I feel better. I feel kind of . . . amazing, actually."

"You look different," Phoebe says. She's been quiet for so long I had almost forgotten she was standing there. "You look not sick."

"She's right," Kamal echoes. A flash of silver. I can see him wanting to believe. "You look . . . better."

"If ARNS is triggered by a person's emotions being out of control," I say, "then it can be stopped by their rational mind bringing them back into balance. That's what Nam meant. And Evans said it too. I can stop it. Anyone can stop it. If they know how it works, if they use their rational mind to create a new belief, a new truth."

Silence as we all take it in.

I pick up my phone and open x.chat. I write to Nam: **I know what you meant. I know how to stop it.** Send.

"What are you doing?" Phoebe asks.

"Writing to Nam. Telling him I've figured out what he was saying."

"If he made the videos and the videos are the cause, then he's behind it all," Kamal says. "Nam created ARNS."

Before I can say another word, Nam responds. "He sent me another poem." I read it once to myself, and a second time out loud.

> "Like brothers, they set out to reach
>
>   the edges of the earth
>
> To topple cedars, slay a beast, live
>
>   an eternity past birth
>
> One, he died a tragic death, his
>
>   friend was left alone
>
> The serpent smiled and shed her skin,
>
>   taking his fortune for her own."

"It's—" Phoebe stops herself. Her shoulders are drawn down. Her brow is tense. She looks like she is trying to make herself invisible.

"Do you know what it means?" I ask.

She half nods. "It's Gilgamesh," she says. Her voice sounds as heavy as her face looks. Kamal and I stare at her. "It's *The Epic of Gilgamesh*. Gilgamesh and his friend go looking for an eternal-life potion and the friend dies, but Gilgamesh finds it. He stops on his way home to bathe in a river and a snake slithers by and takes it. The poem is about *The Epic of Gilgamesh*."

My mind starts weaving the threads. "The resurrection of Lazarus. The Indian gods looking for eternal life. Gilgamesh looking for eternal life. The poems aren't about stopping ARNS. They're about stopping death. All death."

Another jolt of revelation hits me.

The man at Lux with the long dreads, his words as I rushed down the aisle: "Death no more." I look at my phone, at Theodore Nam's name on my x.chat interface. The letters seem to leap from the screen and float in front of me. My eyes begin to rearrange them in my head. The *d* comes forward, then the *e*, *a*, *t*, and *h*, and on like that until the meaning of the cipher's name is clear. Like the poems, Nam's name is a puzzle.

"It's an anagram," I say. "Theodore Nam. It's an anagram for 'death no more.'" I flash back to the story in the Montana paper about Nam and his death. "He was a man who supposedly killed himself because all his friends died before him. He's a cautionary tale. He's fiction. The message is that when people die, our lives are destroyed and our loneliness becomes unbearable."

Phoebe's eyes appear to shrink into their sockets, which makes the rest of her seem to get smaller and smaller and smaller. A flash of blue and before she even speaks, I know.

"Yes," she says after a long pause.

She is a part of this plot.

"Yes?" Kamal snaps. "Yes, as in you know that, you've known that this whole time?"

Phoebe looks away.

Anger rises in my chest like a hawk spreading its wings. My heart pounds. I spin, dizzy with purple light. I pull off my mask. "You could've saved him." I can barely breathe. "You could've saved everyone."

"You have to know that I was young when I met him," Phoebe pleads. "Practically a child. It was right after Blackout. I had lost everything. When I came out here for the protests, he offered me solutions. He understood what I had gone through. He had lost his own parents at a young age. And he had a vision for the world that made sense to me. I believed we could change the course of civilization and that the consequences of that were worth it." She pauses. Tears paint lines down her cheeks.

"How could you lie to me, to us, every single day? You could've saved my father," I say again.

"I know, and I'm sorry. But I don't believe it anymore. I know it's wrong now. The part of me that died with my parents, I don't know, it's like it's been brought back to life. I can feel pain again, but it's like I can handle it now. I look at you, Lu. I see how strong you are, how you just keep moving forward. You keep searching, eyes and heart wide open. And I want to be like that. I am like that, or I was. And I want to be again."

Kamal is seething. "You get that you are partially responsible for the deaths of, what, hundreds of thousands of people as of this moment? Ultimately millions? Including Lu's dad, probably my parents, our friends. So that's great that you've changed your mind now, but it actually doesn't matter, like, at all."

"You're right," Phoebe replies. "I can't undo what I've done. All I can do is try to help now. That's why I told you what the last poem means. That's why I'm telling you the truth now."

I bury my gaze in her. I want to understand, but I don't.

"You do realize he wants you, Lu. He sent you the poems and the messages as tests. He wanted to see if you could uncover the truth that has eluded the entire world. And if you passed the test, whether you'd be part of what comes next."

It's like swimming in head-high breakers. As soon as you make it through one, another hits you with full force.

"What you said on the train was right. ARNS is the groundwork.

He's brought the world to its knees through grief. That's the terror. Next he will bring relief from the terror—immediate relief but also lasting relief." She looks up at the cloudless sky and clarity slams down like lightning as my whole body trembles with the smell of fresh-cut roses.

"He becomes a hero with the cure and then—" I begin.

"And then when everyone is still reeling from their loss, he offers them the thing they will want most."

"Eternal life," I mutter.

"Eternal life."

"Who is he?" Kamal asks.

Phoebe and I ignore the question.

"He's figured out the basics of how."

"But it's also a certain kind of future for humanity," I add, filling in the blanks as shards of colored light swirl around me like I'm under a disco ball. "That's why the virus works the way it does? Empathic, deeply feeling people must be gotten rid of?"

"That's right," Phoebe says. "He thinks they're unpredictable; they make poor decisions. They cause damage and erode order. He'd actually be surprised you got sick. He pegged you as a pure intellectual. I guess he was wrong."

"Yeah, guess so," I say quietly.

"Who is he?" Kamal asks again.

"Thomas Bell," I say evenly.

On some level, I realize, I have known it all along.

CHAPTER 16

"We need to get the fuck out of here," Kamal says. His focus is on me as though Phoebe no longer exists. "They said at the meeting tonight that planes are being grounded as of tomorrow."

"I can probably get a car," Phoebe offers.

"We aren't going anywhere with you." Kamal's voice is like ice. "You're a terrorist."

I turn to Phoebe. "Where is he?" I ask.

"He could be anywhere," she says.

Kamal puts his hand on my shoulder. "Are you well enough to walk?" I stand up slowly. My head rushes with heat. *It's just waves*, I think.

"Yes," I tell him, still looking at Phoebe. Pain and guilt hang off her like a suit of heavy chains. But underneath that, as if through the openings of the links, a bright light shines through—a glimpse of her unbroken soul.

I have every right to hate her. I want to hate her, but in that moment I realize, she is also a victim of Thomas Bell's madness. He preyed on her hurt and weakness, on the same desire for peace and purpose we all have. If I think about what my father would say to her, it's that we all deserve the opportunity for redemption. "I can't forgive you right now," I tell her. "But I believe that you see it differently now."

"Don't go," she says.

"We have to." I grab my pack, turn, and head down the path.

Kamal and I wind our way from alley to alley toward the gates. "To be clear," he whispers as we pass the vegetable garden, "you just cured yourself of the deadliest virus on the planet."

"The virus isn't deadly," I whisper back. "It's our belief about the virus. I cured myself of that belief, yes. And now my body has no reason to destroy itself."

Kamal tugs at his mask around his neck. "We should put these back on. Just in case."

I stop walking. "You don't trust me?"

"I don't trust Thomas Bell." We put on the masks and continue. I want to yell to everyone that they can stop ARNS with the power of their thinking and a leap of faith, but then I freeze. How crazy would that sound? I need a way to show people, not just tell them.

"I'm sorry about your dad," Kamal says softly as we exit the front gates onto the empty industrial streets of downtown LA.

"Time is such a—I don't even know what the word is," I say. "How often do I bargain with time, asking for more, or wishing it would speed up? My father died less than twelve hours ago. If I knew then what I know now, I could have saved him. If time had behaved a little differently maybe he would still be alive."

"Or maybe you'd be dead," Kamal counters.

"I guess that's true." I stop again. We stand under the buzz of streetlamps, a hot breeze whistling through the palms high above. "We need to do something. I need to get people to understand what is actually happening."

Kamal searches my face. "What happened back there, when you closed your eyes? It looked like you disappeared to somewhere else."

"I did, sort of. It was like I went inside myself, inside my body. I pictured the virus trying to attack me. And then I used my mind to disarm it."

"Okay," he says slowly. "Assuming that's not quite as bizarre as it sounds, how can you get other people to do that?"

"I have absolutely no idea." However powerful I might've felt as those squealing red balls vanished into nothing, now I'm just a girl with a dead father and a strange condition standing on a street corner three thousand miles from home. "We should just figure out a way back to Brooklyn."

We keep walking.

"It's nearly midnight," he says, thinking. "I suggest we find a hotel, take an actual shower, sleep, maybe even eat something. Then try and find a car in the morning."

My eyes brighten. "You had me at shower," I reply.

It's a four-mile trek across a desolate downtown to The Ritz. Darkened office towers loom empty and ghostly over everything. We pass a stretch of homeless people camped out along the sidewalk, their stray shopping carts piled high with trash and old clothes. An empty suitcase lies sprawled against a chain-link fence with a scrawny dog asleep inside. It all looks like it was here long before ARNS. I wonder if the people here even know the difference.

It's 1:00 a.m. when we arrive and I'm pretty sure I've never been so tired in all my life. We peer through locked doors at a lone, masked receptionist behind a desk.

"May I help you?" Her voice breaks the still air, pinched through an intercom.

Kamal pulls out his Black Amex and holds it up against the door. "We need a room, please," he says.

A moment later, a massive block of a man appears in a security guard uniform. He squints at Kamal's card, then opens the door. There's no one else in sight.

"We'd like the best room you have," Kamal tells the woman behind the desk.

Within minutes we are on our way up to a three-thousand-square-foot suite that seems to overlook the entire world.

We walk into the room and a white-gloved bellman begins turning on lamps. "Apologies, but our dining options are limited in light of the situation," he says. He has trouble looking at either of us. My chest starts to feel warm. "But we do have some items. They are marked on your in-room menu."

Kamal hands him a twenty-dollar bill. "Thank you."

The bellman nods and heads for the door.

"Wait," I say. He stops and turns back. I stare at him, not sure at first why I called him. "Do you know anyone who's sick?" I ask finally.

He looks down at his shoes. His shoulders form a cave around his chest. "My wife, I think. She's a nurse. When she came home from her shift this morning . . . She's . . ." He can't finish the sentence.

I pull up my mask, sensing it will help if he can see my face.

"I know this is going to sound like the craziest thing you've ever heard. And I know I look like I've been sleeping on the street for a week, but you have to believe what I'm about to say. Can you trust me?" Heat is building behind my ribs. "I'm not crazy; I'm not on drugs. I'm just really smart. Okay?"

"Okay," he replies. His voice is tight, his eyes narrow.

"Okay?" I insist.

"Yes, okay," he says, more sure.

"You have to believe it completely, with, like, your whole self. ARNS is real, but it's not real. It kills you by messing with your brain chemistry. When you really understand and internalize the truth of that statement, the symptoms will reverse."

The bellman stares at me.

"Tell your wife she needs to tell her brain that she is not dying, that she is healthy and going to survive."

I pause, searching for a sign of acceptance in his expression. I try to will the warmth I am feeling toward him somehow, like with the man who stole our car.

"You have a good night, ma'am." He turns and walks out.

"Fuck," I blurt out as the door closes behind him.

I go over to the terrace door and walk out onto the deck. Kamal follows. He pulls off his mask and looks at me. He's standing so close I forget everything but his smell for a second.

"I don't know what's next or what to do, how to help people or stop this. I feel like an idiot," I tell him.

"You're not an idiot."

"I'm scared."

"Me too."

Alone together, our faces bare, it's like we are right back to that night in my garden. The dawn threatening to arrive, my mother's raspberry bush overflowing with fruit, the quiet drone of the earth's motion underscoring everything.

And now, all these months later, his hand is on my face. Soft, but firm enough that I lean into it just slightly. I feel the roughness of his skin. I smell his smell on his fingers.

"Are you sure about all this, about the cure?"

"I don't have proof, if that's what you're asking."

"It's not. I'm asking if you're sure."

"I am."

"Then we made it," he says, so close he's whispering.

My eyes hold his gaze comfortably, like a marble in my palm. "Made it where?" I ask.

"To the rest of ever." His lips find their way into a grin before he leans in and kisses me.

We stumble back inside. He pushes me up against a window. We're kissing rough, like we'll never get enough. He pulls my shirt off and his warm hands slide along the surface of my skin. My legs start to go numb. Colors flood my view. I tap my foot three times and press my back against the cool glass pane. The smell of pine weaves a cloud around my face.

He pulls his shirt over his head and we fall to the couch. His strong arms flex on either side of me. I wrap my hands around them as his chest hovers and his hips press against mine.

It's just waves. Slow, amazing, overwhelming waves. I want it to stop. I want it to never end.

"I think," he says, breathless after a minute. "We should leave this here. Much as I would prefer not to."

"Okay," I say. My heart is beating like hummingbird wings. Our bodies slowly find stillness and we stay like that, our faces close, everything on fire. My hands trace the curves of his shoulders.

"I think," I begin, "I'm going to take a shower."

He smiles. "That's not going to help my self-control efforts."

I smile back. "That's part of my motivation."

"You're very, very cruel," he whispers. We kiss again. Then I get up and go into the bathroom.

I step into the marble stall. Hot water pours over my skin in sheets. I replay the past ten minutes in quick cuts—glimpses of his face, his body, interspersed with bursts of coral and silver.

The lemon scent of the soap brings me back to the present. I look out through the glass shower door. My eyes shine in the mirror. I feel beautiful. I feel like myself.

I scrub my body clean, then pause on my scar as the soapy water spirals down the drain. I think back to Bell, how he stopped and stared at it. Evans too. The shape or the very existence of it, this rough patch on my smooth skin. It must surprise people.

I dry off and pull clean clothes from my pack. There's my father's knife. I take it out and rest the handle in my palm. I feel its weight, its power. I think back to the face of the dead man lying on the ground. I shiver.

"I ordered food," Kamal calls from the other room.

I put the knife back in my bag and get dressed.

I come out and find Kamal lying on the bed watching the flatscreen. "They're confirming Bell's ID'ed the virus," he says. "They still don't understand how it destroys the nervous system, though."

I stare at the television. An image of Bell in frat boy–handsome, presidential mode. I feel foolish when I think about how badly I wanted to impress him.

"Look at him," I mumble. "In the middle of killing millions of people and he looks like the guy you'd want to be your dad." The word sends my heart into my stomach. I'd let myself forget again.

Kamal clicks off the TV. "Come here," he says. I lie down next to him and settle in his arms.

"Is this weird?" I ask.

"Which part? The pandemic? You solving the greatest mystery of the twenty-first century? The next president being a sociopath?"

I laugh. "No. You and me." My legs tingle as I look at him.

"It's weird that it's normal. Don't you think?" Yeah. He kisses my head. "I'm gonna take a shower too. An exceptionally cold, cold shower." He gets up and goes into the bathroom.

I pick up my phone and open my photos. There's the note from my dad. LU: MAKE SOMETHING OF YOURSELF.

I hear a crash from the other room. I jump up. What the fuck was that? I go into the living room. The terrace door is still open and a small tree is on its side. I go out and stand it back up. The wind gusts and it almost falls again. The leaves shake as I hold its trunk steady.

I look up at the sky. "What?" I mutter. The wind stops and the leaves fall still. I go back inside.

I grab my laptop and take a seat in the living room. As I sit staring at the screen, I imagine my father in his music room. He's at the piano with a blank piece of paper in front of him.

Make something of yourself.

I hear it differently now. It's not an imperative toward success. It's a call to create. It's an invitation to translate myself, my own experience, into something that can be experienced by someone else.

I open my lexicon of sensory episodes. There are 1,143 entries. These are my disturbances, my waves. Emotions, colors, sounds, vibrations, sensations—all of them reducible to wavelengths, to bits of data. All of them, together, a kind of language.

I write a piece of code that converts the lexicon into visual and auditory building blocks—waves of color and bursts of sound that mimic on the screen my past sensing of different feelings. This is the material.

The LightYears analysis of the world's feelings will be the blueprint and the blank screen, the piece of land.

It's a simple program: Take the data of human sentiment generated by a piece of online content and translate it into a flowing, swelling mass of colors and swirls, twisting, intersecting lines, deep drones and mind-bending tones—all according to my lexicon. My unique sensory perception and the world's emotions combined into a single piece of original content.

I put in the Hugo video analysis to test it. Won't compile.

"Shit." I look up to see Kamal in a towel, watching me from the doorway. "How long have you been standing there?"

"A while. I tried talking, but you didn't hear me."

"Sorry." My eyes drift to his bare torso, then snap back to my screen. "I'm trying to do something."

"Okay." He comes and sits next to me.

I fix a couple of errors and try it again. Still not working. More fixes and another test. Now I've got something. I pair my laptop's Bluetooth with the massive sixty-five-inch flatscreen.

"Turn off the lights," I instruct Kamal. He does.

We sit in darkness and I hit Play.

Bursts of red flood us in what almost feels like three dimensions. They surge over each other, like an ocean of blood—wave after wave moving toward us as menacing bass tones moan and whine underneath the visuals.

The red swirls together with purple, yellow, and brown, then the colors gather into themselves, almost vanishing into darkness at the point in the analysis when *#hisnameishugo* first appeared. And then everything erupts again in a heart shape, like a time-lapse flower blooming all at once—the red heart of humanity exploding in every direction, and the warped noise of a whirring engine gurgling into silence.

The data itself—the original text—is invisible, replaced by color and sound, translated by the alchemy of my senses into the expression of an unseen dimension. It's like a message from another world.

I feel ill. It's as if those red raging orbs inside my body have returned. And they are unstoppable. A crushing weight presses down like I'm being buried under a flow of wet cement. I feel feverish, weak, dizzy.

I try to shake it off. I tap my foot and feel the couch. *It's just waves. Choose the light.*

I turn to Kamal and realize he's curled up on the couch. He's shaking.

"It's not real," I tell him.

But my words, my tricks, are powerless. I start shivering. My lungs constrict. I'm coughing. I fall to my knees on the plush carpet. I cling to the edge of the coffee table and glance back out the terrace door. The wind is rattling the glass.

The tree tips over again.

"We need to undo it," Kamal mumbles.

I stare at the tree on its side. I imagine picking it up as Kamal's words register. An impulse courses through me. It's just a fragment of comprehension, like I'm searching for a word I can't quite recall.

What if? I think. *What if.* I look down at the keyboard and back at the final image on the screen, the heart torn to pieces.

I command the program to play the compilation in reverse.

"Look at the screen," I manage to say.

We watch as the broken, disparate fragments of emotion, the waves of discordant colors and the droning, soul-crushing din transform into a rush of beautiful shapes and sounds.

Played in reverse, the tones are vibrant and joyful. They seem to strike my deepest insides, then reverberate through my veins, healing each cell as they go. Rich reds swell into each other. The image of the heart being made whole seems to leap from the screen and dive into my eyes. Red and yellow melt together into the most exquisite shade of orange I have ever seen—it feels like sunlight pouring over my freezing skin.

My breath calms. The dizziness stops. The red orbs once again seem to evaporate into the ether. Separation dissolves and I feel weightless.

I look at Kamal. He's smiling like he's high.

"I feel normal," he says. "Except not, actually. Are we floating?"

"I dunno. Maybe?"

"You made that. How did you make that?"

I scramble for my phone. "I have to get it to Merz."

I draft the message: I'm sending you something. You have to put it up. Forget the votes; just do it. It's a cure. Ask Phoebe if you think I'm crazy. Send.

"It's so beautiful," Kamal mutters as his eyes flutter closed, that smile still plastered to his face. "I love you." He says it so quietly I can't be sure it's what I heard, but my vision ripples silver and my legs go numb.

"Kamal," I say softly. But he's asleep.

I get up and start to pace. The amber light of the city bleeds in through the windows and I'm thinking of Janine. I have so much I want to tell her. I remember how Ron kept on talking to Jordana, how he said she was dead, not gone.

I open my texts and touch Janine's name. My fingers hover over the keys as I try to figure out where to begin. But I can't; there's too much.

Then, a message from Merz: **OK**.

Good. I compress my video and send it. I look over at Kamal asleep. Will he remember what he said when he wakes up? Am I supposed to say it back?

I lay a blanket over him, then tune the TV to FLN, mute it, and wait.

I feel how I used to sometimes before a swim meet. It was like a spark in my belly when I knew I should be nervous but I wasn't. That feeling always meant I was going to swim well.

An hour passes and then another. No video.

I watch the endless cycle of news reports. I think of my dad on our couch, how upset he was about Hugo. Why wasn't I able to save him?

My watch buzzes. Merz: **Video about to break**.

I sit forward with my laptop. There it is, live on Front Line's site. I bring the link into LightYears. A hum fills my head. My heart booms in my ears.

It's a slow build, tracking first overseas where it isn't the middle of the night. Kabul, Berlin, Tokyo. Seconds become minutes and the curves begin to generate. The responses begin to emerge. Words and phrases come bursting to the front of the text cloud.

Bliss. Magical. Connection.

The curving lines bend and arc, then hit a peak. The word *Cure* blazes to the front.

It's working.

I jump up in a wave of orange. It's fucking working.

I go to the windows. Twinkling lights stretch as far as my eye can see, then disappear into the dark void of the ocean way beyond. I picture my father out there in that emptiness. I see him watching what is happening. He's standing shoulder to shoulder with everyone who has ever died, with everyone who has ever lived.

Always together, never apart. Me, him, all of us everywhere. The rest of ever.

I look back at the screen. The data keeps pouring in. The word *Cure* still holds top position. Pervasive Sentiment: *Love*.

Time warps as I stand on the crest of an imaginary wave. Heat builds behind my heart. Separation once again dissolves.

I reach to wake Kamal. He has to see this, to feel this.

But before I can, a banging on the door. I am jolted back to the confines of the room.

An instantaneous spark of blue. I ignore it. For some dumb reason, hunger maybe, I ignore it.

I rush to the door and whip it open. A face, and before I can make a sound, I'm flooded with an avalanche of scent: a heap of just-cut roses.

"Joe," I manage to mutter before everything goes black.

I wake up in the back of a high-end van. It looks like the interior of Air Force One. Leather captain's chairs, a desk, a sophisticated AV system.

Bell's special assistant, Joe, sits across from me. Behind him sits another man with a terrifying, blank stare. I instinctively glance at my wrist in a haze of yellow. My watch is gone.

"Sorry for the drama," Joe says plainly. "Can I offer you anything? Peanuts, pretzels, a beverage?"

"My head hurts," I reply, realizing I've been drugged.

"That's normal," he says. He opens a bottle and offers me two red pills. I stare down at them. He spins the bottle around and shows me the label. "Ibuprofen," he says.

"No thanks."

Joe shrugs.

I look out the heavily tinted windows as we move from one six-lane highway to another. Lights, buildings, the occasional car or emergency vehicle. The road is open; the sky, cloudless. There is nothing to tell me where we are, where we are going, or what's going to happen when we get there.

Then I spot it. There on a wall as we fly past, brightly lit under the acidic streetlamps. A massive spray-painted drawing of a wolf, midstride.

I glimpse it like a camera's open shutter—for an instant. But the image freezes in my mind. My prayer for a sign, answered. That certain spark of something inside me reignited.

Joe's phone buzzes.

He puts in his earpiece and answers. "Got her. Yes sir." He clicks off and turns toward me with his J.Crew smile. "We'll be there soon."

I look at the door. I squirm in my seat. There is no way out except through.

CHAPTER 17

We arrive at the entrance to a deserted marina. The van stops and Joe leads me out. The air is still. The boats clang eerily against their moorings.

We go through the gate at the top of the dock. Rows of fishing trawlers, sailboats, and skiffs stretch out against the black water. And at the end, one massive yacht floats, lit up and glowing like a box of gold.

We arrive at the ship. Its name, Isis, is written across the stern in beautiful jet black. We climb aboard. I scan the rosewood surfaces polished to a shine. Five levels of crisp white decks are capped by a helipad and its shiny black chopper. A pair of small lifeboats hang over the sides, defying gravity.

I follow Joe into the main cabin. Bell is waiting. On one side of the room hangs a large cage. In it, a collection of striking blue birds flutter and chirp.

He stands up. "Luisa. It is so, so nice to see you again." He smiles like I just dropped by for Sunday brunch.

Joe takes a seat behind a desk in the corner and begins typing on a laptop.

Bell motions to the cage. "I can see you're admiring the birds." I wasn't. "They are quite interesting. Come, sit down. You must be hungry." He picks up a large touch-screen device and keys something in. Blue and yellow swirl around me as my heart pumps furiously. I picture my feet digging into sand. "A snack is on its way. Now, come. Sit." He beckons to the couch.

"No thanks," I say. A sudden vibration leaves me unsteady. It's the engine kicking on. The boat is pulling away from the dock. I bolt for the door. Bell watches me calmly as I try the knob. It's locked.

"Lu, may I call you Lu?" Bell asks. I turn back toward him. "Lu. You act like you're in danger. We're just going for a little spin."

A second door opens and a butler comes in pushing a cart laden with food.

We pick up speed and the birds dance around their cage. They want to get out too.

"They're lovely to look at, aren't they?" Bell gazes at them with pride. "Western Jays. They are one of a small handful of animals, aside from humans, of course, that display visible signs of grief. They actually hold what seem like funerals when another bird dies. They stop eating for days. So emotional. I keep them as a reminder of what an un-evolved species looks like, of what humanity would succumb to without my work."

"I guess it's easier to have your enemies caged," I snap. "But if death isn't worth mourning, then how can life be so precious that you're doing all of this to make people live forever? You're too rich to be doing it for money."

He grins. "Have something to eat," he says. I don't move. He shrugs and grabs a gleaming green apple from the cart. He takes a bite. "Life is precious because of its potential. You study physics. You know the value of latent energy. But when potential is constrained, it is worth nothing." The boat rocks as we pick up speed. I grab the edge of a chair. "When people's lives exist in a finite plane, their potential is deadened, innovation stagnates, progress and radical evolution grind to a halt. 'He had so much promise,' they say when someone dies. 'There was so much more she planned to do.' What if 'he' fulfilled that promise? What if 'she' got to see those plans through?"

I dig my nails into the chair.

"You agree with that, don't you?" Bell says.

I do actually.

"But what about the potential and promise of all the people killed by ARNS?" I demand.

"There is not a single significant leap humanity has taken that didn't bring with it loss of life on a mass scale. From the fall of the Roman Empire to the industrial revolution, the civil rights movement—this is no different. Our species is ready to leap into a phase of unprecedented expansiveness, of freedom to reach the full extent of our capability."

"And for all you know you just killed the next Einstein."

He smiles. "Unlikely. Look, freedom comes from the removal of absolutes. I'm a problem solver. I'm going to free the world from the greatest, most absolute problem of them all, from the only true fear that exists."

"By preying on it," I interrupt. I glance at Joe who's nearly invisible behind his laptop. "You're just amplifying a fear in order to assuage it. There's nothing noble in that."

"No?" he looks at me. I can almost see the gears turn behind his crystalline eyes. His voice turns gentle. "How's your father doing?"

I inhale slowly. Colors again. The smell of roses. My feet in the sand. "He died earlier today," I tell him evenly.

"Oh, Lu. I'm so sorry. It's horrible when children are left to make sense of life without their parents. I know what that's like. Wouldn't you like to take that pain away? Or, better, wouldn't you prefer that you had never felt it in the first place?"

I would, but I say nothing.

"We'll put that aside for now," he says. "I'd like you to watch the screen." My gaze follows his to a large television on the wall. He motions to Joe and the screen comes to life with LightYears's feed.

"What the fuck?" I mumble. "You hacked me?"

Over 900,000 people's feelings have been captured so far. The tag cloud swells with words. *Cure* still dominates. *Love* still holds as Pervasive Sentiment. Then, from the corner of my eye I see Bell nod at Joe. With one keystroke, the number of comments freezes. A long minute passes without any change.

"What's going on?" I ask. "Why has it stopped?"

"Just watch," Bell says.

The number begins to drop rapidly. Words in the cloud disappear.

"What the fuck?" I exclaim. The analysis is vanishing before my eyes. "You're scrubbing it?"

They've erased the video from the Internet, along with all traces of the response to it. A small wave of hope that had the power to carry the world to salvation has been swallowed into nothing. I sit down without meaning to. A hiss blocks out the sound of the engine. I struggle to breathe.

I press my feet into the floor, imagine the sand. I look out at the dark ocean spreading beyond the window. The sky above it is just beginning to brighten with the dawn.

Choose the light, I think.

The hiss fades, replaced by the birds chirping.

"Freedom does come from the removal of absolutes," I say after a long pause. "But death isn't an absolute, neither is pain. You can't see that because you're too afraid. People who are afraid or hurting only see one answer to a question. They only want one thing: relief. That's what you're offering, but it's small. It's limited. It's the same song on an endless loop or a 2D rendering."

I'm standing up again.

"Your power relies on the weakness of others. That's not real power. Real power comes from being vulnerable, from *feeling*. If you can't feel, you might as well be dead."

Bell looks at me with a mix of horror and awe.

"You can make my video disappear. You can become president and live forever. You can even kill me. But you will never be free and neither will anyone who follows your path."

"Kill you?" He laughs. "You disappoint me, Luisa."

I stare at him. "You disappoint me too."

"I thought we were going to do great things together." His words spark blue.

"Why?" I ask.

"Why?"

"Yeah. Why did you think that? Why did you choose me?"

"I told you, I'm not going to—"

"I know. You're not going to validate my existence. I know. That's not why I'm asking. I'm asking because it doesn't make sense. You didn't even like LightYears. So why would you choose me and send me those poems and lead me right into the center of what you're doing? I don't get it."

I catch him glance down at my knee. It's so quick I almost miss it. But I don't.

"You have no idea," he says quietly, "what you're capable of."

We hold each other's gaze for a long moment. I notice the engine has stopped. I look out the window. We are anchored at least a mile offshore. More light bleeding up from the horizon.

"I'm powerful," he continues, "because I know how to exert power in the right place at the right time. I always find a way to get what I want."

He stares through me. Another flash of blue.

Then he drops his apple core onto the cart and stands up. "You must be tired," he mumbles. Without another word, he walks out.

"Let's go," Joe says, rising to stand.

"Go where?" I ask nervously. Moments later we're walking down the boat's narrow corridor. We arrive at the door to a bedroom and he leads me inside.

"Breakfast is served at eight. I'll be back to get you," he says.

"And then?" I ask.

He pulls the door closed and locks it from the outside.

I sit on the bed and gaze out the window. He always gets what he wants. But what does he want from me?

My hands move to my bare legs, my knees. My finger absent-mindedly traces my scar. One thing is clear: I have to get off this boat.

I leap to my feet. I open the closet, the drawers, not even sure what I'm looking for. Extra blankets and pillows, an ironing board, an old toothbrush.

I go back to the window. I press down on the handle. Locked.

I look closer at the casing. The glass is held in place by six wide-faced screws. I dig the edge of my fingernail into the groove of one. I try to twist it. Not happening.

I sit back on the bed. I catch my reflection in a mirror on the opposite wall. The edge of the chain around my neck shining silver against my skin: My necklace, the smooth flattened coin I made with my dad on the train tracks as a kid. I pull it off and go to work on the screws. One by one, they come tumbling out of the frame. I heave the heavy sheet of glass aside and climb out.

The sun is visible now, but still low. I brace against the morning chill and tiptoe along the deck. I duck past a couple of darkened windows, then stop. Footsteps on the walkway above. They recede and leave behind the sound of the sea sloshing against the boat's belly. A gust of cold wind. Pink and yellow flash before my eyes.

I reach the stern deck. The current is calm, the air still. I stretch my arms overhead. I think back to that first day in the car as the four of us left the city. I remember how my eyes found Kamal's in the mirror, how I silently asked him to hold me and keep me safe. I glance down at the waves. I ask the same thing of them now.

I take in a massive breath and I step off the edge. My body arcs through the air—a momentary challenge to gravity before it breaks the surface of the sea.

The freezing-cold water sucks all the oxygen from my lungs. I come up gasping and let myself bob with the chop.

And then I start to swim. I pull and breathe, kick and glide across the waves in a perfect rhythm. My arms and legs work to propel me. The natural power of the ocean helps me float. The sunlight beams across the water, warming my face with every turn of my head toward the sky. The glorious morning air fills each cell and atom of my body, guiding me forward. I am alive.

I picture Janine diving into the darkened pool at night, how our weightless moments underwater made all our cares fade away. I see my father standing on the edge of the pool, drilling me on my strokes.

There is no separation between me, the water, the air, the sky, the sun, the mountains, the dead, the living. No separation between pain and the beauty pain illuminates.

I swim forward, stroke after stroke. I can see the shore getting closer, but the current is suddenly stronger. The swell is picking up. Soon the land disappears, then reappears with the rise and fall of bigger and bigger waves. *Hold me. Keep me safe.*

My legs start to feel heavy. Yellow bursts pop across my view as I wonder, *Can I make it?* The rest of ever. Kamal. Is he still lying there on that couch? I swim a little harder. The ocean pushes back a little more.

I'm close now. The waves are starting to break. They're easily eight feet high, maybe higher. My chest burns with the effort of just keeping my head above the surface.

I scan the empty beach. There's no one. I paddle into a cresting wave and let it carry me toward the shore. If I time it right, I can get in without getting crushed.

But I don't. I ease back when I should go for it and I am pummeled. I tumble like a rag doll in the dryer, losing all sense of up. I need air and there is none. There's only water, holding me down.

Finally, the wave releases its grip and I manage to surface and inhale half a breath. My heart is pounding to the rhythm of yellow flashing light. I look up. Another wall of water bearing down. I shut my eyes as it crashes and slams me to the ocean floor.

Total darkness.

CHAPTER 18

I wake up in my own bed in Brooklyn. There's a foot of snow on the ground and more falling. I sit up, confused. How did I get here? How is it winter?

I throw on black sweatpants and a Harvard sweatshirt. It smells like Kamal.

I move toward the door and realize: I'm woozy. My head is aching. I stumble to the bathroom for some water. Better.

I come back to my room. There's something strange about it. It's familiar, but not quite the same. Was that puffy chair always there? I don't remember that purple candle on my desk.

I pause to look at the wall of photos. Dozens from before I dyed my hair. Only one after, from the morning I left—two hemispheres of time. I barely recognize that old version of myself.

The wind rattles against the windows, shaking me with it. I go downstairs. A Christmas tree stands in the living room, presents arranged underneath. My mom is reading on the couch. It surprises me to see her there.

"Good morning, sweetheart," she says warmly.

I go into the kitchen.

Ben is making Dad's banana bread. "'Sup, dude?"

"Hey," I say. "What day is it?"

"Uh?" He pours me a cup of coffee. "It's Christmas Eve?"

I grab the coffee and sit down. "I must've been dreaming something," I say. I go back into the living room. "I'm going to the pool," I tell my mom.

She looks up. "*Cariño*, the snow. The storm is getting worse."

"It's just snow, Mom." She goes to the window and looks out at the yard. Loose flakes gust from the trees' heavy branches. "I'll be careful," I assure her.

She smiles. "I know you will." She comes over and gives me a hug. I let her hold me. I don't want to let go.

She pulls back and looks at my face. "Have a good swim. And don't be gone too long," she says.

I walk past my father's music room, then turn and go back. All the sheet music has been put away. The piano lid is closed.

I go upstairs and get my swim gear. I pause on the landing and go up to my dad's room. I open the closet. My mother's clothes fill it. Nothing of my father's remains.

I tumble down the stairs and head for the door. The photo of the four of us from Ben's graduation hangs framed in the hall. I stop and look at my dad's smile, my own.

I miss him, like a thud behind my ribs.

I walk to the subway under a darkening sky, snow steadily falling. I descend the stairs. The roar of a train pulling away fades into the distance. I stand and wait on the empty platform, staring out into the tunnel's blackness.

A rush of warm air blows toward me like the bellow of an angry beast. I step back, frightened.

A moment later, I hear a voice. That same voice that told me to go to California, so quiet it's barely there: "The time is now."

What?

Another blast of warm air and another train comes swiftly into the station. The doors open right where I stand. I get on, sit down, and ride alone in the car seven stops.

I come up from belowground and walk the eight long blocks to St. Francis College, where my father always took us to swim in winter. The snow is coming down in thick sheets. The grinding rumble of a passing plow is the only sound.

I change into my suit and step under the shower on the deck. My body is so cold, the icy water feels warm.

I have the pool to myself and I take my first lap slowly. My limbs are stiff, but I find my rhythm like always.

My breath fills the space where my father's instruction would've been. The shadow underneath me is like the ghostly imprint of Janine's body swimming alongside mine.

I imagine an empty seat at Christmas dinner.

I swim a mile and a half and climb out. I return to the locker room. The radiators hiss warm air. A small TV chatters in the corner. I take off my suit and watch news of the presidential campaign in full swing. Bell is up in the polls, they're saying. They call him a "hero" for curing ARNS.

It's strange to me that so much time has passed, that I could have no memory of it. There must be nearly a million people with stories about a phantom video that cured them of ARNS symptoms. Does anyone care about that? Or is it like tales of aliens landing in empty fields and old bridges haunted by ghosts? Is my cure just a myth?

I come out of the shower and wrap myself in one of the too-small towels they give you. Bell is still on the television.

"America is ready for tougher, smarter leadership. We are ready to innovate in ways our parents and grandparents only dreamed," he says to a crowd of supporters at a rally. "The time is now." A chill as his words echo the voice from the station. I pick up my pace.

The water from my wet hair drips down my back and as I wrap my towel around my head, I feel a presence.

I look up at my naked reflection in the mirror. The flattened coin around my neck. There's no one there.

I ride the elevator up from the pool. I imagine Bell being found out. I picture him jumping to his death from the balcony of his apartment. Then I flash to him standing outside my front door, calling to me to help him. I shudder as the elevator doors open.

The snow is blinding and the wind is like a wall pressing against my body. I make it two blocks and realize the remaining six will be impossible. I notice a small shop across the street. It looks open.

I push through the brightly painted door and greet the smell of cinnamon and ginger.

The space is brightly colored and lined with shelves filled with an array of ornate gold and silver statues. I move closer and see they are the statues of Indian deities.

"Good afternoon," calls a voice. I turn to see a heavyset Indian man behind a counter at the back of the store. "Would you like some chai?"

"Yes, thank you," I reply. I pull off my gloves and rub my hands together.

"This is not a day to be outside," he says, smiling.

"No," I agree. I take off my hat. I'm drawn to the statues. Men with elephant heads, monkey heads, women with multiple arms seated on flowers or riding on lions—they are vaguely familiar from the stories I read as a child.

The man approaches with a hot, steaming mug. "You like the murtis?" he inquires.

"The statues?" I reply, presuming to translate the word I do not know.

"They are statues, yes. But they are also the gods and goddesses themselves. We make no distinction between the deity and its image." I nod and sip the chai. "Is there one that calls to you?" he asks.

"I don't know."

"Each of us can find an archetype in these entities. There is great power in choosing and working with your archetype."

I pace alongside the shelves, looking at each one carefully. I stop in front of a bronze sculpture of a woman with eight arms riding on a lion. "That one," I tell him.

"Ma Durga," he replies. "Pick her up. Hold her." I set down my mug and lift the statue off the shelf. A shock radiates up through my hands and arms. I place her back down, startled.

"Don't be frightened. She's just letting you know she's real." His smile puts me at ease.

"Who is she?" I ask.

"She was created by all the other gods and goddesses when the demon king Mahishasura was granted a sort of immortality by Lord Shiva. They created Durga to vanquish him. She is goodness in a fierce form."

I pick her up again. I hold her.

"In each arm she holds a tool given to her by the others to use in her quest. She heals through firmness *and* compassion."

I study her eyes.

"You must take her," he offers.

"I'm sure I can't afford her."

He wraps his hands around mine, still holding the statue. He closes his eyes. "She's yours," he says softly. "Please, take her. My gift."

"No, I can't," I protest.

"You already have. Please."

"Okay," I say. "Thank you."

"Put her someplace where you can sit near her and look at her."

"You mean, like, meditate?"

"Well, yes. But nothing so formal. Just *be* with her. She will rub off on you, so to speak."

I look outside. "It looks a little better," I say. "I need to get home."

"I shall thank the snow for bringing you here," he says, beaming.

"Me too." I put Durga in my bag. I thank him again, and step outside.

The snow is still falling. The banks are higher now and it's difficult to walk. I make it to the next corner, but the wind picks up into a howl. My view dissolves into total whiteout. I stop moving.

I close my eyes. An image of me and my brother hanging my father's Christmas stocking flashes across my mind. How can it be that my dad won't be there to open presents with us in the morning? I clutch my bag. My hands grab for Durga's solid shape. My face braces against the chill.

When I open my eyes, I'm surrounded by white. But it's not snow. It's fog. Dense, opaque, enveloping fog. I look down and the snow is gone, along with the paved sidewalk of the city. Instead, a dirt path lies under my boots. I can see only a couple of feet in any direction and all other sensory perception is nonexistent—there are no smells, no sounds, no colors.

Am I dead?

I begin walking forward, compelled once again by something other than logic. I follow the path up a steep incline, as the colorless cloud floats all around me.

As I climb, I hear the sound of a child laughing. The gentleness of that singular sound keeps my fearful thoughts at bay. As the ground levels off, the moisture in the air begins to thin. The smell of woodfire fills my nose. I breathe it in. It's comforting.

The fog is all but gone and in its place comes a rush of rich color as I enter a grove of impossibly tall, majestic redwoods—the kind that have been there for centuries.

Their age, their beauty. I stop and look up as sunlight flares through their wispy boughs like the flickering light of an old projector.

People and moments begin to play in front of me like the images across Jordana's eyes on the train. Janine flying down the bike path on the bridge; my father's hollow expression as he lay dead in his bed; the choir at Lux bursting with life; wolves in the woods; Kamal's mouth on the back of my neck, his eyes narrow in the darkness; the ocean churning underneath me as I swam away from Bell.

And then the images dissolve into a shimmering beam of light, shifting and taking the shape of what I eventually recognize as my own form rocketing through the void of outer space. My skin is illuminated by starlight. My whole body glows in a glittering wave.

The light emanating from my figure grows more and more intense until it explodes into a blinding flash, retracting, pulling everything in the surrounding landscape with it—the trees, the path, the sky.

Everything except me.

I'm left in a darkening abyss that is losing light by the second, like a star collapsing into a black hole.

Then, the sound of a flame igniting and the blink of a candle in the corner of my eye. I look down to see myself holding a freshly extinguished match, still smoking.

Standing beside me holding the candle is Evans Birkner.

She's much older now, her face wrinkled and her hair gray, but her light eyes and clear skin remain as luminous as ever.

I jump at the sight of her. My body is trembling.

"Hello Luisa," she says in her husky voice.

"Am I dead?" I blurt out.

She smiles. "I would venture to say you have never been more alive."

I tell myself to wake up, certain now that I must be in the grip of a dream. But nothing happens.

"When you arrived at Lux," she continues, "we thought you had realized who you are. But your questions, your uncertainty. We saw you had not. But now it is time." She pauses. The candlelight dances across her face. The sound of distant voices whispering.

"Time for what?" I ask, sensing the answer is already somewhere inside my mind even if I can't access it.

"For you to remember your future," she says plainly. "He threatens everything. He must be stopped. The girl who refracts the future of the world through a different prism, who holds her heart and her mind as one —it is she who can lead us where we need to go. We are ready for *you*, Luisa."

"Me?"

"Will you answer our call?"

I swallow and look past her image into the blackest point of nothing. Before I can form a single syllable, I feel the smoothness of wet sand under my feet. My legs are heavy, but I'm walking.

I blink and I'm on a beach. I hear crashing surf behind me. I turn and look out at the waves. I see a small dot on the horizon. Bell's Isis.

My heartbeat slows steadily as the sun climbs out of the east.

My right hand reaches for my aching head and my mind begins to offer explanations for what just happened. The wave. I hit a rock. I almost drowned. Grief. Fatigue. Hunger.

As I become ready to dismiss everything that just happened as mere hallucination, I feel a tug of awareness pulling me toward my left palm.

I look down. I open my cold, wet hand and there, pressed against my skin, is the half-burnt stub of a matchstick—a smudge of black ash sweeps across the grooves in my flesh.

I hear Evans's voice again as I hold the match between my fingers: "Will you answer our call?"

In an instant, my mind shuffles through a hundred different replies, all dismissive and doubting. But then, a quiet voice, born from gathering all the light deep inside. That voice manages to climb onto the shoulders of my psyche. Its wise heart surveys its surroundings and recalls a future that has already happened, yet is just about to. As I stand alone on the beach in the morning sun, it is that voice, detached from time and space, uncomplicated by insecurity or peril, that emerges from my mouth and utters a simple, unqualified "Yes."

ACKNOWLEDGMENTS

This book would not exist without two very special women, Carey Albertine and Saira Rao of In This Together Media, who packaged it. They took a chance on me and shepherded *Light Years* from the very start with their keen creative input, astute big-picture insights, and caring support. My deepest thanks are for them.

I am also exceedingly grateful to Jess Regel of Foundry Literary + Media, who found the book a happy home and endured the endless anxieties and questions of a first-time author with kindness, patience, and sage counsel.

And to Jacquelyn Mitchard, who leaped to publish the manuscript two days after receiving it and provided the exact right input I needed to "find" the book and bring it to its final form. To work with an editor who is herself a brilliant artist was a true privilege and she will always be a critical part of my story as a writer.

To Mark Merriman, who made me feel heard, sane, and taken care of. Thank you times one million.

To my genius publicist Megan Beatie, and to Mara Anastas, Jodie Hockensmith, Sarah McCabe, and everyone at Simon Pulse who brought the finished book beautifully into the wider world.

To Kassie Evashevski and Mary Pender, the best!

To Genevieve Gagne-Hawes, who, through her genius critiques, taught me how to write.

To Rosemary Graham, who, through her genius critiques, also taught me how to write. She has become the kind of artistic mentor I have always dreamed about and I am so grateful to call her family as well as friend.

To Francisca Alegria, Eoin Bullock, Erin Dicker, Arielle Fenig, Michael Fressola, Keith Gordon, Rachel Griffin, Jeff Matlow, Michelle Miller, Liam O'Rourke, George Paaswell, Kay Reinhart, Ellen Ross, Sarah Trouslard, and Liz Wyle who read various drafts and parts of drafts and provided feedback and encouragement along the way—you are each a part of the book's DNA and I am so thankful for you all!

To Marshall Lewy, who gave me a game-changer of a note. Thank you, brilliant friend.

To Jennifer Niven and Mitch Larson, who gave me my first and most-cherished blurbs and who inspire me so deeply as writers and humans.

To Erin Alexander, who designed a thoughtful, kick-ass cover.

To Katie McDonough, whose copyedits were so intelligent and precise and polished the book to become the best possible version of itself.

To the following generous souls who answered various research or publishing questions and/or provided helpful insights about math, science, technology, and/or various aspects of human existence: Jenny Ghose, Dean Gloster, Dr. Rachel Gordon, Jason Jones, Daniel Kohn, Jillian Lauren, David Lubensky, Robert Marshall, Rev. James Martin, Jynne Martin, Hannah Minghella, Dr. Bradley Perkins, Douglas Rushkoff, Graham Riske, and Stephanie Simon. Thank you so!

To the following authors whose work inspired me while I was writing: Leigh Bardugo, Joan Didion, Clarrisa Pinkola Estes, Michio Kaku, Barbara Kingsolver, Madeleine L'Engle, Edan Lepucki, Meghan O'Rourke, Amanda Palmer, Carlo Rovelli, John Sarno, and Rick Yancey.

To Nicola Behrman, Jessica Gelson, Stephen Malach, Sara Murphy, Philip Schuster, Stephanie Swafford, and several of the people also mentioned above who believed in my creative abilities even when I wasn't so sure and have always encouraged me to keep going.

To Kelly Wheeler, who lovingly helped to take care of my children while I wrote. You are our family.

To Gretchen and Peter Haight, who made it possible for me to devote myself to this project.

To Tessa Petrich, who is a rockstar. Thank you!

To my grandmother Ruth, who passed away just before the book was finished. You will inspire me for the rest of my life.

To Phil Hoffman, who taught me too many things to list, but chiefly that all creative work must be personal. Oh, how I wish you were here to read this book.

To my children, Wren and Zephyr, who show me daily how much wisdom, power, and beauty kids possess.

To my husband, Nicholas Griffin, who complemented the efforts and impact of every single person on this list with his unwavering confidence in me; his beautiful, expansive, and creative mind and heart; and his patient wisdom. Everything this book is is because of everything you bring out in me.

To my many extraordinary teachers, some of whom I include here by name: Beth Bosworth, Stanley Bosworth, Gail Brousal, James Busby, Manoj Chalam, Ruth Chapman, Maria Cutrona, Matthew Derby, Jonathan Elliot, Jim Halverson, Heather Hord, Victor Marchioro, Mike McGarry, Jack McShane, Barbara O'Rourke, Paul O'Rourke, Robert Perry, Bob Rubin, Leslie Thornton, Leslie Yancey, and most especially Michael Bernard Beckwith and Kelly Morris, without whose inspired teachings this book would be half of what it is.

And lastly, to the girl who codes, who creates, who cares and fights and loves fiercely with her whole heart, to the girl who holds the entire universe in the palm of her hand, and to the rest of us who see her: I wrote this book for you.